BODY LANGUAGE

ISBN: 978-1-7367707-2-6

Printed in the United States by Monponsett Press

Acknowledgements and Thanks

To my family, for bearing with me as I set out on another,
even stranger, writing journey.

To my friends and family who served as early readers,
for their feedback and enthusiasm, which makes my books
better and the effort more worthwhile.

To my editors, David Abrams, Alison Murphy and Emery
Rosansky, for their sharp minds and sharp pencils.

To Grubstreet, for keeping hope alive for
writers of every kind.

To Sturbridge Coffee House and Cedar Street Cafe,
where much of the early writing was done.

To Robert Frost Mountain Cabins, where I holed up for a few
cold, dark months to write the remainder of this book.

Chapter One

ANDREA UNCROSSED HER long legs, tanned from years in the African sun and streaked here and there with small white lines, where the inevitable wounds from jungle life had been left to heal undressed. She crossed them the opposite way and drummed her fingers on the soft arm of the plush white couch. The bald man sitting on the identical couch opposite her ignored these showy efforts at impatience. He kept his gaze lowered to the glass coffee table between them, and Andrea watched the reflection of the ceiling lights ripple unevenly across his shaved scalp as he turned his head back and forth, scanning the pile of documents laid out on the table. From time to time he'd hold a page to the light in his thick, crooked fingers, as though looking for faint markings or perhaps for some sort of invisible ink. It was all for show: Andrea knew his cryptography expert had already reported the documents were free from any codes or cyphers. Some of the pages he inspected were clearly printouts from a computer, and some were handwritten in Andrea's hasty, child-like penmanship.

He glanced up again, holding Andrea's eyes, attempting to impress her with some sort of silent judgement. She met his eyes blankly, denying him any response. After a moment, admitting defeat in their wordless battle, he slid all the papers back into the manila envelope from which they'd come.

"Satisfied?" Andrea asked.

"They seem to be clean," he said. "Although if it was me deciding, you wouldn't be sending them at all."

"It's not you deciding it because you have no imagination."

"You must really still hate this guy. It must be some story, between you two."

"You don't know the half of it," she said.

Those words were true enough, she thought, although she knew the meaning the bald security man would take away from them would be wrong. He did not know Andrea's story with the man to whom the package would be delivered. It was a story of five amazing years of struggle, hope and love. Five years that had ended in 48 hours of shame, rage and, finally, death.

And then, even worse, silence.

But still, the worst memory of that time was sweeter to Andrea than the best day in the three years since. The bald man did not know that. Andrea had decided he did not deserve to know something so precious as that.

"So that's what all this is for, just to poke a stick in this fellow's eye?" the man said, gesturing to the envelope he'd rifled through earlier, and the name she's scrawled on it as part of the address.

"I figured it would get his attention," she said. But what she thought was far more desperate. *It has to. Or everything else will be a waste.*

"You and Stanley have an even more twisted sense of humor than I do, Mrs. Reston." His English was good, but his words were clipped. Like most Belgians, he spoke several languages, and managed to portray a sense of arrogance in all of them. He drew out the syllables of her new last name, perhaps getting used to it himself, perhaps trying to belittle her with the emphasis. Either way the name sounded as disgusting coming from his lips as it felt in her heart.

"That would be *Doctor* Reston, to you," she said.

He smiled thinly. "Still, I would not want to cross you."

You already have, Andrea thought, but she kept her face neutral. She'd gotten very good at that over the past year, offering nothing to the eyes watching her every move and reading every message she sent, the ears she knew listened to every sentence she uttered.

He sealed the envelope, glancing at the long line of stamps across the top. "Where did you think this was going, to Mars?"

"It's been a while since I've actually mailed something," she said, faking embarrassment. "I didn't know how many stamps it needed."

"These should do the trick."

"I hope so," she said.

They have to, she thought.

"I'll bring it down to the front desk," she said.

"Nice try. You stay put. I'll have the bellhop come get it."

The presidential suite was easily 2,000 square feet. CNN was playing on a huge TV mounted on the far wall of the sitting area, the volume turned down. As they waited in silence for the bellhop, video footage flashed onto the screen of people in BioHazard suits, carrying body bags to a waiting pickup truck. Andrea froze, trying to tear herself away from the screen, knowing too well what the story contained. But she couldn't look away, and a small corner of her mind told her that she deserved to have that image be the last in her brain as she completed the final step of her plan.

It struck her than even three years after she'd watched Alan Wright walk away from her, it was still him that she wanted to turn to in her moments of doubt or pain. It seemed a lifetime ago that she could actually do that, to lean her head on his shoulder, to scream or cry or just be silent, as they tried to get a comfort that no one could fully give in the face of the waves of suffering they were attempting to staunch. And now, staring at the waves of suffering she'd helped to unleash on the people she'd worked so hard to save, she'd decided it was a comfort she had no right to seek.

And then it struck her hard enough that she sucked in a hard breath; soon enough, the seeking would be over. Forever.

The text across the screen read *Ebola Outbreak Spreads in the Congo*.

The bald man noticed her expression and glanced at the body bags on the screen as well. "You have to break a few eggs to make an omelet. Isn't that the saying?"

"They're not eggs. They're people."

The man shrugged. "It's the Congo. They've got plenty of people to spare."

"It should not be happening."

"That's rich, coming from you," he said. "It is your work, after all." He smiled thinly. "Those are your eggs getting broken, no?"

She pressed her lips together so hard they turned white, rage and guilt both washing through her. Then she breathed deeply, letting the heat in her face cool, using her rising anger to push away the panic that played in the shadows of her mind, using her breath to transform her lurking terror back into the cold hate she had built over the past year.

Hate for Stanley Reston, the man she'd married only a few hours earlier, whose reckless vision she knew had unleashed the Ebola crisis on the people of the Congo.

And hate for herself, because she also knew that despite her best intentions, it was her own weakness—her trust in Stanley, and her heedless rush to discovery—that had made such a terrifying scenario possible.

The doorbell to the suite rang, and the bald man handed off the package to a young bellhop.

"When will the mail go out?" Andrea barked at him, too quickly.

The young man flashed her a smile regardless. "You just made it. They pick up in 10 minutes."

Andrea tried to give herself a bit of solace as the door closed behind the bellhop: the package would be on its way; the rest would be up to Alan Wright—and the feelings she had to believe were still mirrored in his heart from hers, despite all the evidence to the contrary.

The metallic click of the door locking shut left her with only one more task—and with that thought, the panic clawed its way back into the forefront of her mind, no longer content to stare at her from the shadows.

She made herself sit still for five minutes. Enough time, she felt, to make it impossible for the bald man to retrieve the package, if he was sharp enough to consider such a thing. Then she stood and walked toward the sliding door that led onto the balcony, suddenly feeling disconnected from her body, operating almost as if by remote control, willing her flesh to do something that betrayed every primitive instinct it possessed. "I'm going to get some air," she said. Somehow the voice she heard—*her* voice—sounded relaxed, despite the thousand other voices suddenly screaming in her head.

The bald man shrugged. "Suit yourself. But leave your phone."

She pointed to her iPhone, still sitting on the arm of the couch. He just nodded.

She slid open the glass pane and stepped out into the cool, late-September air. The suite was on the 30th floor, and the city of Boston glowed in front of her. She barely felt the chill that cut through the thin fabric of the brightly-colored sheath she still wore from her wedding to Stanley only hours earlier. The voices in her mind screamed more loudly, more insistently, more desperately, trying to tear away her will and her courage. Her heart hammered in her chest and she realized she'd stopped breathing.

She fought to focus her mind on the simplest of actions; one step forward, then another. And on the package, and the belief that the man who received it would see the truth in it and do what she was asking of him.

The plexiglass barrier that ringed the balcony, separating her from the open space beyond was chest-high, but was open above to ensure the best view of the city beyond. It was meant to keep the hotel guests safe; no one expected the wealthy people who could afford such a view to be threats to the people below.

Or to themselves.

She dragged the small plastic table she'd found on the balcony over to the plexiglass panel. A glance over her shoulder showed the bald man still sitting on the couch, hulking over his own phone as he pecked out a message of some sort. She'd guessed correctly that he would assume she was cornered on the balcony, unable to get out of his sight or communicate with anyone else.

With her right hand she felt for the wedding ring Stanley Reston had placed on her left one only hours earlier. But her thoughts went to a different ring, a simple steel band that had been slipped over her finger years earlier by Alan, when they had exchanged identical rings and vows in a hot, windowless room in the Democratic Republic of the Congo, bare toes curling in the soft dirt floor while a handful of friends looked on in witness to a wedding ceremony that was a mashup of Christian ritual and local tradition.

Andrea wondered if Alan still had his ring. And if he ever looked at it.

Unknown to Stanley or his security chief, that other, simpler ring was now in an envelope downstairs in the house-keeping lost-and-found. She'd given it to the hotel staff at the reception, claiming she'd found it on the ballroom floor, scribbling a hasty note to accompany the steel band, and stuffing both into an envelope she'd taken from one of the "thank you" cards scattered on every table. She'd done all that while Stanley had chatted nearby with a handful of guests, oblivious to her, her loving new husband also having decided that she was no risk amid the throng of loyal guests, and the ring of undercover security guards watching her every move.

She worked Stanley's gaudy ring off her finger, the voices rising even louder in her head, her blood roaring like a cataract, the combined cacophony rising to a crescendo that was almost physically unbearable; she knew she had only moments before her resolve collapsed entirely. She tossed the ring high off the balcony, watching it glitter for a moment in the lights from the city before it disappeared into the dark. She hoped someone in need would find the diamond-crusted gold band on the sidewalk below and perhaps use it to change a life. Then she stepped up onto the plastic table, which twisted under her weight. She turned her head just in time to see the bald man look out at her, his eyes widening, the sudden realization of his error dawning on his face.

She thanked the twinkling stars wheeling overhead for that final bit of satisfaction, and then she rolled herself over the railing, and out into the night sky.

Chapter Two

"FUCKING AFRICA?"

Frank put his hands to the sides of his head as the words exploded from his mouth, as if he needed the pressure from his palms to keep his head from exploding, too. Frank was in his late fifties. He still sported a military haircut, although his military fitness had turned to a bit of thickness around his waist and in his face. His close-cropped white hair had thinned enough to show pink skin underneath, which was turning brighter as he got more upset.

"Don't say it like that. It's hurtful to them," I said, hoping some levity might offset his anger.

"The biggest deal of our lives is in front of us and you want to go to Africa to dump out a vase?"

The levity was gone. "Jesus, Frank. It's not a fucking vase. It's *Andrea*."

He held up his hands and took a breath, walking himself back from the line he'd charged across. "I'm sorry. I know why you're going, and yes, it's a noble thing to do. But the key word there should be *was*. Shouldn't her *new* husband be doing this?"

"She had a will—it's clear, I guess—I'm the one she wanted."

"It's got to be a mistake."

"She updated her will two weeks before...the wedding." I stumbled over the words. A reason Frank didn't need to know. "She didn't change that part. Her lawyer sent me the document."

"That's strange."

"Maybe, but it's not a mistake."

I left out the part that the scattering of the ashes wasn't nearly the strangest request she'd made of me since her death.

"Okay, but can't it wait a while?"

"No."

"Jesus, Alan. You could die over there, and then the deal is screwed," he said, rubbing his temples again.

I shrugged, knowing he was right on both counts. But I wasn't changing my mind.

Frank was my Chief Operating Officer, and over the two-plus years we'd worked together, directness had been one thing we'd always had between us. He also had two decades in the Marine Corps behind him, so his honesty usually came wrapped in a four-letter word of some sort. I'd told him over too many drinks one night what I'd done that ended my marriage to Andrea; how my parting gift to her and the DRC had been three dead men sprawled on a dusty road two hours north of the capital city of Kinshasa.

They were men who had deserved to die—I'd believed it then, when I'd pulled the trigger, and I believed it still, as I watched Frank try to rub away the implications of my trip back to that place now. Those men had taken so much from Andrea, I'd felt no remorse when I pulled the trigger, and taken their lives from them.

They'd still gotten the better end of the deal, in my opinion.

But Andrea hadn't seen it that way.

I still had not forgiven those men.

And she had never forgiven me.

Those men had been leeches. They made their money through bribes to allow us to deliver medical care to the very people they were supposed to represent. But even leeches had friends—in their case even more despicable men who'd taken their cut from the extortion and corruption they enabled; those other men would have seen my actions as a threat to their power and income. Those friends, if they were still alive, would like to find me back in the DRC.

They would not be forgiving, either.

I realized Frank was still looking at me, waiting for a response.

"I appreciate the concern, even if it is more for the deal than for me," I said, rolling my eyes. "But I need to do this. I know the timing could not be worse. This is the best I can do to make things right. With her."

"Your team has worked on this deal for a year. They deserve some loyalty, too."

I felt the jab but pressed on. "I'm not changing my mind. I can't."

I didn't tell him I'd already changed it back and forth probably a dozen times the prior night, alternately crying at what I'd lost and cursing at what Andrea had asked me to do.

He met my eyes and I guess he saw the resolve. And probably the pain. He took a breath and nodded.

"You get killed over there and I'm just flushing *your* goddamn ashes down the toilet at the bus station," he said. But the anger was gone.

Frank knew a bit about loyalty and old debts, too.

I nodded. "It'll be quick. Up to Bikoro and Lake N'Tomba, then back to Kinshasa and on a plane to Paris. In and out in a few days."

He scowled, but I could tell now it was from concern as he started working the problem. "Your entrance we can control. It's your exit I'm worried more about. We'll need you alive for the final negotiations. You know that. It's be two weeks from now."

"I know." The deal Frank was worried about was an agreement to sell one of the companies from our investment portfolio to Zestra, one of the world's biggest biotech companies. It would be the first billion-dollar deal for the fledgling venture capital firm I'd founded after my return from the DRC.

"The team's worked for a year on this deal," Frank said.

"They know the drill. They can keep it going while I'm gone."

"You're taking a big risk."

"I'll be OK."

"I wasn't just talking about you. This is life changing for half the folks on this team. You don't come back in one piece, it's their money you're risking too."

"I'll be back. Count on it."

Frank scowled again. "You're leaving the people who you told to trust you to go back to a place you swore you'd never set foot in again. Forgive me if 'counting on you' isn't a phrase I think I can sell to the team right now."

"She's dead, Frank. That wasn't on my list of things to count on. And for whatever reason she wanted me to do this. It'll be OK."

"Let's hope," he said, giving up on the argument. "When do you leave?"

"Kara's working on the visa now. I figure three days."

"Kara must be pissed. She spends her whole life keeping you organized and now she has to worry about you staying alive."

"I can't say I blame her. I still can't believe I'm going to be carrying an urn full of ashes halfway around the world to a place I'd thought I'd never see again."

Frank shook his head again. "Join the club."

Chapter Three

I PACKED LIGHT. A week would go quick, and the less I brought, the less there was for anyone to steal. September and October marked the beginning of the rainy season, but a look at the weather had shown no sign of the torrents that could fall so hard it felt like standing under a waterfall. I brought a lot of small bills. "Tipping" was expected and essentially required to get through the airport and government processes. Even police directing traffic would sometimes demand a small payment with the threat of a bigger fine for some fictitious violation. I wasn't worried about changing my currency. American money was, as usual the world over, the accepted vehicle for bribery and corruption.

I spent a few minutes staring at my watch drawer. The watches had been my reward in the past few years; I bought one for each successful deal I'd closed in my Venture Capital fund. I'd tried a few on as I got ready for the trip, but as I'd slipped the glittering timepieces on and off, I felt like a woman trying to decide which pair of designer heels to bring on a climb up Mount Everest.

I'd finally put them all back and gone to the hallway closet instead. I dug out a shoebox I'd stashed on the upper shelf years before. It held the only souvenirs of my five-plus

15

years in the region. Old travel documents. A faded bandana. A money belt I'd never used. And under all that, a simple analog watch, a gift from Andrea, displaying the 24-hour military time common in Europe and Africa. It had a sturdy steel bezel and a stained canvas band. The watch had run down on the plane the day I'd left Africa, three years earlier, and I had never rewound it. I'd simply tossed it into the box with the other items, leaving the hands forever marking time at five minutes before midnight on that terrible blur of a day.

When the page turns.

That had been her ask to me the night we had first spoken, standing on a rooftop bar, looking out over Kinshasa after a series of briefings we'd coincidentally attended with our teams, and a couple of gin and tonics we'd had by ourselves afterwards. *Wait with me until midnight. When the page turns, and a new day begins.* It was her favorite thing to do, she'd said, as a light breeze pulled the sweat from our skin and pushed strands of her hair toward the moon; a chance to renew hope, she'd said, and put aside whatever troubles had marred the day just ended.

Her favorite thing, on her good days at least.

I just held the watch, unwilling to wind it. Its hands had last turned at a moment when the flame of our anger and pain were all we had left, but it had been, nevertheless, a time when Andrea was alive, and before either of us understood that that final argument before I left for the airport would be the last time we'd ever speak.

I knew the watch deserved better than to be called back to service into a world where Andrea no longer walked. But I suddenly felt as though I needed it again where I was going, for a lot of reasons I couldn't fully explain. So I took a breath and wound the spring, afraid the crown would break off in my hands. Against all odds, it spun smoothly, as though I'd just taken it off the day before. I set the time and strapped it on my wrist. It was lighter than the massive, jewel-encrusted ones I'd grown used to, but it was still solid.

It was also waterproof, and the hands were luminescent for telling time in the pitch dark of an African night. Better to tell the stroke of midnight, she'd said.

When the page turns.

Chapter Four

THE BOX SITTING between my feet seemed bigger to me, somehow, than its size should allow. And lighter; far too light for all it contained. It was no larger than a Johnny Walker gift box, but the room around it seemed to twist in some way, the sterile space distorted by the gravity of its presence. That room was the Delta First Class Lounge at Logan Airport, where I was waiting on my flight to Paris and then on to my final leg, a flight that would take me and the box back to Africa, to the Democratic Republic of the Congo.

We'd both go there, to Lake N'Tomba. I would return to Boston, empty-handed, a week later.

At least that was the idea.

When I looked around the lounge, I felt as though everyone there—exhausted businesspeople and jaded tourists—should have their attention forced to the box in some ancient, subconscious way. Instead, they kept their attention pulled tight around themselves the way people did in public spaces, drawing it close and focusing it out through the lens of their phone screens towards some distant, more pleasant digital world.

All the passengers but one, it turns out: a little girl, blonde hair tied back in red ribbons, curled up next to her mother in one of the plush padded chairs scattered about the room. The girl also had a tablet in front of her. Occasional faint noises of children's games reached my ears across the open space between us. But every few minutes she'd glance over at the brown cardboard container flanked by my shoes. It was a curious, wary look she gave it, as though she knew what that box contained, but was not sure she approved.

Children and animals, my grandmother had always said, are the creatures best able to see ghosts. As I watched the little girl flick her eyes over to the box now and again, studying it with unease but not alarm, I thought my grandmother was right.

Because inside the cardboard box was a plastic urn. Plastic to allow the airport x-ray machines to scan it. In the urn were Andrea's ashes.

In those ashes, I thought again, as I put a glass of whisky to my lips, were all that remained of the most beautiful, meaningful years of my life.

I wished I could believe that they'd been the best years of Andrea's life, too.

Deja vu was all around me. I'd always connected through Paris on my trips to the DRC and had spent countless hours in the Delta Lounge waiting for that flight. The Belgians had colonized the country—formerly known as Zaire—but France still had complex ties to the region, including a language and direct flights from Charles de Gaulle Airport to N'djili Airport in Kinshasa. N'djili had been the site of an important battle in the Second Congo War, when rebel forces advancing on the capital were pushed back by the Zimbabwean army, which was supporting the local government, at that time led by Laurent Kabila. Ultimately, nine African countries had been drawn into the conflict, and by the time the war and its aftermath were declared over, nearly five and half million civilians were dead, mostly from disease and starvation.

But "over" was an optimistic word for that declaration; the misery had continued as rival powers inside and outside the country battled for control of the nation's mining riches. That never-ending tragedy was what Andrea and I had gone to the DRC to confront, and it was that mission that had first brought us together.

She'd been there as a doctor and scientist, specializing in infectious diseases and researching new genetic therapies. I ran operations for the same non-profit that had funded her work. My job had been to engage the government, the rebel forces and other aid organizations operating in the region after the war to try and ensure security for our volunteers, safe transit for our supplies and access to the people we were there to help.

Andrea had done nothing but good in her work as both a caregiver and advisor to the people she served. Mine had been a dirty business on all fronts, a mix of intimidation, bribery, negotiation and endless frustration. I'd felt at the time that it was my job to get my hands dirty so Andrea and her colleagues could keep theirs clean and focus on the medicine.

In the end, I knew, I'd gotten my hands far dirtier than I'd ever thought possible.

As I waited for the minutes to tick down to boarding time, my mind twisted its way through those memories, a part of it alternated between pretending the box was not there at all and feeling an unnerving inability to take my eyes off of it: an entire person, the best person I'd ever met, larger than life, who'd cast a shadow across three continents, now shrunk down to the size of a liquor box, sitting next to my carry-on bag and all my regular travel possessions.

Wallet. Tickets. Passport. Dead ex-wife. Everything a man needed for a week in the Congo.

From time to time I felt like I should talk to the box; to Andrea: to ask her why, after three years of silence, she'd requested that I be the one to spread her ashes on an African lake; to ask her about the strange package I'd gotten in the mail, two days after her death—a package that had ripped my heart out and added a second reason for my trip to Africa; to ask about her wedding, only two weeks past, to a man I'd once considered anathema to us both; and finally, the question that I still could barely form in my mind, never mind bring to my lips—to ask her why she'd stepped off the balcony of that honeymoon suite and into the cold Boston sky, 30 stories above the pavement, still wearing the bridal dress from the ceremony only two hours earlier.

But I had no idea how to begin those conversations.

And I really did not want to cry again that week.

Chapter Five

I SLEPT DURING most of the flight from Boston to Paris. We touched down about 9 in the morning, Paris time. I had a layover at Charles De Gaulle Airport. I didn't think Frank or Kara would be in the mood for a 3 a.m. wakeup call, but there was one call I had to make, to someone I was sure would be awake.

Thomas Kinsley had been one of my best friends during my years in the DRC. Born to wealth in a London suburb but called to help those he could, he was a prodigious fundraiser in the wealthy haunts of Europe and an equally ferocious advocate for the people of the DRC in the most remote corners of the jungle. He ran one of the more effective Non-Government Organizations, or NGOs, which provided health care services in the north and east of the Congo. Easily three inches taller than me, and 30 pounds heavier, dreadlocks down to his shoulders, he cut a figure that was tough to forget, whether he was wearing a suit from Seville Row or a pair of canvas pants and a stained bush shirt.

"Alan, so good to hear from you, so sad for the circumstances," he said, when he picked up the call. His voice had always held humor and optimism, his accent a mix of London sophistication and Congolese lilt. I could picture his quick smile and penetrating eyes. It struck me suddenly how much I had missed him.

"The same to you on both counts—perhaps even more," I said. "You saw her all the time. I haven't seen her since…" I let the words trail off.

"I know," he said quickly, stepping in to rescue me from finishing the sentence. "But that doesn't matter now. I got your message. I cannot believe you are coming back to the Congo."

"That makes two of us."

"You should not come," he said. "You are in danger here."

"I'm hoping people have forgotten about those times."

"Some things have changed here, but the corruption, not so much." There was a pause. "Send me the urn. I will spread her ashes. You can return to Boston and your business."

"I thought about that, actually. But she asked me to do this. Besides, I'm already halfway to you."

I waited through another pause, as though he was considering my words—or maybe his response. When it came, the force in it was almost physical. "Go home, Alan. This is no place for you anymore."

I felt my face flush, and I could hear the anger rise in my voice. "I know I left in a bad way. But I need to be back here. I need to do this."

He sighed, a long hiss on the phone line. "Okay, then. Call me when you're settled in the hotel. I will arrange a lunch. Much to catch up on."

I disconnected and shoved the phone into my bag, angry and a little embarrassed, realizing the gulf I'd left between myself and my old friend seemed greater than I ever imagined, and wondering if he felt I had gotten too soft for a week in the Congo.

The flight to Kinshasa was about eight hours. We'd land in the evening and I wanted to be tired enough to get some sleep once I got to the hotel. I skimmed some business plans I'd been sent by companies seeking my investment, barely seeing the text, but using the work to stay awake. Every few minutes my mind would leave the business world entirely, wandering back over the prior three years. Memories of my time in Africa came and went: the crush of people; the smells of unwashed bodies and sickness; the humidity so thick that it felt like you could swim through the air. Through it all I could see Andrea, smiling, grimacing, laughing, working with her patients or her lab studies, tirelessly battling the infectious diseases that ravaged the region generation after generation, war or no war.

As the pilot announced our final descent into N'djili Airport a sense of foreboding crept over me. I watched the ground spool by as we made our approach along the Congo River, the brown and green grassland giving way to a scattering of shacks that quickly turned into endless seas of tin roofs and bright spots of color I knew to be laundry, washed in metal tubs and hung out to dry. That image had been one of the most omnipresent from my time in Africa. It had seemed to me that every village had been awash in clothing, hung on lines, on poles, in doorways and alleys over muddy paths. The DRC of my memory: a country of abject poverty, hopeful people and endlessly drying laundry.

Our approach took us over the city. I spotted a few new taller buildings, but not much else seemed to be different. As we banked for our landing, I saw Brazzaville, capital of the Republic of Congo, rising up on the far side of the river. The two capitals were only a mile apart, separated only by the muddy river water and a single word of naming.

The airport had no jetways, so we walked down the metal stairs from the Airbus A330 and onto the tarmac. The heat struck immediately, the air so wet and warm it felt like a dog's lick. We reached the first passport checkpoint, the first of the lines that I knew would occupy the next few hours. There'd be lines simply to check that I had my passport and other lines to be sure the passport was valid. Lines to check to see if I had my vaccinations. Lines for customs and baggage claim. And at each line a chance to hand money to somebody for something—whether it was paying a local official to ignore a misplaced vaccination certificate or rewarding a local hustler to end a tug of war for your luggage as they offered to carry it the hundred feet to your vehicle.

As I navigated the lines, Thomas' words rang in my ears. Many things seemed exactly the same as I'd left them. The surly officials. The slow pace. The cacophony of French, Dutch, Lingala and a dozen other local languages and dialects. But some things were different. The arrivals terminal itself was new, and actually quite nice, an unexpected bit of air conditioning raising bumps on my glistening arms as I finally passed through it to the lobby.

Standing in the lines, I could still feel the unease flipping my stomach, but a sense of melancholy had joined it. I thought of my last trip through N'djili Airport, on my way out of the DRC. Andrea's horror and three dead men lay behind me in a village outside the city, and I'd had no idea what lay ahead for me. Only after I'd boarded the plane to Paris that day had my anger cooled, and the chill realization set in that I might never see Andrea or the DRC again.

Now, three years after that day, I found myself stepping out of N'djili Airport once more into the fading Congo sunlight, the heat, dust and smell of the land already soaking into my skin. And all that remained of Andrea was tucked into my carry-on bag next to my shaving kit and a change of clothes. My guilt and regret were as frozen in my heart as the hands of the watch on my wrist had been stopped, at five before midnight, on a page that could never turn.

I was in the DRC once more, this time carrying what was left of the love of my life.

I figured that made my prediction slightly more than halfway right.

In the airport, a part of me had expected to be pulled out of one of the many lines and dragged down to the police station or into a secluded alley for my actions three years earlier. But all the looks from airport officials and the machine-gun-wielding national police soldiers had been typically cold and anonymous. I started to think that three years, an uncaring government and the chaotic state of affairs in general had apparently rendered my actions moot to all but me. I shouldered my way through the crowd of locals shouting offers of help and rides and climbed into an official taxi. And just like that, sitting in the sweltering back seat of a rattling, decades-old Toyota, I was on my way into Kinshasa. Traffic was heavy as usual, but I was in no rush for the next few days to arrive anyway. I was mired in a swamp of memory and prayed to myself that the bar at the hotel would still be open when I got there. Staring into the distance and lost in thought as the shacks gave way to small homes, then storefronts, offices and apartments, I didn't notice the set of headlights that followed us, mirroring our slow weave through the evening rush.

Chapter Six

I'D REGISTERED AT the Hotel Memling. It was one of the nicer hotels in Kinshasa, near the business district, but not the obvious choice for aid workers or tourists. I figured I enjoyed at least a chance of anonymity there. The white marble floors and dark wood paneling were comforting and very western, counterpointed by a colorful mural of Congolese life that covered the wall space behind the reception desk. I hung up my clothes in the room, which was actually two rooms; a bedroom and a sitting room with a desk, couch and side table. Once the clothes were away, I paused for a minute, not sure what to do with my less-traditional cargo. I finally decided to remove the urn from its cardboard sarcophagus and put it on the shelf over the desk in the sitting room. The urn's blue and yellow trimmings felt incongruously festive, but they also made it look right at home against the bright colors of the curtains. I convinced myself it was a proper place of honor, but I knew the spot I'd picked also meant I wouldn't wake up staring at it in the middle of the night.

I had enough ghosts to deal with already in the DRC.

I went downstairs to the dining room and ordered a plate of chicken and rice. I devoured it in minutes, realizing how hungry I'd been and remembering the savory flavors of the Congolese dishes. The hotel bar was called the Cockpit Bar. It was still open after dinner, so I chased down my meal with two whiskeys, slumped in one of the soft leather chairs off the bar, surrounded by model airplanes and other flight-related paraphernalia.

Sinking deeper into the chair after my second scotch, I checked my phone. Thomas had left a message inviting me to lunch the next day. I texted him "yes" and he replied that he'd pick me up around noon. There was a string of emails related to the due diligence process with Zestra, which seemed to be moving forward according to plan.

I settled my tab and headed up to my room, hoping I was tired enough to sleep through the night. I glanced at the urn on the shelf as I entered the room but resisted the semi-drunk urge to say goodnight to it, or to Andrea, or to my grief or to whatever it was that that blue-and-yellow bit of plastic represented. Fortunately, the long trip and the scotch did their work, and I was asleep in a matter of minutes.

Thomas' Mercedes pulled into the circular hotel drive a bit before noon the next day. His driver swung open the rear door and Thomas greeted me with his trademark smile, patting the seat next to him. I climbed in and we nosed out into the chaotic traffic. We worked our way slowly over to Le Boulevard de 30 Juin, the main artery in Kinshasa, named after the day the country had finalized its independence from Belgium in 1960.

"We will go to one of my favorite restaurants to welcome you back, my friend," he said. "It's in Ngaliema."

"It's a bit of a ride, no?" I said. Ngaliema was one of the municipalities on the west side of the city.

"It's worth it, don't worry. It's out of the way. No one will bother us there."

"Nobody seems to care that I'm back," I said, thinking of my easy trip through the airport.

"That's good," he said. "Let's keep it that way. Also, I have made arrangements for the ceremony the day after tomorrow in Bikoro. A few of Andrea's local friends wished to be there also."

"Thanks." I felt the relief—I hadn't wanted the complexity or visibility of making those sorts of arrangements myself.

"You have it with you?" he asked cautiously.

"Yes. In the room."

"Quite a thing to travel with, I'm sure," he said.

"I never thought I'd be back here with her," I said. "Especially not like this."

"I still wish you had stayed home," he said, drumming the back of the passenger seat nervously.

"You okay?" I asked.

"Yes," he darted me a smile. "This traffic gets to me. How a country this poor can have so many cars I'll never understand."

"We brought many of them," I said.

He barked out a laugh. "That's true. Cars, bars and brothels flourish whenever the NGOs come to town."

As we worked our way towards Ngaliema, we passed signs on our left for the *Palais de Marbre*, the Marble Palace. It had been built by Mobutu Sese Seko, president and strong man, who'd taken power in the Congo in a coup with the aid of the U.S., whose goal was to blunt Soviet influence in the region. Seko had renamed the country Zaire. He lost power to Laurent Kabila in the first Congo war. Kabila renamed the country the Democratic Republic of the Congo. He ruled through several dubious elections and multiple protests until he was assassinated by a bodyguard in the Marble Palace in

2001. His son Joseph took the reins of government, brutally cracking down on protestors and adversaries and still hanging on to power long after the constitution allowed.

So went politics in the second largest country in Africa.

We left the main thoroughfare and navigated down a few side streets, the tarmac giving way to hard-packed gravel roads, until we arrived at the restaurant. Thomas hadn't been kidding—it was definitely out of way, at the end of a wide dirt track. It looked nice enough, with a tidy flower garden out front, but hardly seemed like a place that would be the local favorite of a man who'd dined at the tables of the finest chefs on three continents.

Thomas led me to a table near a wide-open side door. "A good breeze here," he said. The restaurant was fairly crowded for mid-day. Several young men stood at the bar, sipping iced teas. Within a matter of seconds, I realized I was the only non-African in the building.

So much for not standing out.

Thomas ordered for us, plates of Moambe with both chicken and fish, rice and sweet potatoes, and bottles of ice-cold Turbo King, a local beer I remembered all too well. Aid work was insanely stressful, lonely and often dangerous. Booze and sex both flowed freely around the NGO facilities and operations. In the countryside where the power was turned off at sundown, and the night was black as ink, those diversions were often the only escapes from the horrors and helplessness that we'd all been immersed in day after day.

In the restaurant the breeze and an armada of ceiling fans running at full speed kept us cool enough and pushed the flying insects away as we ate. The waiter dropped off another round of Turbo Kings, the cold bottles sweating in the humidity. Thomas and I touched glasses.

"How is the work?" I asked.

Thomas nodded. "It is going well. We are on the verge of some breakthroughs," he said. "Genistar is working with the government and us NGOs in new ways. Their vaccines will make all the difference."

I raised an eyebrow. Genistar was the company Andrea had joined over a year earlier. It was a behemoth in the biotech industry, the product of multiple mergers and a few blockbuster drugs. Andrea's husband of two hours, Stanley Reston, was the CEO; she'd become the Vice President of Clinical Care.

"New ways?" I asked, stabbing at a piece of chicken.

I could hear my own skepticism and it was clear Thomas did, too. With everything I knew about Genistar, I could not envision that company in the role of benevolent savior, nor could I picture Andrea working there. I decided that if she'd committed herself to Genistar, it was because she'd moved that massive company in a better direction through her sheer will and stubbornness. I felt a bit of my old pride in her swell at that idea.

The fact that she'd committed herself to Stanley Reston in the process was something I still preferred not to think about.

"We were in the dark ages only a few years ago, my friend," Thomas said. "Trying to treat patients one at a time, with not enough medicine and too few people. A hundred sick and dying for every person we could help. Trying to undo what decades of deprivation and depravity had done to those people." He was growing more animated as he spoke, slapping the table hard enough to make the silverware jump. "We treat them for malaria, they come back with yellow fever. We treat them for yellow fever, they come back with

33

measles. We treat them for that, then the rebels conscript them for the mines and they never come back at all. All these years we have been pissing in the ocean hoping to raise the waters." He shook his head and took a hard pull from his beer. "An ocean the size of the universe, Alan. We were wasting our time."

"What choice did we have?"

"We didn't have one then. But now we do. The genetic treatments. The new vaccines. They will change everything."

I nodded. "They will over time. But you still need the access to the people. And the equipment and the support from the government. And permission from whoever controls the countryside at that moment."

Thomas leaned in close and locked his eyes with mine. He flashed a smile, but this one was almost smug. "But what if we didn't need those things, eh? Then we could treat a thousand people at once. Ten thousand. Ten times *that*. We could *prevent* diseases, not just Band-aid them. We could eradicate at least some of the misery these people face."

"You'll always need those things," I said. "The genetic treatments are expensive, and the research is still unpredictable. I've seen tens of millions of dollars lost in a day when a sure-fire clinical trial comes back a failure. Who'll foot *that* bill?"

He studied me critically. "It's not all about the money here, Alan. At least not *everyone* thinks that. Genistar is funding it all, with help from Chinese investors. Stanley Reston himself is involved."

"Stanley Reston never does anything for anyone but himself. He's nobody to trust."

"Andrea thought he was."

"Not the Andrea I knew."

"People change, Alan. You did."

Maybe I was feeling defensive, but I was sure I could hear recrimination in his voice.

We sat silently for a moment. Then Thomas touched my arm. "I'm sorry, I should not lecture you," he said, more gently. He pushed his chair back from the table. "Speaking of change, we are not as young as we once were, eh?" he said with a laugh. "Two beers and I need to piss."

He gathered up his phone and disappeared into the depths of the restaurant. I followed his path with my eyes for a minute, assuming I'd be making the same trip shortly. With my gaze pointed that way, I saw the three young men at the bar watch his exit also, as they slid off their bar stools. Even in the DRC, Thomas wore his wealth plainly; in this case, it took the form of gold chains and diamond earrings. I started to push myself back from the table, thinking they were planning on intercepting him at the toilets in the back. One of the three followed Thomas down the narrow hall towards the back. But the other two turned and rushed me instead. I realized, too slowly, what was happening and spun around, looking for the open door, but they reached me before I could take my second step. I felt hands on my right arm. I let it go limp, spinning backward and jamming my left elbow into the side of the head of the man. I heard a sharp yelp as I twisted my arm free. I felt a stab of pain in my right shoulder; in the strange slow-motion time warp of sudden danger, a corner of my mind still had time to note to itself that I wasn't as flexible as I once was. I ignored the pain and tried to figure a way to reach the open doorway and a chance at safety beyond. Everyone else at the bar started shouting and shoving their way out of the room. I looked around frantically for Thomas, but he was still out of sight.

Then the other two men were on me. I snapped my head forward, catching one of them in the nose, hard enough to cause a grunt but too high to break the bridge. He responded with a punch to the side of my head. I saw stars for a moment and lost track of the two men, so I just guessed where the one closest to the door was and took a swing. I got lucky and connected, hard. He fell back and I started sprinting for the door as my vision cleared. I could see the freedom of the parking lot ahead of me when arms wrapped around my legs from behind and drove me to the hard-packed ground. I kicked back and made contact with flesh, but the grip stayed firm. I twisted onto my back, hoping for better leverage for my next kick, only to find myself staring into the muzzle of a pistol.

"Get up," the young man holding the weapon barked in French. The other two men took advantage of my sudden focus on the gun to grab my arms and haul me to my feet. They dragged me through the doorway and across the dirt parking lot and into a waiting SUV, the pistol always trained on my head. The gun-wielder slid into the seat on my right. One of his partners—the one with the quickly-swelling nose—jumped in on my left. He wrapped zip ties around my wrists and pulled them tighter than he needed to, grinning as he saw me wince when the straps cut into my flesh.

The SUV rocketed off along the unpaved road. I heard the wheels spinning momentarily on the dry gravel. Pistol Man turned and smiled at me with a mouth full of gold teeth. "Some people want you to know they remember you." His smile turned to a crooked leer. "From how much they are paying, I think they really must have missed you."

The vehicle veered left around one corner, then right around another, working back towards the highway. With each turn I was jostled against either Pistol Man on my left or the door frame to my right, flames of pain shooting up from my wrists as the bounces dug the plastic ties deeper into my flesh. My mind flashed back to Thomas' warning not to return, and to the three bodies in that dusty road three years back. I'd hoped a few years was enough space to make me safe.

Unfortunately, as they say, hope is not a strategy.

The SUV made another turn and the lines of pain flowed up my arms. I cursed myself for my own recklessness. But crazily I found myself thinking of the urn sitting on the shelf in my hotel room, and Andrea's final wish to me. I was going to let her down, I realized. As I was slammed once again into the doorframe, I wondered crazily for a moment what would happen to the urn if I never returned to my room. Would it sit forever on the shelf, guest after guest admiring its pretty details with no idea of the sad contents it held? Or would the staff eventually find it and toss it unceremoniously into a trash bin, Andrea's final resting place becoming the dump on the edge of the city? Those thoughts tortured me more than any worries about what the men we were about to meet intended to do with me.

Pistol Man turned to me, the crooked smile still pasted on his face. He was starting to say something else when suddenly we were both slammed into the seatbacks in front of us, then bounced back hard into our seats. The pain in my wrists made me see spots again.

"*Que faites vous?*" Pistol Man shouted at the driver. The driver pointed forward. I followed the direction of his outstretched finger and saw the reason for the sudden stop; a white Range Rover was sitting crosswise in the road ahead. Our driver threw the car into reverse, then cursed again. I couldn't turn all the way around but from the corner of my eye I saw a gleaming white shape emerge from the cross street as another Land Rover pulled out from a side alley to cut us off from behind. The two men in the front seat of our SUV jumped out, the one on the passenger side grabbing a dusty Russian-style assault rifle from the floorboards. By the time they rounded the open doors three men from the leading Range Rover were already out of their own vehicle, using its bulk as a shield, and holding far more modern-looking automatic weapons. A fourth man emerged from the Range Rover in front of us. He was wearing pressed khakis and a deep blue collared golf shirt and looked more like an investment banker on his lunch break than a gang leader in central Africa. He held a handgun in his right hand. He let the pistol dangle casually at his side but with a sort of grace that made it seem even more dangerous. He called out something to my captors in Lingala, one the local languages I could recognize, but not understand.

Pistol Man dragged me out of the car and pressed the muzzle of his weapon against my temple. He shouted back, also speaking Linagala, but the men behind the Range Rover didn't move or lower their weapons. Pistol Man and the man in the perfectly blue golf shirt went back and forth that way for a bit. Then the man in the golf shirt rolled his eyes and stepped out from the cover of the vehicle. I felt the muzzle of the pistol digging deeper into the side of my head as he approached, still dangling the pistol and apparently not the least concerned about the weapons aimed in his direction. He stopped directly in front of us, and in a blur his own pistol was up, pointing into my captor's left eye, so close I could feel the side of the barrel against my left check, smooth and warm.

"Let him go," he said, in French this time.

"Leave now," Pistol Man hissed back, in French. He tipped his head towards me. "I don't care if this one's alive or dead. I get paid either way."

"I do care if he lives," his adversary said, his tone almost conversational. Up close I could see he was younger than I'd thought, maybe late twenties. His obvious air of command added a sense of years to his appearance. He shrugged, meeting the other man's stare. "But you? I don't care so much about you."

They stood that way for a moment, giving me time to wonder how loud the gun nestled against my cheek would sound if the man in the golf shirt fired first. And whether I'd even hear the sound of Pistol Man's weapon before the bullet entered my brain, if he ran out of patience instead.

"Perhaps everybody lets me go and we all live?" I said, in French. The young man in the golf shirt actually laughed. "A good suggestion." Then his eyes swiveled back to my captor and the humor left them. He said a few terse sentences, in Lingala. The tone was brusque but without anger.

After a moment I felt the muzzle of the pistol come away from my skull. Pistol Man snarled something in Lingala but stepped away from me. He shoved me towards the front Range Rover and shouted to his men. They all piled back into their own vehicle. The Range Rover behind them backed up into the side alley, making room for them to retreat. They did just that, tires spinning again in the gravel. Dust swirled around the space between the two remaining vehicles. I debated making a run for it, but there were still three assault rifles pointed in my general direction from the front, and I assumed several more from behind.

The leader of the new crew reached out a hand in greeting. I shook it reflexively with both hands still painfully restrained by the zip ties. In a flash, the pistol was gone and he had a glittering knife in his hands. My heart skipped a beat staring at the wicked-looking weapon, but he cut my bands with a graceful move, so quick I didn't even have time to flinch.

"I am Atombe," he said, emphasizing the long French "ay" at the end of his name.

"What do you want?" I said in French.

He replied in English, "Nothing."

"I can guess who they worked for," I said, motioning my head in the direction of the departed vehicle. thinking of three bodies lying in another gravel road several hours to the north and three years in the past. "What about you?"

He smiled. "I work for you."

Chapter Seven

I JUST STARED for a moment, trying to make sense of what he'd said. "I didn't hire you."

The young man named Atombe laughed. "Perhaps we've rescued the wrong man then. But that's a question for my boss, not for me. I'll take you to our offices now. And we'll patch up your face on the way."

He sent one of his men to the other vehicle to create space in the closer one for me. He sat in the passenger seat and I sat in the second row, next to one of his men.

"Were those men with the government?" I asked.

He shook his head.

"Why did they let me go?"

"They were outgunned. What choice did they have?"

As we drove back towards the center of the city, I thought to myself how much I'd forgotten about life in this part of the world. I knew Atombe was just being sensible, as had the men in the other cars. While arguments were common and guns were omnipresent in the Congo, surprisingly few disputes ever resulted in gunfire. It was a sort of unwritten rule. Everyone wanted to live another day, and so while everyone was armed, things usually got worked out short of pulling a trigger.

Usually.

"I am sorry for the drama," Atombe said, still in English. "We were watching from the outside of the restaurant, thinking any trouble would come from that way. Those men were already inside. I don't know how they beat us there."

The image of Thomas disappearing down the hallway, the third attacker behind him, sprang into my mind. I pulled my cellphone out of my pocket and dialed his number. It went into voicemail.

"We need to go back to the restaurant," I said to Atombe. "My friend was there. There was another man following him."

He shook his head. "I'll send the other car there. I am supposed to keep you out of danger, not drive you into it."

"He's my friend. I don't want to leave him."

"My guys are good. If he's there they'll take care of him. If not?" he gave a fatalistic shrug. "We're paid to watch you, not him." He smiled politely, but his eyes stayed locked on mine, and it was clear that was the end of the discussion. I realized the look he turned on me was the same look he'd given Pistol Man. It was a hard look to ignore.

We were soon back in heavy traffic. I could see the driver and the other passenger continue to scan the vehicles around us, keeping watch in case the kidnappers decided to mount a counterattack. But in the crush of lorries, bikes and overloaded cars jamming the roadways I didn't see how anyone could even get close enough for that.

I tried to quiz Atombe more, a million questions in my mind, but he just shook his head and told me his boss would fill me in. In a half hour we'd covered the few miles back into the city center. We navigated off Le Boulevard de 30 Juin and down toward the water. We passed the U.S. Embassy on our left and I got my bearings. Then the vehicle stopped in front of a plain-looking office building closer to the Congo River. Atombe hopped out of the passenger seat and opened the door for me. He ushered me into the building. One of his men accompanied us while the other sped off with the vehicle. I saw no directory of company names either outside or inside the unfurnished lobby area. Atombe pushed the button for the lift, which arrived quickly and silently. We took it to the third floor. As the door opened the cool rush of air conditioning hit my face. The elevator opened onto a small set of offices which could have been in New York or San Francisco. Modern desks were scattered about in an open area to my left. Ahead were doors leading to a handful of private offices which, I guessed, looked out onto the river.

"You want a coffee, or some water?" Atombe asked. "Or maybe a whiskey?" He added with a laugh.

I shook my head.

"Wait here," he said, and headed off toward the private offices. The other man remained by my side. In a minute Atombe returned and led me toward the far office. He swung the door open and ushered me in. I scanned the room from right to left, my surprise growing with every second, taking in the leather-covered sofa against the right wall, the padded chairs and glass coffee table facing it, the view of the muddy, fast-moving Congo with Brazzaville in the distance through the tall windows in the back, and finally the desk to the far left. The desk was a simple flat plane of dark wood, but with a very modern set of technology sitting on it. Two Toshiba monitors were mounted on swivels, driven by a laptop on the desk. A printer sat behind the desk against the left wall, partially blocked from view by the man rising up smoothly from the leather office chair behind the desk.

He was Caucasian, which was another surprise. Well-tanned from the equatorial sun, but Northern European, I guessed. He had short brown hair cropped in a military style. He wasn't particularly tall, perhaps an inch or two shorter than me, but he seemed to occupy the space around him in some way that made him appear bigger, or somehow more "there." Like Atombe he wore tan khakis but with a long-sleeved cotton shirt, the sleeves rolled up to the forearms, just tight enough to hint at muscles on his chest and arms that rippled without bulk. He moved gracefully around the desk and reached out his hand.

"I'm Marco," he said. "I'm glad to meet you, Mr. Wright."

"I'm glad to be here," I said, still feeling the muzzle of the pistol against my skull.

"Sorry for that. It should not have happened."

"Who are you?" I asked.

He looked at me, some surprise on his face. "I run a private security firm here. Your company hired us to keep watch over you while you were here. I'd assumed that was your usual practice."

"I didn't hire you."

"We got a call from someone named Frank. He said he was your Chief Operating Officer."

I scowled. "He is." *I should have known*, I thought to myself.

Marco shrugged. "The wire transfer went through and he gave us all the releases. So, we took the job. Frank said not to contact you unless needed, so we just tailed you from the airport and again to the restaurant. I figured you wanted your privacy."

"You're right about that," I said.

"Frank seems to have made a wise decision by hiring us," Marco said.

I shrugged. "He gets lucky once in a while."

Marco waved me to the couch and then sat, leaning forward, in the leather chair next to it. "Not many folks know how to reach us. Frank got to me through some friends we share. We usually wouldn't take the work on that short of notice, but Frank came…" he paused for a minute, then nodded to himself, "…well recommended, I guess, is the best way to say it." He smiled, a charming, easy smile. "Plus, he doubled our fee."

"Do you know who those men were who came after me?"

"If I'd had time to do my usual assessment before you arrived, I probably would. But I was going to ask you that same question."

I thought for a moment but decided there was no reason to say anything other than the truth. "I got on the wrong side of some people in this country the last time I was here. It was not long after the war. I was hoping their friends had forgotten by now."

"What happened?"

I told him the story. About Andrea's desperation to help a village of dying people; about the various forms extortion can take; and how those men had taken advantage of her desperation in the worst possible way.

And how I'd found them and made them pay.

"How many men?"

"Three."

"They deserved it?"

I thought of Andrea's bruised face, and the way she tried to move without letting me see the pain from the worse injuries underneath her clothing. "Yes."

He shrugged. "Okay, then. Thanks for being honest."

I studied his too-casual reaction. "You already knew all that."

"Some of it—not all of it. Frank told my friend you may have some enemies and why; my friend relayed that information to me. I just wanted to see whether you'd be open with me. Like I said, I didn't have time for my usual background check. If you lie to me, I can't keep you safe."

"That's a lot for him to share," I said, annoyed.

"He trusted his friend. His friend trusts me. That's how it works."

"And now I should trust you. Why?"

"Because you're not dead right now."

I nodded. "Fair enough."

The door opened and Atombe stuck his head in. "Your friend Thomas is okay. He was still at the restaurant. Beat up a bit, he said, but nothing too serious. He said he will call you in a few minutes."

"Your friend. Who is he?" Marco said, eyes narrowing.

"He runs an NGO in the region. Huge money raiser. I've known him since my first time here.

"A good friend?"

"Yes, why?"

"The guys who grabbed you were already inside the restaurant. That's why my team didn't spot them. Those men knew you were coming."

"Thomas and I went through a lot of shit together here," I said. "There's no reason he'd want to see me hurt. And nobody could bribe him. He's got more money than God."

Marco considered my answer. "Maybe next time you pick the restaurant, eh?"

For the first time I picked up his accent. "You're Canadian?"

"Yes."

"You're a long way from home."

"In every way you can imagine." He stood. "We'll get you back to the hotel. Then you can book a flight back to Boston. We got you out of this mess, but I have to think those men will try again. I don't want my people to be in a firefight every day you're here."

I thought of the urn and shook my head. "I'm not leaving. I have something I need to do."

"Spreading your ex's ashes? Frank told me why you're here. Delegate that to us. It'll get done. I promise."

"I need to see it happen."

"You're crazy," Marco said. "It's a plane flight to a dirt runway, no communication for any of it other than satellite phones, and even those don't always work. And a thousand places for an ambush once we get there if anybody feels like it."

I walked over to the windows. The Congo River was narrower here, but still nearly a half-mile wide, and fast-flowing. It was the source of life and commerce for so much of Central Africa. Andrea had dedicated her life to what lay up that river. I thought for a minute of all the ways she could have died in Africa. Disease. Accident. Violence. She'd survived it all, only to take her own life half a world away, while the stragglers from her wedding reception still mingled in the ballroom below her.

Andrea's life could have ended a thousand different ways in Africa, most of them bad, and all of them as old as humankind: disease, violence, accidents. What drove her to end it herself, jumping off that balcony in Boston, I still did not know, and I was afraid I never would. Regardless,

47

she'd made two requests of me: the first was to scatter her ashes in the lake at Bikoro; the second one was a request I'd discovered, in the most bizarre way possible, days after her death. I had not shared that one with anyone, even Frank.

I turned to Marco. "Did you ever make a promise to a dead person?"

A shadow crossed his face. "More than one."

"Did you honor them?"

"Always." He answered directly, eyes unwavering.

"I made my wife a promise. I intend to keep it."

I actually didn't know how strongly I meant those words until I said them. The sights, sounds and smells of Kinshasa had triggered so many memories. Of great times and terrible ones, but most of all of Andrea. I could picture her walking the streets of Kinshasa, turning heads as she moved. Her love for the energy, the life of this crazy city evident in her eyes. I could see her, cradling a baby girl in her arms as the child fought for every breath, tiny chest pushing hard for another minute of life. I could imagine her, sitting cross-legged on the floor, chewing absently on a pencil as she ran diligently through her lists, packing for another month out in the country, eager for another fight with the most brutal circumstances created by nature and man.

Three years earlier, I'd felt nothing but guilt and rage when I boarded the plane to Paris. This time, I had come to realize with my wrists bound in the car, and the gun held to my head, I would die before I would leave the Congo feeling that way again.

"I thought she was your ex?"

I smiled, Andrea's memory burning bright inside me, the ring she'd worn at our wedding cool and heavy in my pocket. "Me, too."

He thought for a minute. "Okay, we'll take you to Bikoro. Then we're done."

I nodded, not contradicting him. He, in fact, would be done after we'd finished in Bikoro. My second task, however, would take me a few miles further inland, deeper into the countryside where Ebola terrified the population.

I'd decided I would maker that second trip without him. If my pursuers wanted to track me through Ebola country, so be it.

My phone buzzed.

Friends.

Thomas.

I answered and we filled each other in briefly on our relative mishaps. "One day in Kinshasa and I already let you down," he said. "I am glad you are okay."

"You, too," I said. We agreed to meet for breakfast at my hotel the next day.

"Rest up tomorrow," Marco said, once I'd finished the call. "No sightseeing. We'll head to Bikoro first thing in the morning Monday. In the meantime, I'll keep a detail on the hotel."

"Are you going to report the attack to the police?"

He laughed. "No. They'll just ask for a fee to investigate. And I'd rather not call even more attention to you. I'll find out who those men were myself."

He called for Atombe to drive me back to the hotel and had another young man bring some bandages and antiseptics for the cuts on my wrists. A third brought the car around and served as driver. Atombe sat in the passenger seat, with me in the second row. The car windows were tinted, both so no one passing could see the occupants of the vehicle and so the air conditioning would have a chance against the heat and humidity. At the hotel, Atombe accompanied me to my room.

"I don't need a babysitter," I said.

He looked at me, one eyebrow cocked. "How are your wrists?"

I just scowled, but he'd made his point.

He laughed, a good-natured, infectious sound, and clapped me on the shoulder. "Let us do our job, Mr. Wright. We're very good at it." Then he left me there, heading downstairs to take up guard duty, I assumed.

Chapter Eight

I LINGERED IN the shower, soaking off the sweat and dust from the chaos at the restaurant, then called back to Boston to check in with Frank. He screamed into the phone for a few minutes when I told him what had happened, but then took a breath and updated me on the progress of the Zestra deal.

"Who's this guy Marco?" I said after we'd finished the business update. "What's his deal? Why's he here?"

There was a pause. "He'll tell you if he wants to. But you can trust him."

"How do you know that?"

Another pause. "He comes... highly recommended. Let's just leave it at that."

After I hung up with Frank, I poured a scotch from the minibar and dropped onto the couch in the sitting room. Andrea's remains kept watch from the shelf.

I wondered what Andrea would have thought of my day; when we'd been together, I'd felt invincible, keeping the petty bureaucrats in line with one hand while holding the local warlords at bay with the other, organizing the logistics of travel and the delivery of supplies while she managed the doctors and healthcare workers. Now it seemed I needed a small army of guardians just to get through lunch.

When we'd been together.

That work had been exactly what I'd hoped it would be when I'd signed up for the job. Three years of business school and five years at a management consulting firm had cooled my blood and drained my energy; I'd wanted something different; something raw and meaningful; days filled with blood, sweat and tears. Something as far as I could get from the sterile, clinical talk of wealth creation and capital deployment. My dad, whose contacts and reputation had helped me land that consulting job, just shook his head when I'd told him my plans. *Well, if you have to get that out of your system, now's as good a time as any*, he'd said, after the arguments, as if the desire to do something meaningful in the world was the professional equivalent of a 24-hour bug.

The aid work was far harder than I'd ever expected, but I found it was humbling and exhilarating to be able to help people who were struggling to secure their next meal rather than their next promotion. I'd felt an intense gratification in the face of a smiling child or relieved mother and before long I found myself wondering how I'd ever gotten satisfaction from my prior life, where success was measured in the invisible movement of ones and zeros from one computer to another as millions of dollars changed hands, my firm getting rich carving off a few percentage points along the way.

And while I'd gotten everything I'd hoped for in the job, I'd gotten far more than I deserved when I'd met Andrea, three months into my assignment. I'd first seen her at one of the parties we'd held to burn off stress and grief, a mix of ex-pats and locals where everyone was dancing and sweating and drinking, the music courtesy of a battery-powered boombox, the lights a combination of candles and lanterns, in a concrete building that pushed into the edge of jungle itself.

She'd glistened with perspiration, long brown hair in braids, green eyes sparkling as she danced with a few of the local women in the center of the dirt floor, a bottle of beer in her hand.

She had been beautiful.

I did not speak to her until three months later, at the conference in Kinshasa, when we'd wound up at that rooftop bar as crossed midnight and into a new day.

When the page turns.

Whenever I was with her after that I'd see the world through her eyes as well as my own—more vibrant, more alive than I could have imagined. It had sustained me for a while; enough where I could overlook the frustrations and heartbreaks that became as inevitable as the rains, and enough where I could help her when the dark periods struck her; hard days of anger and melancholy.

She'd told me once, during an especially bad day, about her childhood—and the monster her mother had brought into the house in the form of a boyfriend, when Andrea was only 12 years old. Andrea had left the house at 18, and never gone back. I'd always wondered after that whether her insatiable drive to understand and repair the human body had been born from that time, in some way; if somehow she thought the ability to heal other people would be enough, in some way, heal herself.

Staring at the urn on the shelf, I was afraid I had that answer now.

But none of it—the work, the love, the tears, and especially the way she had ended it, helped me understand the two requests she'd made of me.

The first one I'd complete in Bikoro, when I handed her ashes to Lake N'Tomba.

The second, the one I'd kept from Marco, was even harder to explain. That request had been revealed to me wrapped in in the most excruciating, unexplainable experience I'd had since I'd left Africa—watching a video of the toast Andrea given at her wedding. It had been a speech to her new husband on the one hand but, I'd come to realize, contained a message meant for me, quite literally, on the other hand.

I finished the scotch, retrieved my laptop from the bedroom and powered it up. I found the video file of the toast easily enough; it was still on my computer desktop. I clicked it open and Andrea's figure filled the screen, her bridal dress from that day spilling gracefully from her shoulder, a microphone in her hand, her impossibly green eyes darting over the crowd. I let the video play without sound, letting myself get lost in her gestures, the gentle sway of her body as she'd spoken to her assembled guests. I could watch it now, end to end, without anger, almost without grief, which had not been the case when I'd seen it for the first time. Or the second.

The video had been in the confusing package I'd received two days after Andrea's suicide; a plain manila envelope mailed to my office, the address handwritten, far too many stamps lining the top of the package. There had been no return address. I'd pored through the contents, their meaning dawning on me in a slow, torturous layers as I skimmed page after page. The envelope was stuffed with Andrea's wedding planning documents: table layouts, menu selections, song lists, invitations. Some were typed, some hand-written.

I'd thought at first it all had to be a mistake—that the envelope must have been meant for someone else, winding up in my hands on a day fate's cruelty took an especially ironic turn. But the handwriting on the package was Andrea's own—I knew that without question. And scrawled across the face of the envelope above the address, a single line; *Alan—everything you need is here.*

Kara had given me the package when I'd arrived at the office that day. Heart thumping in my chest, I'd flipped through the odd, painful collection of documents in disbelief. As I'd pawed at the papers my mind reeled, remembering, through the myriad of details, an event I'd never wanted to even imagine. Then a hard plastic rectangle slipped out from between two brochures for wedding photographers and skittered across my desk; it was a USB drive. I slipped the drive into my MacBook. It opened up and showed only one file. I'd sat back in my chair, not believing what I saw as I read the file name. It was the video of her wedding toast. *Her wedding toast.*

I'd thought about just pulling out the USB drive and just tossing it and the folder into the trash, turning my back on the pain and anger just as I had when I'd left the Congo three years earlier. But even in my grief and hurt I knew, in the end, I couldn't just throw it away. Some part of Andrea was in that video. Some part of the hole in my life that had been left wide open for the past three years.

In the end the decision was simple, because it had been made for me five years earlier, the day I'd met Andrea.

I'd hit "Play."

It was a shaky recording, taken from just above table height, probably with a cell phone. But the audio was clear, and the video was good enough to remind me how captivating she'd been. The dress had been colorful, reds and blues, with hints of African patterns in the stitching along the hem. It fit her slim figure with the casual grace she'd always carried. I'd barely listened to the words, seeing her image moving on the screen, knowing now that she was gone. Maybe she'd changed inside in the years since we'd been together, but it was hard to believe that as I watched the video. Her body swayed slightly, in a way that reminded me of the first time I'd seen her. Her graceful hand held a microphone, long fingers wrapped tight around it.

Her hands.

I'd stopped the playback and rewound it a bit. And watched it again. She'd held the microphone in her left hand for the toast, Stanley's engagement ring glittering. Her right hand stayed low, fingers on the table. She kept it motionless, positioned between a flower bouquet to her right and the wine glass in front of her, out of sight of most guests but visible to whomever had recorded the video. It was the stillness that had drawn me to that hand—Andrea had been expressive, and her hands were as much a part of her speech as her voice. The stillness drew me to the hand, but then something else caught my attention and stopped my breath. On the middle finger of that quiet hand I could see a dark band. It was tiny on the video, but somehow I already knew what it was. I froze the video and enlarged it. Then did it again. Until I was sure. It was the ring I'd given her the day we'd married. A simple steel band made in a village we'd frequented. It had cost less than ten dollars. And she had cherished it.

Until she hadn't.

I'd let the video play. At one point she put down the microphone, waiting for the applause to finish. Both hands disappeared under the table for a moment. When they reappeared the ring was gone.

What the hell.

I played that part again. The way she'd held her hand the ring wouldn't have been visible to Stanley, who was seated on her opposite side. Or to anyone else not sitting along the sight line of the camera that had captured the image. She had positioned herself perfectly; it could not have been an accident.

She'd wanted the ring to be seen. But not by everyone. Just, I was certain, by whoever shot the video.

And, therefore, by me.

What the hell.

The video had approached its end. Andrea had nodded toward the band and they began to play. She closed her toast asking people to think of where they'd been when they'd heard that song for the first time. It had been our song. I'd heard it with her in a coffee shop in Zurich, while we sipped espresso and waited on a train back to Paris. On my laptop screen she raised her glass in toast, and then the video ended, the same way her life had ended for me; a jarring, unexpected cut to black, followed by silence, and questions.

I'd sat and stared at the computer screen for a while, the final frame of the video still frozen on it. Then I'd called the hotel where the wedding had been held and asked them to check to see if anyone had lost a ring that evening. I told them it would have been on the rug near the head table. A dark steel band, I'd said, sized for a woman.

The hotel didn't call back that night, so at 8 a.m. the next day I found myself staring at the hotel's main entrance, unable to keep myself from measuring the distance from the portico's roof, where the news said they'd found her body, to the honeymoon suite far above.

The hotel had already eliminated any evidence of what had happened that night. Guests came and went through the main doors, oblivious to the incredible life that had ended on the flat roof just over their heads. It made me angry to think that they could erase her final moments so efficiently.

I wondered if she'd been cold in those last minutes, looking down from the balcony in that sheer dress, her blood still thin from the years straddling the equator. Had there been goosebumps on her flesh? Did she feel the bite of the wind? What could she have felt at all, to make such a decision possible?

I could not imagine it. And I could not stop from trying.

Once in the lobby, I asked for the lost and found and was directed to the bell desk. I told the man there what I was looking for. "It's just a piece of steel," I said. "But there's a hundred-dollar reward if it's found."

He came back a few minutes later, holding an envelope. It had been opened then re-sealed with tape. "Your lucky day," he said. "The bride herself turned it in. Girls downstairs were working that night. She told them she'd stepped on it when she took her heels off to dance."

I'd ripped the envelope open again. The ring was there, and a note, scribbled on a bar napkin. I took out the ring first. It was lighter than I'd remembered. Black with a gold filagree. Wider than most women's rings. But she'd like it. Easier for everyone to see, she'd said. I turned it over in my fingers. There was no inscription. The man we'd bought it from had no such equipment. At the time we'd never thought we'd need one. Why bother to inscribe in words what was already etched on our hearts?

I realized I'd stopped breathing. I took in a lungful of stale hotel air and slipped the note out of the ruined envelope. Andrea had written it. The script was unmistakable. It was one line. "Please return this to its original owner," it had said.

"Yeah, the lady left that note for the staff, I guess," the bellman had said. "Not sure who else she thought we'd return it to."

I was barely listening, staring at the note. She'd signed it with three initials. AGW.

My breathing stopped again. This time it felt like my heart did as well.

AGW. Not AGR. Andrea Gallard Wright. Her married initials. Married-to-*me* initials. Not married-to-Stanley-Reston initials. I saw them, in her curlicue handwriting, and three years fell away like a curtain cut from a stage rigging. I could see the endless plains and jungles of the Congo. I could feel the steaming heat that seemed to emanate from everything: the sun, the ground, the air, the buildings themselves. And I could see Andrea, plain as day, hair pulled back out of respect for the wind. Her smile bright, even as she tended to the most wretched cases of illness and injury that nature could concoct, and man could amplify.

"Well, I'm glad we got it back to you," the bellman said, pointedly.

His words broke me out of my reverie. I gave him the hundred.

Please return this to its original owner

At first, I'd thought she meant those directions for the hotel staff—that they were to return the ring to me. But I realized quickly that made no sense- how could the hotel know who that might be? Which meant the instructions

59

were not for anyone at the hotel: they were for me. And that meant the owner she was talking about was Lufua. He was the sorcerer, witch doctor and priest who'd made this ring and the matching one I'd worn for three years. He was also the man who had married us in the large room that served as his church in the village of Makoua, an hour north of Bikoro

For reasons I could not understand, she wanted the ring returned to Lufua.

If he was still even alive, he would still be there, in Makoua. So Makoua became the second stop on my journey, the one I'd make after I'd said goodbye to Andrea for the final time at Lake N'Tomba.

Sitting in my hotel room in Kinshasa, I played the video again. I watched Andrea smile and move, trapped in time, the steel ring still on her finger. She'd seemed nervous in the video, which was unlike her, even drawing an irritated glance from Stanley when she'd misspoken the name of one of the guests, thanking him even though he'd not been able to attend the wedding. The first name by which she called him tweaked a memory in the back of my mind, but as she corrected herself and moved on my mind did the same, wondering if the nervousness she was showing meant she'd already made the decision to end her life.

Seeing her face as I breathed the thick equatorial air of the Congo, I wanted so much to believe that those intervening years had never happened; that she was still alive; that on some crowded Kinshasa street, tomorrow or the next day, I'd hear the carefree sound of her laugh and we'd meet again, bathed in sunlight, all pain and guilt forgotten.

But the urn facing me from across the hotel room told a different story.

Chapter Nine

I woke around 7 under protest from my body, which still insisted it was the middle of the night and had decided to remind me of the abuse it had taken the prior day. I showered and then checked my phone, catching up on some emails that had come in during the night.

I worked my way downstairs just after 9. The hotel lobby was bustling with a mix of Kinois, the name the city residents gave themselves, and foreigners of a dozen nationalities. The mineral riches of the DRC had brought interest from all over the world for 300 years, and misery to the people of the Congo for just as long, ever since King Leopold II of Belgium had brutally enslaved the population in pursuit of rubber, gold and ivory. The modern tactics of colonialization used money, not terror, to exert control; the Chinese alone were investing billions of dollars across Africa through their "Belt and Road" initiative, often putting the recipient nations into debts they could not repay, giving the Chinese huge leverage over their "partners."

In the lobby, I spotted a young man in dark pants and a white polo shirt studying his phone in a far corner of the open space. He looked bored, glancing up regularly from his phone, but from his vantage point he could see both the front entrance and the doorways that led out to the pool area, which were the only ways into the hotel other than the elevators. I figured he was part of my protection detail. He smiled at me as I approached, confirming my guess.

"I'm Henry," he said in French. "Marco said you would be staying in the hotel today?"

"Marco said that. I didn't. I'm having breakfast here, then going to visit someone."

"You have friends in the city?"

"We'll see." It was an odd answer, I knew, but the best I could give.

"Where?"

"We can talk about that later."

I'd accepted that Marco and his team were there to keep me safe, but I still wanted some things to stay within my control. I headed towards the dining room. Henry followed discretely behind. Thomas was already there, his white cotton shirt open to reveal several loops of gold around his neck. He stood to greet me. "We are lucky to be alive," he said warmly. "You especially. You did not tell me you had hired private security."

"I didn't know I had. I guess some people back home do like me after all."

"Very fortunate," he said.

I ordered a Western breakfast. Thomas had fruit and a croissant.

He leaned towards me, lowering his voice. "What happened yesterday is why I said you should not come back here. There's no reason you needed to do this for her."

I thought of Andrea, and the echoes of her that bounced back at me from every corner of the city. "I've got more reasons to be here than I thought."

"Clearly other people know you are here, too. I assume you'll let me finish the task, and get yourself back to safety?" He said it urgently, almost hopefully.

"Speaking of knowing that I'm here. Those men were at the restaurant when we arrived. They knew we were coming."

Thomas nodded. "I have fired my driver. I can only assume he told those men where we were going. I'm sorry for that."

"Did anyone else know?"

He shook his head. "But that does not matter. What matters is getting you out of here. I have already reserved a flight to Bikoro for tomorrow morning. I will spread her ashes. You have my word."

"I'm going to Bikoro."

He scowled, but I could see nervousness, too. "Those men may try again."

I shrugged. "You don't have to come."

He locked his eyes with mine. "Stanley will be there, you know."

"I know. He called me, in Boston. He said it just an oversight on Andrea's part, leaving this task to me in her will. He said it should be him doing it."

"A lot of people would say he's right. She was his wife."

"She was mine first. Regardless, I told him I didn't think it was a mistake." I gave Thomas a wry smile. "Actually, his call is probably what made me decide for sure that I'd do it."

"You're still that angry?"

I know what Thomas meant. Years earlier Stanley and I had crossed paths, and swords, competing to acquire a hot biotech startup. He'd won that contest, in ways I'd considered underhanded. It had taught me something about Stanley, but it was not a grudge I'd carried for long.

"No. That was just business. Besides, the acquisition was a bust. He actually saved me money."

"Then why not let him do it?"

I paused for minute, deciding how to share with him the thing it had taken me some time to admit to myself. "I guess I didn't realize until I got the news, about her death, how much I really missed her. This—this request—is the last connection I have to her. I didn't realize until Stanley offered to do it how much it mattered to me."

"Do you think it *was* just a mistake?"

"She meant it. I'm sure of it."

"Why you? I mean no offense, my friend, but you said you have not spoken to her since you left here."

"Thanks for reminding me."

He studied me for a minute, seeming to weigh his next question. "Did she tell you anything else? Give you any other reason to come?"

I thought again of the video and the ring, but decided those thoughts were for me alone. They were, in some ways, the last private moments she and I would have together. I just shook my head.

He picked at his fruit for a minute. "So be it. Don't say I didn't warn you. But I will go with you."

We sat in silence for a bit, finishing our food.

"Stanley and Genistar seem to be everywhere I look these days," I said.

"They're very involved here," Thomas said. "I told you. They are the only big drug company that's taken an interest in the problems we face here."

"The Ebola vaccine. You think there's a return on their investment?" Developing-world diseases such as Ebola were usually ignored by the multinational drug companies because there were no wealthy patients or big insurance companies to pay for the prescriptions.

His face darkened, as it had in the restaurant, surprising me again with the suddenness of the change. "All returns can't be measured in dollars, Alan. What we've been doing here—me, Andrea; you, when you were here—it doesn't work. It doesn't scale. It depends too much on people that don't give a damn about the people we're trying to save. Genistar has new thinking. I'm willing to bet on that."

"You and the Chinese."

"Don't knock the Chinese. They're putting money into this region in ways the Westerners never did. Ports. Railways. They're not colonists."

"There are lots of ways to colonize," I said. "There's always a price to pay."

"You spend one day back here and now you want to judge us on how we're trying to improve these people's lives?" He was not even trying to contain his anger anymore. "The Congo has paid a price for three hundred years. It's time for a change. If that takes some bold thinking, then so be it."

"I won't argue with you there," I said. King Leopold II might have died before World War I, but the echoes of his greed and cruelty still reverberated in the Congo. A memory of a cocktail party years back flashed into my mind, where a group of Americans were decrying the brutality of Congolese rebel groups for their practice of cutting off the hands of the people who defied them. "Only in Africa," one of them had said, shaking his head, as if such backward cruelty was a unique flaw of that troubled continent. I explained to the group that that practice was in fact a European import. King Leopold's administrators had given every man in the Congo a quota for ivory, gold, rubber or whatever else they produced to enrich his wealth. Those who came up short would have a hand or foot cut off as motivation to the rest. If the man needed both hands to do his work effectively, then his wife or children would suffer the consequences instead. I told them about a photo I had seen of one such man, sitting on a wall, contemplating the severed hand and foot of his five-year-old daughter, almost doll-like in their delicate size, laid out in front of him as a reminder of his lack of productivity.

I wasn't invited to their next party.

Thomas took a breath and regained his composure. "I will see you at the plane tomorrow," he said. "We'll say goodbye to Andrea and then you can go home."

He left, but I stayed at the table for a bit longer. Thinking over Thomas's words, I felt as though I'd become some sort of intruder to him, no longer connected to the work we had done together. I wondered how he'd become enamored by Genistar and Stanley Reston. And how Andrea, so single-minded and independent, could have fallen under Stanley's spell as well, enough to go to work with him. And marry him.

But then again, the Andrea who'd become part of Genistar was a woman I could not pretend to know any more.

I put that thought out of my mind, signed for the breakfast, and headed out to ruin Henry's day.

Chapter Ten

HENRY WAS SITTING at a table in the corner, holding a copy of *L'Avenir*, one of the more popular daily newspapers in Kinshasa.

"Get the car," I said to him. "I'll meet you out front."

"I can't do that."

"I'll give you directions on the way."

He shook his head violently. I figured that while I was talking with Thomas he'd called back to the office and gotten some instructions. I guessed they did not include letting me take him on a blind drive through Kinshasa.

"I'm the client, Henry. If you want, have Marco call me. Or he can come, too. But we're going. Or I'll call an Esprit de Mort and get there on my own. You can chase me around the city, at least until one of us dies."

Henry blanched at that thought. "Esprit de Mort," French for "Spirit of Death," was the slang name for the rundown, rattling taxicabs of Kinshasa, which had earned the name through the steady stream of spectacular accidents and deaths they caused for their passengers. "I'll get the car," he said. "Don't come out of the lobby until you see me."

I saw the white Range Rover appear a few minutes later and met him at the curb. He came around and opened the second-row door for me but I climbed in the front instead. "It'll be easier for me to direct you from up here," I said. The truth was Kinshasa had changed a lot in the years I'd been gone and I wasn't entirely sure I could find the place I was looking for—especially since I'd never actually been there myself.

I directed him to head south out of the city center on the Avenue Luombo Makiadi, working our way out of the business district, past the football stadium and into the endless rows of ramshackle housing and dirt roads that were home to 10 million people in Kinshasa. Henry was getting increasingly nervous. He made two calls to the office as we got further and further from the city center, explaining generally where we were headed. After his second call my phone rang.

"What's up, Mr. Wright?" It was Marco, calm but forceful.

"I'm checking in on an investment."

"Not many places to invest your money, out where you are," he said.

"Depends on your kind of investment," I said. "Don't worry. Henry will be safe."

He laughed, but without much humor. "Tell Henry where you're going. I've got another car shadowing you as best they can, based on your general direction."

"Are you in that one?"

"No, but Atombe is."

I considered my options, but Marco didn't wait for a response. "For God's sake, Mr. Wright. If we wanted to kill you, Henry could pull over and do it right now. All you're doing is making our job harder." He paused for effect. "Hell, if you keep this up, maybe I'll have him do it anyway."

"Your customer focus leaves a lot to be desired," I said.

"So does your cooperation." There was a pause. "Look, we're really just here to help. Can we drop the guessing game?"

I could hear the exasperation in his voice but also what sounded like actual concern. "Okay," I said, and described the place I was looking for.

I was surprised when he said, "Oh, for Chrissake. At-ombe knows it. Henry does, too." Next to me Henry nodded in confirmation, but a nervous look crossed his face.

"See, isn't my way easier?" Marco said.

"Okay, we'll try your way for a while."

I hung up. Now that I didn't have to struggle to find landmarks, I could focus on the sights around me. We'd passed from the glass towers and stone government buildings near the hotel through the suburban homes of the wealthier residents, and now we were in the shantytowns that ringed the city center. Kinshasa was the biggest French-speaking city in the world, and one of the fastest-growing cities on the planet. Unfortunately, government corruption and political unrest meant growth was not accompanied by any sort of infrastructure investment or public services. Health care and education were almost non-existent.

The roads away from the city center were merely dirt tracks between rows of concrete or plastic and sheet-metal structures. Garbage was piled in almost every open space. The splashes of color I'd seen from the airplane were all around me now—lines of clothes strung on thin cords or draped over walls, drying in the sun.

Henry picked his way around the adults walking along the roadside, carrying everything from water jugs to furniture on their heads. In some places young kids played in the street, kicking soccer balls fashioned out of rags. Eyes flashed up at the expensive vehicle, but no one made any attempt to challenge us. Cars like the one we were in generally belonged to government officials or wealthy expats. The National Police in the DRC were brutal, and while crime between Kinois out here would be ignored, the locals knew better than me that any attempt to rob a government vehicle would be a quick path to a beating or death.

We came to a wide, open space fronting a brick building which was much larger than the structures around it. While I'd never seen it in person, I recognized it instantly and felt a burst of excitement and pride. But those were quickly washed away by a wave of sadness, which drained away in its turn, leaving the usual residue of guilt.

I'd spent three years thinking I'd never actually see the building. One I'd helped to build with wire transfers from the other side of the world, but that Andrea had no doubt passed through a dozen times. Now I was in front of it. And Andrea was gone.

I wondered suddenly if any of the footprints in the dust were hers.

A group of kids, easily 20 strong, filled the dusty yard. The older boys and a few girls kicked around an actual soccer ball, brand new and jarringly bright in the sunlight. The rest of the kids sat in the shade thrown by the building. The building itself was well-constructed, with barred glass windows and even some struggling plantings against the foundation. I studied the condition of the roof and the structure, happy to see all looked good. There were two doors to the building, steel doors separated by an expanse of brick and a row of windows. The door closer to us opened and Sephora appeared. She was in her late thirties, short and round, with

70

long black hair tied behind her head with a piece of string. She wore a colorful dress, but left her hair plain, which made the patch over her left eye stand out even more starkly. She strode briskly towards the Range Rover, a wide smile on her face, wiping her hands with a white towel. As I stepped out into the sunlight on the passenger side, she froze, the towel falling unheeded to the dirt. She put a hand to her mouth. I stopped as well and waited, giving her a chance to get her head around my presence, wondering how she'd react. I knew she appreciated my money, but I wasn't sure she'd appreciate my presence. Sephora's kindness was legendary. So was her anger. I wanted to see which one would win out before I got any closer.

She didn't give me a chance to wonder for long. She broke into a slow trot, colliding with me hard enough to make me take half a step backwards, and wrapping her arms around me. The children crowded around, eager to see who their special visitor was.

"Alan, I am so sorry to hear about Andrea," she said quietly in my ear, in English. "I am sure you miss her, despite all that happened."

"More than I ever thought," I said, my throat suddenly closing tight.

Sephora had always had a way of bringing deep and unexpected emotion out in me. It was her kindness and optimism, and her utter lack of pretension. She challenged you to be better for the world around you, without ever saying a word.

Which was why I hadn't talked to her since the day I'd boarded that plane to Paris.

Her parents had died when she was very young, she'd told us soon after we'd first met; she'd said did not know

71

how. She'd gone to live with her grandmother and aunt, who'd already had too many mouths to feed. She'd been beaten for any manner of childhood failing, from forgetting a chore to a disrespectful glance. One such session had cost her left eye. Eventually, when some of her cousins had fallen sick, her grandmother and aunt had branded her a sorcerer, accusing her of causing the illnesses in her family, and sent her away. She'd become a Shegue, a street kid, one of tens of thousands in Kinshasa. She'd lived on the street for a year or more, fighting and running to protect her life and her maturing body from the older street children and at times the federal police themselves. Then she'd been taken in by a home operated by a local church. They'd performed an exorcism on her and, hot wax dripping on her arm, she'd confessed to witchcraft, knowing it was the only way to end the pain. Satisfied the demons were purged from her body, and happy for the show she'd put on for the parishioners, the minister and his wife had taught her to read, write and figure, and had given her shelter and food, as long as she cleaned their home. Once she'd mastered reading, she'd pursued it voraciously, tearing through books about medicine, and science, history and religion. She'd become an administrator for the church and started outreach programs to save other kids that had been branded as possessed like she had.

That's how we'd met her. Andrea liked to visit the homes for the Shegues in Kinshasa or the other big cities, bringing them whatever medical supplies we could spare from the clinics we managed, plus food we bought ourselves at the local markets. Andrea's face would light up whenever we set foot in one of the centers, or when we stopped in our travels so she could give food or money to street children who sometimes, at first glance, appeared to be not much more than piles of rags on the roadside. Andrea had known better than I ever could what monsters those children faced every day. She'd face her own, in a nice house in suburban America.

We'd met Sephora at one of the homes she was managing and taken an immediate liking to her irrepressible spirit and keen mind. She'd shared with us her lifelong dream to open a new kind of shelter for the Shegues based on education and medicine. When I sold my first company back in the States, I'd set up a fund to let her fulfill her dream. She was a relentless, creative whirlwind, tackling the seemingly endless obstacles thrown in her path by government bureaucracy, corrupt officials and failing infrastructure. I'd only known of her progress through photos and phone calls, but it had been miraculous. Now she operated four centers, each able to care for 50 or 60 children at a time. The centers offered food, basic healthcare, and basic education in reading, writing, math and trade skills such as carpentry or weaving. They also offered something equally valuable: safety. Many of her earliest charges were now emerging from her programs to make a living and start families of their own. Her success was a drop in the bucket compared to the 20,000 or so street children estimated to live in Kinshasa at any one time, but it was a start.

She looked up at me, right eye shining from tears. The she stepped back and put her hands on her hips, a bit of the anger rising in her voice. "You should have called."

I smiled ruefully. "I'd sort of forgotten how to do that."

"Yes, you have."

I looked at the building "You've put the money to good use, I'm glad to see."

She rolled her eye at me. "Money is no substitute for connection."

"I know. But it's been the only one I had."

"You have forgotten how to be a friend, too?"

I just looked at her, unable to put into words how true that statement was. I was, once again, realizing just how much I'd forgotten in my days in Boston.

She paused for a minute, clearly considering what to say next. As I'd hoped, kindness won out.

"But you are here now. I will show you around."

While were talking the second Range Rover pulled up. Atombe stepped out and approached us. "Bonjour, Mademoiselle Sephora," he said, with a mock bow. She smiled in return and gave him a hug of his own.

I looked at him, my eyes asking the obvious question.

"When we have free time, we stop in on these centers," he said. "Just to let the locals know that these places are to be respected. Not just Sephora's, but others, too." He smiled and winked at Sephora. "Although hers are my favorite ones."

Sephora clucked and shook her head at the compliment. "Atombe and the others make sure everyone knows these children are to be left alone," she said. "And Marco intercedes with the Federal police when we need help. It works, for the most part."

Atombe looked questioningly at me in turn. "Sephora is an old friend," I said. "We met a long time ago."

"Not so long ago," she said with mock indignation. "I am not so old as that." We all laughed. I realized it felt good to laugh, and how easily Sephora could bring joy out in even the most difficult of circumstances.

"Come in," she said, motioning towards the door.

I turned back to invite Henry. Atombe touched my arm. "Let him stay in the car," he said. "The Shegues frighten him."

"He believes in the stories?"

Atombe shrugged. "Henry won't say he believes anymore. But he doesn't *not* believe either, you know? It is our religion, after all."

While the people of the Congo were mostly Christian in name, the often-violent intersections of local beliefs—which included mysticism, magic and sorcery—with the Christian traditions of exorcism and redemption had resulted in a unique religious mosh pit of beliefs and practices. Local churches made significant money charging for exorcisms and other ceremonies to identify and ward off evil spirits, which oftentimes were thought to be most powerful when they inhabited children. Stories of packs of witch children flying over the cities at night, or children waking from their sleep to eat the flesh of their parents or siblings were common and often taken as faith. Oftentimes when a child was orphaned by war or disease, their relatives would brand them a Shegue, claiming the child had caused the family's troubles through sorcery, and send them out of the house. They claimed it was to protect themselves from the evil, but in reality, they were often just saving themselves from an extra mouth to feed. That had been Sephora's fate.

We went inside the center. There were two big rooms, separated by a short hallway that had bathrooms and a door marked "Private." Plastic chairs were set up in rows in the two bigger rooms, facing a blackboard, and locked drawers lined the back wall. Thin pads, rolled up and tied with twine, were stacked against the side walls in those two rooms. Each pad had a name written on it. "The big rooms are classrooms in the day and sleeping rooms at night. One room for the boys, the other room for the girls," Sephora said. "And my room in the middle to keep them apart."

She told me about the progress of the children, the relationship with the local police and religious leaders, and the general state of Kinshasa and the DRC. "Some things are better since the wars," she said. "But others are the same or worse. We will see what happens after Kabila leaves."

We finished the tour. Atombe and Henry headed back towards the cars. Atombe had said he'd drive me back to the hotel. Henry would trail us in the other vehicle.

I lagged behind with Sephora. Once Atombe and Henry were out of earshot I turned to her, and took a breath, asking the question I'd held since the moment I'd set eyes on her. "Did you see her much?"

She smiled sadly. "I wondered if you would ask. I used to. Many times the first year after you left. But not for a while."

"What was it like, for her. After."

"She was angry. And sometimes she'd get blue. For days sometimes. You know how she was. The work always brought her back. But after she got mixed up with that big company? She came by once or twice, but never again. Not for almost a year."

"What changed?"

Sephora shrugged. "The last time I saw her, she seemed excited. She said that soon everything would change. That she was on the verge of something amazing. She didn't say what it was. And she never came again."

"I wish I hadn't left." I surprised myself by saying it out loud, but that was the effect Sephora had; all pretense went out the window around her.

"She missed you, too."

"I'm sorry." I gestured at the building behind me as I said it, but she knew I meant it for much more than just my lack of phone calls.

"I know. But it was not your fault. Or hers."

I smiled and hugged her tight, partly as a goodbye, mostly so she wouldn't see the doubt in my eyes. Then I met Atombe back at the car and climbed in.

"So, you are the one," he said, as we worked our way back towards the city center.

"One what?"

"One who helps pay for all that," he said, motioning with his head back towards the place we'd just left.

"I help out, yes."

He just nodded, considering that thought.

"But sending money is easy," I said. "You do the harder part, I think."

"This is our country. It's our job to do it. Why do you help?"

I stayed silent for a minute. "I did some things in this country I am not proud of."

He continued to study me. "Most people who come here can say that by the time they leave. Most don't try to do anything to make up for it." He paused for a moment, hesitating over his next words, then spoke again. "Marco told me what happened last time you were here. Is this your way of paying your debt for those men?" He seemed more curious than judgmental.

I shook my head, both sad and angry, thinking about the urn on the shelf. "I owe them nothing. This debt isn't one I can ever repay."

77

Chapter Eleven

MARCO WAS WAITING in the lobby of the hotel. He was wearing khakis again, and a solid blue shirt, sleeves rolled up to his forearms as usual. "You have a few minutes to chat?" he asked casually, although I didn't think he intended to give me much of a choice.

We took a table in the Cockpit Bar. I ordered a beer. Marco nodded for the same.

"Drinking on the job? I ought to report you to Frank," I said, laughing.

"Just being polite to a client," he said. The bottles arrived and we clinked the necks together, then and sat back in our chairs. The bar was mostly empty in the early afternoon. It would be full in a matter of hours, once the offices and embassies emptied out.

He took a drink from his beer. "I did some asking around. Nobody in the government seems to have any interest in you."

"Somebody dragged me out of that restaurant."

"Yes, they did." He spoke in a calm, measured way, with a confidence that almost made me forget it was my neck we were talking about. "But I don't think it's connected to the things you did last time you were here."

"The guy in the car said that some people remember what I did here. It has to be tied to that."

"Did the men you killed have a connection to the mining companies or other multinationals?"

"No, I don't think so."

"But other people knew what you'd done here, right? Or could find out?"

"I guess."

"Your ex-wife knew."

I felt the anger rise. "What are you saying? That she lured me back here just to have me killed?"

He raised his hands. "I'm not making judgements. All I'm saying is the guys who tried to take you weren't working for local people. They were hired by a Westerner. Somebody who clearly knew about your past, based on what you told me that guy said to you in the car. That narrows the range of possibilities, don't you think?"

"That one's not possible."

"What about her new husband?"

I shook my head. "Stanley probably doesn't like me much, but he runs a global corporation. He's not going to have me killed just because Andrea chose *me* to bring her ashes here."

"Anything you did back in the States that would maybe give someone reasons to want to mess with you here?"

"Nothing I can think of," I said.

"Okay," Marco said, acknowledging my answers but clearly not accepting them. He had a way about him of just sitting still, but somehow occupying more than just the space around him. In some undefinable way his strange, calm presence reminded me of the urn on my hotel room shelf. I also got the sense that he would be impossible to rattle and hard to fool. I realized I took an unexpected comfort in that.

He took another pull off his beer. I noticed that despite his regular, enthusiastic pulls on his beer, only a fraction of the beer was gone from the bottle. He was still on the job, after all, I realized.

"Thomas has offered to fly me with him to Bikoro," I said.

Marco just shook his head. "I arranged for a plane and a pilot I trust. I don't fly anybody else's planes in this country. Your friend can come with us if you like."

"You worried about my safety again?"

He shook his head. "I worry about my own. The airlines here haven't gotten much better since you left. Neither have most of the private rigs."

I nodded. The year I'd left, the local airlines had been second only to Russia in the number of crashes. I wasn't surprised it hadn't changed much. "I'll let him know." I paused, wondering how Marco would take the next bit of news.

"I'm not coming back with you, though," I said.

He tipped his bottle towards me in mock salute. "That's the confidence I was hoping for."

"It's not that. I have another stop to make after that. A few hours north of Bikoro."

"That's crazy. You can't get there. It's all blockaded."

"It's okay. I can hire a car in Bikoro. I'll talk my way through somehow. I sort of want to do it alone anyway."

"The night life's not what it used to be up there. Not since they lost electricity anyway. And the Ebola thing hasn't helped."

"I've got another promise to keep," I said.

"You seem to make a lot of those,"

81

"These are the first in a long time, actually. I sort of got out of the habit."

I waited for his pushback. To my surprise he just nodded solemnly. "It's a hard habit to keep. And hard to let go of." He studied me for a minute. "I'll get a car arranged for you. Let Atombe go with you from Bikoro. But if the police or military turn you back, you don't try anything, okay?"

I nodded.

He dropped a few bills on the table. "I'll also have somebody around the lobby tonight." He paused and locked eyes with mine. "You are eating in tonight, yes?"

"Yeah. I have some reading to do."

He said goodnight and slipped out of the dining room, moving so smoothly that if the room had been full of water up to his waist, I don't think he'd have left a ripple.

I ordered grilled chicken and vegetables from the waiter and asked that the food be sent to my room around 6, with a couple more bottles of beer, then I headed back upstairs.

I had time before dinner, so I put on a pair of shorts and a T-shirt and found the hotel gym. It was nothing elaborate, but there was a phalanx of treadmills facing a TV, and a reasonable set of free weights. Back in the States, I'd felt like I was in decent shape, but faced with the younger, fitter men in the restaurant I was embarrassed by how slow and weak I'd gotten over the years. I knew I'd never be 30 again, but I felt the urge to keep working off whatever rust I'd brought with me.

I spent a half hour on the treadmill then turned to the weights. The burn in my chest and arms felt good. I pushed myself harder than I should, part of my mind lecturing me that sore muscles would not be any help in the next few days if trouble came for me again. But I didn't stop. Part of me realized, as the sweat formed rivulets that turned quickly to streams along the hollows of my nose, that it wasn't just embarrassment that was driving me. It was a need to burn off the feelings of anger and grief that were building, feelings reinforced by every smell, every sight, every mention of Andrea's name in this country. And that need was laced with a desire to burn the pain of Andrea's loss into my most basic memory, deep into the sinews of my muscles and the rhythm of my heart, so far down into me that I'd never again forget what she'd meant to me.

Finally, when the salt from my sweat was stinging my eyes so badly that I could hardly see, I hit the "Stop" button. I went back to the room and showered.

Just after 6, there was a knock on the door and my dinner was wheeled in. I ate the chicken and vegetables, washed down by the first beer, then opened the second one as I spread out the contents of the envelope from Andrea again, using the bed as my workspace.

I thumbed through the pages. Handwritten notes on music choices that seemed pulled straight from my past with her, the memories of them plucking at the strings of my heart. The table layout caught my attention again, so calculating in the names and the priorities. The choice of guests was too political, the food choices too frivolous (Swiss chocolates on every table? Andrea hated chocolate). I spotted the name of the guest she'd gotten wrong in her toast; Doctor Huang. He was listed as chief scientist for Genistar, and a guest of honor, even though it was clear from the video that he'd not attended the wedding. His name seemed an especially odd one for her to get wrong since she must have worked closely with him, which perhaps explained Stanley's ire at her gaff. The thought of Stanley's public displeasure made me angry in a way I did not expect; I realized I resented the idea that, even before their wedding day was complete, he was already reducing her to nothing more than some creature he felt he had the right to judge and admonish.

As much as I struggled with the contents of the envelope, I had no doubt they were authentic. The hand-written notes, underlined and starred in her unique style, the absentminded doodles in the margins—all proved that to me. But, while the papers may have been born of Andrea's wishes, they were like the contents of the urn to me; they were Andrea, but not Andrea at all. And like the ashes in that plastic container, I found I could neither fully embrace their meaning nor let myself turn away.

I'd felt that same sense of odd duality watching the video, but I'd assumed that it was me—that I had been trying to strain the new Andrea, Andrea *Reston*, through the filters of my memories and the recollections of the woman I had known; to force her back into that box, that time. But looking at the papers laid out on the hotel bed, the feeling seemed more than that, somehow. I was staring at a mosaic of images, of statements that didn't seem like her and that didn't tie together in any clear picture I could understand, but that resonated somehow, as if at a frequency just below my understanding. The way the package was delivered, the contents themselves, the strange way she'd led me to the ring; it felt as though it was all supposed to mean something more to me, but it was a message I could not decipher.

My mind wandered back over the years, to an outdoor table in Mbandaka, a few hours north of Bikoro. Andrea and I had been sitting together, in the cooling air of the late afternoon. We were both exhausted, returning from a trip along dirt roads no better than goat tracks, coming back from the east, where the fight had been raging. The human carnage had been almost unbearable. Hunger, disease and violence had killed tens of thousands in a matter of months, with more to come. Our efforts, and those of the other NGOs, were almost laughable in the face of the scale of the suffering.

We'd sat in silence, each nursing a bottle of beer.

"I'm sorry, I've got nothing to say to make it any better," I'd said to her eventually, feeling I needed to fill the quiet. "I can't even find words for any of it."

She'd just looked at me and smiled, a tired, wise smile that lifted my heart at a time when I'd thought nothing could lift it. "It's okay," she said. "You don't need to talk for me to know."

We'd sat in silence for a while more, but I realized then that the silence was nothing to fear. It was a warmth that enveloped us like a blanket. An open space that created room for a deeper kind of communication. In that moment I'd felt a connection to Andrea through the faint breeze that came from the west, ruffling her hair before touching mine. It was in the fading light that bounced from my skin to hers. In the rising of her chest and the falling of mine as we shared the same air, and the same feelings.

I'd never felt closer to anyone. Or more hopeful for the world, despite the horrors we'd just seen. In that moment I felt it was a connection that could never be broken.

Back then I would have known instantly anything she'd intended, her meaning clear from a single word or a quick glance across a crowded room. But now, lying on the bed, surrounded by the documents, I felt at once closer to her than I had in years, yet reminded more than ever of how much space had grown between us.

I rolled off the bed, walked out to the sitting area and dropped onto the couch. I looked up at the urn sitting on the shelf. I studied it, trying to avoid the feeling that it was studying me, too.

"Any ideas?" I said finally, raising an eyebrow towards it.

I was met by silence. Which, I decided, was better than judgement.

Chapter Twelve

WE MADE IT to N'Dolo airfield around 9 in the morning. A dozen fragile-looking propeller planes were scattered about aimlessly on the grass like cows out to pasture. To anyone unfamiliar with air travel in the DRC the motley mix of aging, dilapidated machines would seem more like a junkyard for discarded aircraft than the backbone of the DRC's domestic air travel industry. Those planes however, and others like them, were key to transport in a country that was two-thirds the size of western Europe, but with almost no highway or rail system. The planes bracketed a runway that was really nothing more than a half-mile strip of tarmac. There were no runway lights or radio towers in sight.

As humble as it was, N'Dolo held one of the most horrific records in aviation history. About two decades earlier, an overloaded Russian plane on lease to Africa Airlines overshot the runway at takeoff and slammed into the busy Simbazikita street market just beyond the airfield. Four of the six crew on the plane survived, but more than two hundred people simply out for a day of shopping were not so fortunate. The images of the aftermath had been heartbreaking and surreal, with the giant tail of the plain still intact, jutting out of the smoking ruins of the market. The crash had set the world's record for the most ground fatalities from an accidental airline crash.

I hadn't checked, but I suspected the record still held.

Atombe pulled the car through a gate that looked to have been stuck open so long it was generous to even call it a gate any longer and turned directly onto the taxiway. A twin-engine Cessna was idling halfway down the runway in front of a low building with a rusting corrugated roof. A hand-painted sign hung on the building read "Main Terminal." There were no other buildings in sight. It seemed someone in the DRC air transportation business had a sense of humor. The Cessna we approached was clearly not new, but it was cleaner and better-kept than anything else on the airfield. Atombe brought the car to a stop next to that plane and we climbed out. Marco shook hands with a tall, lean African man with salt and pepper stubble dusting his cheeks. Marco waved me over and introduced him to me as Alfonso, shouting to be heard over the steady drone of the engines. Alphonso had a relaxed but firm handshake and nodded in greeting as we shook. "Good day to fly," he said. I decided to take his word for it.

We tossed our gear into the back of the plane. I had a small duffel bag and the urn, now safely back in its cardboard box. I settled the box carefully between the duffel and the fuselage where it could not be jostled. Atombe dropped a longer bag next to mine, struggling with its weight, but mindful to avoid the box with the urn. He tucked a case of water into the storage bay as well.

The plane had six seats, with four set aside for regular passengers. Marco sat in the copilot seat. Thomas and I sat in the second row, with Atombe alone behind us in the third row. Marco and Alphonso shared a laugh at some private

joke I could not hear over the drone of the engines as Alphonso went through his pre-flight checklist. Alphonso's
motions were precise and practiced, and Marco was relaxed.
The seats themselves were comfortable and clean, as was the
rest of the cockpit. My confidence levels rose a few notches.
Once we were buckled in Alfonso spun the plane around
towards the runway. He taxied to the far end and we were
airborne in a matter of minutes.

We curled around the eastern edge of Kinshasa and
headed north. The sea of tin roofs and splashes of color below
quickly gave way to green treetops and brown fields. I realized I'd forgotten the sense of scale that came, flying over the
DRC in this way. The massive expanse of jungle canopy was
endless, dissolving only when it met the haze of the horizon.
The sun, clawing its way up the eastern sky, glittered off the
mile-wide belt of the Congo River to our left. The powerful
river snaked north as far as the eye could see, and south to
the Atlantic Ocean, nearly 3,000 miles in length. Smaller rivers cut steep valleys into the plateaus below us. We leveled
out and headed north towards Bikoro as the breathtaking
view spooled out below our wings.

I'd probably done that flight two dozen times in the
past, ferrying supplies up to our main hospital in Bikoro and
satellite clinics in Makou and a few other locations closer to
the border with the Central African Republic to the north.
Every time I'd made the trip I'd struggled to imagine, looking down at the beauty of the country, how a landscape
that always seemed so peaceful could be home to so much
misery. Horrors almost too grim to witness played out daily,
in secret under the cover of the trees below or exposed to the
sky in the open plains to the north and east. Now, making
the trip these years later, I thought again of Andrea, pitting

herself against the evils that stalked this enormous nation, fearless for herself and endlessly hopeful in her ability to make a difference. She'd had a self confidence that came from humility, not ego; a conviction that she'd be successful not because she deserved to be, but because she needed to be, for the people she wanted so desperately to help. Sometimes that sense of responsibility boiled over into rage or frustration with the government or even with her fellow medical professionals—more than once I'd had to help mend fences between her and the administrators or other doctors she'd angered. And sometimes the ghosts of her past reached out and pulled her down into bouts of depression that drove her deep into herself. But her anger and pain were fleeting, and her passion was constant and impossible not to see. She ruffled feathers, but she never made enemies.

As the plane ate up the distance to Bikoro, I realized that a quiet melancholy had been slowly creeping over me. When I released Andrea's ashes into Lake N'tomba I would be letting go of my last connection to her. She'd be at rest, in a place she called home. I'd return, I supposed, to my life in Boston. But that seemed such a hollow future when laid against the epic scale of the land below me, and the equally limitless scale of Andrea's ambition to rid it of the diseases that ravaged it.

Andrea's remains, carbon and dust, sat safely tucked in the bay behind me. But for a moment I thought I heard a faint, joyous laughter over the thrum of the engines. Andrea's laughter, echoing up to me from the trees below.

Maybe, I thought, we could still speak in silence.

We stayed at altitude for only 30 minutes or so before Alphonso tipped the nose down slightly. I felt the lift in my spine as we began to descend. Ahead, and to the left, I could start to make out another shimmer of sunlight off water; a sheet of silver tucked between our glide path and the Congo River.

Lake N'tomba.

We closed the final distance to the lake in less time than I would have liked. Flying over the countryside I was just starting to feel like she was back in my life somehow, and I realized I was not ready to say goodbye again. But despite my reluctance the lake grew in size and clarity by the minute. It was a massive expanse of water. Soon it would pull her remains down to its depths, holding her forever. It was a fate she'd wanted, I know, but it was one I still resented for her.

Or maybe just for my memory of her.

Bikoro was a big town for this part of the country. Nearly 10,000 people lived there, pulling sustenance from the lake or farming the lands nearby. There had been an effort by some foreign aid organization to build a commercial fishing center in Bikoro, providing capital for processing equipment and new fishing rigs. It had stalled then faded, like so many initiatives did in that region, a victim of corrupt officials, an unstable political landscape or perhaps just the misguided enthusiasm of foreigners, attempting to imprint on Bikoro a shape of the world as they thought it should be.

Alphonso set the plane down gently onto the dirt airstrip and taxied to a small parking area where a white Toyota SUV waited. We unpacked our bags and tossed them into the back of the vehicle. Marco instructed Atombe to stay with the plane. He nodded. I saw Atombe pull a rifle out of the long bag he'd packed and slide it into the passenger side of the plane. Bikoro was far from the paramilitary groups that operated in the Northeast regions of the DRC, or even the poachers who'd recently killed two rangers and a journalist in the center of the country. I assumed Marco was still thinking of the men who'd come after me in the restaurant only a few days earlier.

In a matter of minutes, I was watching Bikoro roll by. The town was a collection of concrete and wood houses, criss-crossed by dirt tracks, and it seemed as though nothing had changed since the last time I'd seen it. Along the bank of the lake, fingers of land pushed out into the water, creating protected inlets where fishing boats were moored. A few large buildings still held fish processing facilities, the remains of the foreigners' efforts at commercialization years earlier.

The town square held a bustling market. Open-air stalls hawked vegetables and fish, bolts of bright cloth and various herbs and bits of jewelry. The air smelled of boiled fish and wood smoke. People milled about, mostly women, haggling over prices while keeping half an eye on the small children playing in the open spaces between the merchants. Life went on in Bikoro, despite the naive foreigners, the corrupt local officials, the shifting political climates, sudden violence and even despite the specter of Ebola, ravaging villagers only a few hours hike to the north. Life *always* went on in the DRC, it seemed to me, despite the best efforts of man and nature to disrupt and destroy it.

"I have hired a boat for us," Thomas said to the driver and to Marco. "It's on the north edge of the town." He turned to me and lowered his voice. "As I said, a few of her friends from the region are here. You may remember them. And Stanley, of course."

Of course.

Chapter Thirteen

THE DRIVER WORKED his way to the north end of the town, the ragged shoreline on our left, navigating around knots of people and the deeper ruts in the road. We passed a dozen hard-worked fishing boats, their hulls streaked with rust, before coming to two knots of people standing near a dock almost at the far edge of the waterfront area. One of the groups was one white woman and two men who appeared to be locals; there were six people in the other group, all Westerners, I judged, by the clothes. This larger group clustered around two black Toyota Land Cruisers perched on over-sized off-road tires. The big SUVs had extra gas cans mounted on the sides and banks of floodlights on the roofs. They exuded a combination of exorbitant cost and raw power that made me think they'd be at home either on a military base or in the garage of some internet billionaire's beach house.

Stanley Reston was with that group, standing a bit apart from the others, his red windbreaker unzipped as the day was already growing warm. What hair he had was close-cropped on the sides, and he was fully bald on top. The lack of hair, and his high cheekbones, gave him a monkish look that I'd always thought fit his personality. He stared out at the lake, seemingly lost in thought. I wondered if he was thinking of Andrea.

As we drew closer to the dock, I realized I did recognize the people in the smaller group, as Thomas had said I might. The two local men were Ernest and Rambe. The third person was an Italian woman named Theresa. Ernest and Rambe had worked with Andrea and me in Makoua and Bolenge further to the north. Theresa had replaced me as mission director when I'd returned to the States. I was shocked to see her still there. Most mission directors lasted a year or two at most, leaving either to chase higher ambitions or to flee the frustration and burnout that was a staple of the job.

All three wore the red shoulder patches and white jackets that marked them as aid workers and healthcare workers. The identification provided a fragile bit of protection in the safer parts of the country, although I'd read that recently the rebels in the east were threatening the healthcare workers on that side of the country, even as those workers tried to keep the Ebola breakout there from becoming a full-fledged epidemic. Three members of Doctors Without Borders had been killed in the past month alone, and two employees of WHO were still missing.

I introduced Marco to my three old friends then shared hugs and smiles. Thomas went to find the ship's captain.

"We never thought we would see you here again," Ernest said in English once we'd finished the hugs and back slaps.

"I never expected to be back," I said. "I thought the Congo had had enough of me."

"It seemed as though you had had enough of the Congo instead," Ernest said, but without anger.

"Do you go home after this?" Theresa said, her English thick with her southern Italian accent. She had been young to be a mission director three years earlier, all passion and fire. Now I could see the creases around her eyes, the effect of the tropical sun on her skin and the relentless pressure of the job. Her hair was still black, a mass of unruly curls kept short for convenience.

"I may stay a few more days," I said, thinking of my trip to Makoua. "Then back to Boston."

"Andrea was my idol," Theresa said. It hit me like an accusation of some sort, but I let it pass. These people had continued to work with Andrea in the past few years. I had no idea what challenges they'd shared, what they'd fought through together. I knew the camaraderie that living and working in the Congo built between team members who were isolated from almost everything else they knew, surrounded by death, illness and cruelty.

"She was my idol, too," I said.

Theresa nodded somberly, seeming mollified by my words.

"How are things further north?" I said, turning to the two men. "I want to see Makoua again."

Their faces darkened. "You don't want to go there," Ernest said. "The Ebola outbreak is bad. Worse than the government says, by far. And even if you wanted to, it's all closed off. Soldiers are patrolling the roads. It's almost impossible even for us to get in there." He tipped his head towards the contingent from Genistar. "It's *their* show now."

I glanced over at the Genistar crew. They looked more like soldiers than scientists, I realized. They all wore the same red windbreakers as Stanley, the Genistar logo embroidered on the right shoulder. They were worlds apart from the kind, selfless people I was standing with, and who I'd known to be Andrea's friends. I wondered briefly what had become of Andrea in the last few years; whether she'd bent Stanley Reston and Genistar towards her vision of a better world for the people of Africa, or whether the machinery of the giant company and Stanley's persuasions had twisted her towards his own view of a world measured entirely by power, profit and loss.

I studied Stanley again and this time he met my gaze. He nodded in recognition. There was nothing to do at that point except to walk over and shake his hand, which I did. He seemed leaner than I remembered, adding to the ascetic vibe, but his grip was strong. Neither of us made an effort to console the other. He reeled off the names of his companions. They each nodded in my direction in turn.

"A long way for you to come," Stanley said, once the half-hearted introductions were complete. His eyes lingered on the box I cradled in my arm. I realized he was probably just figuring out what it contained.

"She asked me to be here," I reminded him.

"An oversight of some sort, don't you think, given how things ended with you?"

"She wasn't one to make a lot of mistakes," I said. "Although perhaps she'd been making more lately, no?"

He ignored my jab and shot back his own instead. "She was happy. Happier than she'd ever been, I think."

I glanced down at the box in my arm. "Clearly."

He flashed a glance at me, visibly stung by that final remark. I instantly felt dirty for having said it. Not because of its effect on him, but because I realized I was making Andrea a pawn in my petty battle with him. I told myself that she deserved better. Especially on that day. Especially in that place.

"I do hope she was happy," I said to him. "I never wanted anything less for her."

Thomas called for us and we all made our way to the boat. The craft he'd hired was no different than the others along the waterfront; 30 feet or so long, the stern rigged with long poles and winches for fishing nets, the open bow area piled with rope netting and dirty floats.

I handed the box to Thomas, who was already on board, before I stepped across the opening between the boat and the unsteady dock. The group from Genistar came aboard as well, crowding the open spaces on the cramped deck. They clustered together around Stanley like a football team waiting to break the huddle. I saw Marco scowl as he looked them over.

"Not the friendliest bunch, eh?" I said.

"Some of them are armed," he said, turning towards me so that none of the group could guess what he was saying. "That seems pretty un-scientific to me. How'd your ex-wife wind up with this crowd?"

"I wish I knew."

I really did wish. The more I looked at them and the more I thought about Stanley Reston, the harder it was to picture Andrea in their company, throwing her talent in with their ideas or values.

Marco motioned towards Thomas. "Your friend is armed, too."

I tried to hide my surprise behind a shrug. "He's a wealthy man. People know that. I'm sure he's had to protect himself from time to time."

"Does he usually carry a gun?"

"Not that I remember," I admitted. "Feeling a little paranoid?"

"That's my job. I told you the guys who came after you were hired by a Westerner. That could be anyone in this Genistar crew."

"It wouldn't be anyone at Genistar. They're a global corporation, not a gang."

"Hard to tell the difference in this country."

We were moving well away from shore now, the chugging diesel engine pushing us along at a steady clip on the flat water. The lake was massive, the far shoreline just a thick streak of darkness on the horizon. Thomas had been standing with the Genistar people, chatting quietly with a man who appeared to be their leader. He left them and joined us. "Did she say anything about where on the lake she'd wanted?" he asked. I shook my head. "I think a little further out would be better," I said. I didn't like the idea of her ashes washing back towards the shoreline, to mix in with the oil slicks and rotting fish carcasses by the docks. Thomas worked his way toward the cockpit and relayed instructions to the captain, who nodded enthusiastically. I didn't know how much Thomas had paid the man, but I was sure this simple boat ride for a strange mix of foreigners would net him more money than a week of dragging nets in the over-fished lake.

Theresa was standing near the railing on the port side, staring out across the water. I moved over to stand next to her,

"I will miss her," she said. "There is no one like her. At least not anymore."

"You're a bit like her," I said. "You're both trying to save the world. She was never afraid of a fight either."

She smiled briefly at the compliment. "It's not just me. It's a big setback for the program."

"Genistar seems to have that covered," I said. "At least according to what Thomas tells me."

Her face darkened. "There's something wrong with those people. All the secrecy. I don't know what it is, but they make my skin crawl. I could never understand why she went to work with them."

"I don't get that either," I said. "She must have thought they could help in some way she needed."

"I guess." She paused, gathering her thoughts or her courage. "I meant what I said. She was my idol. But something changed in her. When you left. She got more frustrated, more angry. Not just when people didn't live up to her expectations, but all the time. She wanted to move faster. She got consumed even more by the idea of ending the diseases here once and for all. It wasn't just about helping people—it was like she needed to finish it all somehow. She lost herself in it." She met my eyes, a mix of regret and compassion in hers. "I wondered if it was partly so she didn't have to think about you."

I swallowed hard. I'd always told myself that my leaving had made things easier for her. Without seeing me, I'd reasoned, she would not have had to remember what I'd done. Or what she'd done. It was almost too painful to hear that maybe that was not the case at all; that maybe all I'd done was turn my back on her when she'd needed me most.

The captain cut the engine, the sudden silence almost a physical force that brought all conversations to an end, and the boat drifted to a stop. We were in the middle of the lake, the shoreline a consistent dark line on the rim of the water all the way around. The masts of a few fishing boats were visible in the distance, but with the engines off and the air still, all I could hear was the lapping of the small waves against the steel hull.

Thomas came over to me, holding the urn, freed from its box once more. "It's time, my friend," he said. I took a deep breath. I'd thought a bit about what I'd say, and how I'd do this. But in the moment, all those thoughts left me. I looked around at the crowd, unsure what to do. Ernest, seeing my hesitation, stepped up next to me. He crossed himself and said a short prayer, in French. Then he offered another one in Lingala. Theresa, Thomas and Rambe crossed themselves, too, and bent their heads as Ernest spoke. Stanley looked on silently, showing no sign he wished to participate in the humble ceremony. The rest of the Genistar crew just shifted uncomfortably on their feet. Ernest looked at me and nodded. I removed the top from the urn, careful not to look inside. I wanted my memories of her to be about her face, her hair, her laugh, and not a few cups of ash and bone.

I stepped to the railing. "Goodbye, my love," I said quietly, the words coming unbidden from somewhere deep inside me. She *was* still my love, I realized, despite the years I'd denied that to myself. And perhaps, I began to think, despite Stanley's presence only a few feet away, I had still been hers. I turned the urn over, my eyes stinging from tears, and released her to the lake. The ashes formed a dark cloud in the blue-brown water. Most sank quickly into the depths, the rest diffusing slowly in a widening circle. I dipped the urn into the water and washed out the last of its contents. I watched for a minute until the cloud and the water became one in color, the ashes indiscernible from the lake itself. Just as Andrea had wanted it.

The captain waited patiently, the rest of the passengers silent in their own thoughts. Finally, I turned and nodded, and the captan brought the engine to life. We headed back toward the shore. The boat seemed to spring more brightly through the gentle waves then, as if happy to be relieved of its sad cargo.

I saw Stanley and Thomas by the rail and walked over to them.

"You are busy in this region," I said to Stanley. "Trying new approaches? Thomas was telling me."

Stanley flicked a glance of reproach at Thomas, then turned his gaze back out to the lake. "We're doing what we can. It's a hard problem. As you know."

"You have honored your promise to her," Thomas said, putting a hand on my shoulder, clearly eager to change the subject. "Now you can go home in peace."

"I'm starting to think I never should have left here," I said.

He shook his head. "This is not the place for you, Alan."

"Thomas is right," Stanley said. "I hear you've got a big deal in the works back in the states."

The negotiations with Zestra were supposed to be confidential, but I was not surprised Stanley had heard rumors. Information was a currency with the investment bankers and venture capitalists who served the deal-making process. And they'd all want to feel Stanley Reston owed them a favor.

"You know how those things are," I said. "Sometimes they work, sometimes they just disappear at the last minute."

Stanley smiled thinly. "Yes, they do. Safe travels, Alan," he said, and moved back to the knot of Genistar people in the back of the boat.

"Why do they have guns?" I said to Thomas. My question seemed to catch him by surprise, but he recovered quickly.

"Everyone is nervous after the killings of the aid workers."

"That's a thousand miles from here."

"It feels closer."

"Is that why you have one?"

He shrugged. "It's like I said, my friend. A lot has changed here. That's why you should go home."

He turned away and walked to stand next to the captain, leaving me alone to contemplate the water. We made good time back to the dock and all split off into our separate groups. Marco's satellite phone buzzed as we waited for the driver to bring the car around. He listened for a minute then said something terse in return. He put away the phone and motioned to me. "Somebody tried to slip something onto the plane," he said. "Atombe's holding them. We need to go now." The urgency in his voice was unmistakeable, and his eyes were brighter somehow, more alert, as he scanned the space around us.

I jogged over to my old friends and said a quick goodbye, then rejoined Marco. I waved Thomas over to me as the driver pulled up. We climbed in. I put the empty urn on the floorboards in front of me.

"Quickly, now," Marco said to the driver, and we headed off. There were not too many vehicles in Bikoro, but there was a line of them as we approached the marketplace, the traffic apparently waiting for a truck to unload some crates. Our driver slowed, ready to wait for the workers to finish their task. "No," Marco said to him. "Turn left here." The driver hesitated. "Now," Marco said, both command and threat in his voice. The driver obeyed. We sped along a narrow road, into a maze of side streets. "Go right here," Marco said, at the second juncture. He gave more instructions to the driver, each followed by "Quickly now." After the fourth turn, we emerged back onto the main road, on the far side of the market.

"I didn't know you knew this town," I said to Marco.

"I didn't. I memorized the streets last night," he said, matter of factly, as though he assumed it was something we all had done. He called Atombe again and told him we were five minutes from the plane. Thomas looked at me curiously at the sudden urgency. "Somebody tried to get into the plane," I said. He just nodded.

We reached the dirt strip in a matter of minutes. Marco had the driver pull right up to the plane. Atombe was standing with the pilot near the aircraft, the rifle in his hands now. The doors to the plane were closed, but Atombe glanced back into the cockpit once or twice as we approached.

Marco handed a few bills to the driver and jumped out, jogging the last few feet to where Atombe stood. I climbed out and followed, carrying the urn. Thomas lagged behind me.

"I stepped away for a minute to piss," Atombe explained to Marco. "Alphonso was having a cigarette over there," he motioned towards the grass field next to the runway. "I look back and I see the rear door is open, and there's somebody pushing something into it. She came out of nowhere." He jerked a thumb in my direction. "She says she's here to meet him."

"Where's she now?" Marco said.

Atombe reached back and swung open the door. Lying across the seats was an African woman in Khaki pants and a white shirt. Her wrists and ankles were wrapped with duct tape. She was slumped against the far window, black hair obscuring her face.

"Why'd you tie her up?" Marco asked. "She doesn't look like much of a threat."

"If we got more trouble, I didn't want to have to deal with her, too," he said.

103

The woman struggled to sit up at the sound of the door and turned towards us. There was a strip of duct tape over her mouth.

"Her mouth, too?" Marco said, surprised.

"That was so she'd stop yelling at me," Atombe said, sounding a bit sheepish.

I barely heard their words. My attention was on the woman. Above the tape they were discussing, a pair of shocking green eyes sparked with anger. They reminded me instantly of Andrea's eyes, full of intelligence and fire.

Below the tape, on the breast pocket of the shirt, was a Genistar logo.

The woman made a noise through the tape, trying to form words. I could not make them out, but they did not sound polite.

"She was carrying that," Atombe said, pointing to what looked like a plastic briefcase in the grass, 30 paces from the plane. "I thought it might be a bomb so I got it away from the plane."

"A bit further away might have been nice," Marco observed drily.

I put the urn down on the runway and walked over to the open door. I peeled the tape off the woman's mouth with a quick tug. She winced in pain, and then took in a few deep breaths.

"My nose is stuffy. You could have suffocated me," she said, glaring at Atombe.

"See?" Atombe said. He was clearly at a loss faced with this very attractive woman, totally incapacitated yet lecturing him like he was a schoolboy. He seemed both mesmerized and horrified.

"Who are you?" I said to her.

"I am Tshala. I worked with Andrea." A flash of what looked like pain passed over her face as she spoke.

Staring at those familiar green eyes and hearing Andrea's name come from her lips, my head spun, as I tried to comprehend such a living, breathing reminder of Andrea appearing in front of me so soon after I'd said my final goodbye. "What are you doing here?" I asked.

"Waiting for you," she said, eyes still blazing. "You took long enough."

"We had something to do," I said lamely, mind still reeling.

Her eyes clouded again for a moment. "I wanted to be there for that," she said. "But I promised her I'd do this."

"What were you putting on the plane?" Marco said. "Is it a bomb?"

"No, no. It's blood," she said. She motioned towards me with her head, her black hair tossing side to side with the movement. "Samples. For him."

Marco looked at me. I just shrugged in confusion, but I'd already decided that she was telling the truth—her grief when she mentioned Andrea seemed as real as mine.

"How did you know I'd be here?" I asked.

"She told me you would come. And that I should give the case to you. She could not tell me which day, but she said it would be around now. And that I should be ready."

"Andrea told you?"

"Yes of course Andrea. Who else would it be?"

"When?"

"The last time I saw her. A month ago."

Chapter Fourteen

MARCO LOOKED AT me again. I stared back, stunned, not from what the woman Tshala had said, but from what it implied.

"How did Andrea know you'd be here?" he said to me.

I looked at Tshala. There was already hurt in her eyes. I knew instantly she'd long ago reached the same conclusion now exploding to life in my mind.

There was only one way that Andrea could have known, almost a month before I'd stepped out of the airport, that I'd return to this place. She'd already been betting, well before her wedding, that I'd be here to spread her ashes.

I took a step back, that thought striking me like a physical force. I did not want to accept the possibility that Andrea had died, at least in part, simply to get me back to the Congo. It was impossible. It was stupid. Other questions swirled in my head, unanswered, perhaps unanswerable. Why hadn't she just called me if she needed me? Did she think so little of me that she was afraid I wouldn't answer? And if she didn't even trust me for that, then how could she trust me enough to know I'd honor her last request, one so outrageous that I'd thought more than once about denying it?

She must have known the risk, I realized. For whatever reason, she'd trusted in me anyway. And while her gamble seemed to be a mass of confusion and contradiction, underneath them all had to be something she felt was worth dying for. I needed to know what that was.

"Get that thing," I said to Atombe, pointing towards the case lying in the field.

He'd not even begun to move when I heard the unmistakable sound of a pistol slide being pulled.

"No. Stay where you are."

The words came from Thomas, who was still behind us. We turned in unison. He was standing a few strides away, the pistol in one hand, a satellite phone in his other. "Drop the rifle," he said to Atombe. The young man glanced at Marco, who nodded almost imperceptibly. Atombe laid the gun on the hard packed dirt. "You, too," he said to Marco, who reached behind his back to retrieve his pistol, crouching to place it on the runway as well, his eyes never leaving Thomas.

"What the fuck, Thomas?!" The anger drove the words out of me, despite the gun pointed in our direction.

He kicked the weapons out of reach, ignoring me. "Kneel down, all of you," he said. We obeyed. The tarmac was hard and hot on my knees. The image of the three men flashed into my mind. I'd made them kneel, too, before I killed them. For three years I'd thought that action had destroyed any trust Andrea had had in me. The idea raised by Theresa on the boat, that I could have been so wrong about what had happened after, still thrummed through my nervous system, concentrating in my gut like another punch.

"What the hell are you doing?" I said trying to get him to meet my eyes. The opening at the end of the gun barrel looked enormous even from this distance, but my anger was pushing away my fear. Whatever Andrea had intended, it was something he was trying to prevent. I had the urge to rush him, to pound him into the dirt, to make him tell me why she'd done what she did. If he even knew.

"Everyone just keep cool," Marco said. I wasn't sure if he was watching me, but his words broke the spell enough for me to realize I'd be dead long before I laid a hand on Thomas.

"I told you not to come back here," Thomas said to me. He sounded both angry and mournful. He held the gun awkwardly, almost uncomfortably. But he kept it pointed at us just the same.

He spoke quietly into his sat phone, then slipped it back into his pocket, putting both hands on the butt of the pistol. "Why did you bring that?" he said to Tshala, his head jerking towards the case in the grass.

"Stanley is out of control. Andrea knew it," she said, green eyes flashing in anger. "You know it, too."

"It's from Genistar?" I asked.

Thomas glanced quickly toward the road leading to the runway, then returned his eyes to us. He didn't answer.

"You work for those assholes now, too?" I said to him, the anger boiling more hotly.

"I told you. They're doing what we never could," he said. "What you decided not to do. It's what Andrea always dreamed of. They're going to cure disease here. Everywhere. For good."

"That's crazy."

"Why? You've become too arrogant back in Boston to think anyone could accomplish something you can't conceive of?" he said. "Andrea knew it could be done. She threw herself into helping. She believed in what Genistar

109

was doing. At least she used to. It was her breakthroughs that made everything possible. *Her* ideas." He shook his head. "But she was too afraid to follow through."

"She was never afraid," Tshala said.

"We had to keep going. We were too close." He said the words quietly, as though he was trying to convince himself of their truth.

"They killed her?" The anger that had started in my chest was a rage spreading through my whole body now, at the thought that her suicide had been faked—or hadn't been a suicide at all. I fought to keep control. I told myself that whatever Andrea had wanted me to do, I couldn't do if I died on a runway in the middle of nowhere.

He shook his head. "No. Stanley would never allow that." The way he said it made me think that killing her had been an option raised at least once, by someone. "She did that herself. I don't know why." His eyes met finally mine. "I wish she hadn't."

A cloud appeared in the distance, behind Thomas. It was a dust trail, thrown up by a vehicle. A vehicle moving very fast. I glanced over at Marco and Atombe. Marco looked relaxed, but his eyes were studying Thomas' moves like a cat watches a mouse. Atombe was keeping one eye on Marco. He didn't seem afraid either. He actually looked expectant, like a spectator waiting for a show to start.

The dust cloud behind him resolved itself into two vehicles not one, a pair of SUVs approaching fast. Black SUVs, with racks of lights on the roof. The Genistar people.

"Those must be your folks," Marco said, his weight shifting slightly backwards, craning his neck as if to get a better look past Thomas, his eyes turning toward the vehicles approaching from Thomas' back. Thomas turned a bit, following Marco's eyes. He studied the oncoming caravan for an extra heartbeat, trying to confirm that the distant vehicles were the ones he expected.

That was all it took.

Marco closed the distance with Thomas in a blur, somehow getting from his knees his feet faster than I could see. Thomas turned back at the motion, but he was far too slow. Marco kept his body low, his left arm flashing out and up, knocking the pistol upwards just as Thomas pulled the trigger. The gunshot was terrifyingly loud, but the bullet whizzed harmlessly over our heads. Then Marco exploded into Thomas, landing three quick blows with his right hand as he drove him backwards and onto the ground. He pulled the pistol from Thomas' limp hand and rolled to his feet. Atombe was already up, the rifle back in his hands. Suddenly more rounds whistled over our heads, accompanied by the clatter of gunfire. The Genistar team had seen Thomas go down, and jumped out of their vehicles, well over a hundred yards away. They'd opened fire from there.

Atombe squeezed off a few rounds in return, taking out the windshield of the first vehicle and causing the shooters to duck behind the vehicle for cover.

Alphonso used the break in the shooting to run around the front of the plane to the pilot's door. Seconds later, the engine coughed and the propeller started turning.

"Keep them down," Marco said to Atombe. "Don't let them take out the plane." There was no panic in his voice, just calm instruction. I was anything but calm. I'd heard the sound of bullets cutting through the air before, when our clinic in the east had been pinned down between government forces and rebels. But then we had been bystanders, not targets. I tried not to flinch at the unearthly hisses and buzzes of the bullets as they flew past.

Atombe fired off more rounds. A few shots were returned, one slapping into the fuselage of the plane, but the pistols our attackers held were no match for Atombe's rifle, either in range or accuracy, and the shooters stayed behind the vehicles, using them for cover.

"Everybody in," Marco shouted, as the engine came up to speed. He jumped into the co-pilot's seat. I climbed in as more shots sliced the air over my head. Atombe backed up around the nose of the plane, avoiding the propeller, still firing, preparing to enter the plane from the far side. One of the black SUVs started moving towards us, two men behind it jogging, using it for a shield as they closed the distance to the plane.

I started to pull the passenger door shut, then saw a reflection in the high grass.

The case was still there. The case that Andrea may have died to make sure I got.

Adrenaline coursed through my body. My skin crawled in anticipation, waiting for a bullet to strike me; the case seemed to be a mile away, with a cloud of bullets whistling past.

But I could not leave it.

I jumped back out of the plane as Alphonso started to turn back down the runway. I heard Marco shout something, but his words were lost in the engine noise and gunfire. I sprinted across the gravel. A bullet pinged off a rock front of me, and I felt the sting on my shins from the exploding stone. I reached the case and turned back towards the plane. I could see Thomas, still prone on the dirt, although I couldn't tell if he was still unconscious or simply trying to stay out of the line of fire. Atombe had the door on my side of the plane opened now. He was leaning out, firing back at the moving SUV, which was now only a few hundred feet away, the driver staying low on the front seat so Atombe could not target him.

I sprinted back towards the plane, which was rolling slowly down the runway, Alphonso trying to keep some momentum without pulling too far away from me. I heard a hiss and felt a tug on my sleeve as a bullet passed through the fabric. Atombe waved me towards him. I saw a flash of color out the corner of my eye as I ran. Andrea's urn, still sitting peacefully on the runway, the blue and yellow details bright and incongruously beautiful amidst the hail of bullets and showers of rock fragments. I slowed for a moment, thinking I could not leave that behind either. Then a bullet struck the fuselage near Atombe's head. He ducked and motioned to me to hurry. He emptied the rest of his magazine towards the SUV to give me cover. I glanced at the urn one more time then turned back and ran to the plane. Atombe dragged me in and we sprawled together onto the floor of the passenger compartment, Tshala still prone across the seats above us. The plane picked up speed, accelerating away from the SUV, pushing Atombe and me hard against the seat supports. In a few seconds we were airborne, climbing fast.

Atombe and I pulled ourselves to our knees. I turned back for a last look at the runway and thought, through the dust and distance, that I could see the tiny figure of Stanley Reston staring up at the plane, red windbreaker flapping in the breeze.

The hard plastic case I'd rescued from the grass bounced onto the floor of the cabin as we settled ourselves. "You need

113

to be careful with that," Tshala said, sounding nervous for the first time.

"You said it's not a bomb," Atombe said, suddenly alert.

"It's not. It's worse," Tshala said as the plane made a steep arc, turning back towards Kinshasa.

Chapter Fifteen

FOR THE FIRST few minutes of the flight Alphonso alternated between checking his instruments for any sign of damage to the plane and yelling at Marco that bullet holes were not covered by the charter costs. Marco laughed at the tirade, a good-natured laugh, and eventually Alphonso was laughing with him. They seemed already to have forgotten the firefight we'd just left. I breathed deeply, trying to calm my racing heart and jangling nerves. My skin still tingled, as though still anticipating the impact of a bullet.

"We have not done anything like that for a while," Alphonso said. "I don't like to move that fast anymore."

"It was good to see you can still do it when you need to," Marco said. "Mr. Wright's company will cover your repair costs, I'm sure." He said it loud enough to be sure I heard over the engines.

"Who wants to kill him so bad?" Alphonso said.

"Apparently everybody he meets here," Marco said.

I'd moved to the third row, giving Tshala space to struggle to an upright position next to Atombe.

"Take this awful tape off me," Tshala demanded. "I'm not a threat."

"Then why is our plane full of bullet holes?" Marco said.

She glared back me as though it was my fault.

"She's okay," I said, already convinced by the pain that I'd seen flash across her face when she'd mentioned Andrea. "We can trust her."

"How about we wait until we are on the ground?" Alphonso said. "We'll be there in twenty minutes. Shooting up the plane from the outside is bad enough. I don't need you wrestling each other on the inside, too."

"Why were you putting that thing on the plane?" Marco said.

"I told you. Andrea asked me to." She twisted her body in the seat to look back at me. "She said you would come here. She said you would be able to help her."

"Help with what?"

"I don't know," Tshala said. "She was scared. Very scared. And angry. I could tell. They never left us alone. But I heard her arguing once. With Stanley. A month ago. She wanted him to stop whatever they were doing. She said it was madness. He told her she was overreacting. She said it was her work and that she should be able to decide. He said it was bigger than her. After that, they watched her even more closely. They watched me, too, but mostly when I was with her."

"What work? What were you doing?"

"We set out to find a way to program DNA to fight diseases like malaria. Typhoid. Even AIDS. Andrea led the project. I helped her. We wanted something that could circumvent everyone who's always been in the way—the rebels, the corrupt officials, even the lack of roads or medical supplies."

That had always been Andrea's dream. Curing disease at a massive scale. Rendering the petty thieves, armed gangs

116

and money-grubbing officials helpless to hinder her efforts. "The *science* is there," she'd always said, "The *people* are the problem."

"That sounds like a good thing," I said.

"It started out that way. But then it changed. Genistar got new investors. New partners. They moved too fast. Andrea and the rest of us on her team were pushed to the side."

"It could save millions of people, what you described," I said, confused.

"That was the idea. But Andrea seemed to decide they were taking too many risks. That something terrible would happen. But I don't know what that was. I wasn't close enough to it. She suddenly wanted to stop the work. All of it."

"What had you built?"

"Andrea found a way to build a platform, a biological platform like a computer operating system. It can be inserted into people and used to reprogram DNA at a bigger scale. Not one person at a time, but many people at once. As many times as we needed to, like downloading a new piece of software. We could use it to treat everyone in the country if we needed to."

"That's impossible," I said. "There's not enough labs. Or medical teams. Or infrastructure."

"We wouldn't need them," Tshala said. "That's the key. We were close to figuring out how to do it without any of those things. That's when she got scared."

Thomas' words from the hotel came back to me. *New approaches*, he'd said, that would solve all those problems.

"So, what's in the case?" Marco asked.

Tshala set her jaw. "Once you let me out of this stuff, I'll tell you."

117

"We'll be on the ground in ten minutes," Marco said.

Tshala slipped into a sullen silence. Atombe sat next to her, alternately eyeing her and the case that sat on the floor between his feet. It was hard to tell which he thought was more dangerous.

I stared out the window, thinking of the urn sitting on the runway. One more connection to Andrea, taken from me. I hadn't thought about what I'd do with it, but when I imagined the people from Genistar, kicking it over, crushing it under their boots, a cold anger settled in my chest. I'd felt that anger before in this country, three years earlier. It had not ended well for the men who'd caused it.

The landing was smooth. Once we'd rolled to a stop, Atombe pulled his wicked-looking knife out of a sheath on his boot. "Time to set you free," he said to Tshala.

"You're going to use *that*?" She said, aghast.

"I've never used it before. But I will try and be careful," Atombe said, finally finding the nerve to tease her. "Or you can stay tied up."

She fell silent, and he expertly cut the tape around her wrists and ankles. She climbed out of the plane and stamped from side to side while rubbing her wrists as the blood flow returned to hands and feet.

"Okay, you're free. What's in the case?" Marco said.

"Blood samples," Tshala said. "Fifty of them, all from different people we'd been treating."

"Why's it important?"

"They are all people who have had the platform I told you about—the platform inserted into their DNA. Andrea wanted you to have it."

"Why not just take it to the government?" Marco said.

118

Tshala shook her head ruefully. "The health minister is working with Genistar. At first the government people supported the work—our work—to help reduce disease. But now they have other motives. Whatever Andrea was afraid of, they won't stop it."

"What about WHO?" Marco said. The World Health Organization was active in the Congo as well.

"They're desperate for Genistar's help. They won't want to believe there's anything wrong. And they are so slow."

"This platform—how do you get it into so many people?" I asked.

Tshala eyed the case again, which Atombe was now carrying.

"They use a virus," she said.

"That's not a big deal," I said. "Lots of genetic engineering is done using viruses."

"They use Ebola," she said. She said it bluntly, but the word, one of the most terrifying words ever spoken in that part of Africa, hung in the air.

Atombe froze, looking down at the case in his hand.

"Every one of those samples has an Ebola strain in it," she continued. "One they modified so that it wasn't deadly. Or so they thought."

"Ebola? Can you really make that safe?" Marco said.

"*Of course not*," Tshala said, her voice rising. "It's bloody *Ebola*." She shouted the last word, eyes wide, fear in her voice. Her tone dropped and she seemed to be staring a thousand miles away. "But they thought they could. They think they can do *anything*."

"How do you know they can't?" I asked, a terrible insight already dawning in my mind. *They wouldn't have*, I thought.

Even though I already knew in my gut that they had. It fit too well.

"They thought they had it right already, a few months ago. They experimented on a village north of Bikoro. It was supposed to help prevent measles. A controlled experiment on the village. But it mutated. Or evolved. Or just got angry. Who knows? It's bloody Ebola. It does what it wants. It started killing people. And started spreading."

"They *caused* the Ebola outbreak?" It was Atombe who put words to what I'd already feared.

"I think so. They were testing the virus. But the kill switch they built into it, to disable it if things went bad, didn't work right. So, it spread. That's why they shut the area down. They don't want anyone to know what they did."

"We need to get back to town," Marco said.

"You just can't drive a hundred samples of Ebola into a city of ten million people," I said. "You could kill half of them in a week if it gets out."

"We need to take it somewhere." Marco said.

"I'll do it," Atombe said. "I have friends outside the city. I can take it there."

Tshala gave me a hard look. "Andrea wanted me to give them to *Alan*."

"It's okay," I told her. "I trust them."

She eyed the three other men, clearly not sharing my confidence. "The samples are on dry ice in the case. They need to stay frozen. If they stay that way, then they should be safe."

"Okay," Atombe said. "I can do that."

"I can drive the rest of you back to the city," Alphonso said. "I'll sort out the plane tomorrow."

Atombe opened a hard-shell case containing a medical kit and other supplies in the back of his Range Rover. He dumped the contents out into the rear compartment and packed the medical case into the larger case, sealing around the edges with tape, securing it tightly.

"That'll do," he said and climbed into the driver's seat.

"Call when you get there," Marco said.

Atombe nodded and sped off. The rest of us climbed into Alphonso's Toyota and headed back towards Marco's offices. Marco put Tshala in the front and sat behind her, still wary.

"What's the kill switch?" I asked Tshala.

"She called it a molecular lock. Some sort of unique chemical compound. They can use it to neutralize the virus somehow, in case things go wrong. When the virus comes in contact with the molecule in the compound it shuts down. At least they thought it would. It didn't work right. That's what Andrea was trying to do at the end. Get it right."

"So that's what Andrea was afraid of? An Ebola outbreak? That's what she wants me to stop?"

Tshala shook her head. "I think she was afraid of something worse than that."

"What's worse than that?" I asked.

"She couldn't tell me. They cut even me off from her over the last month. She just said she'd send you something that would help. Everything I just told you is all that I know."

"All she sent me was her wedding documents," I said. "That's a pretty strange way of telling me."

"I don't understand either," Tshala said, frustrated. "But she told me she'd given you something that would help."

"It's not like we had a code or anything."

"It couldn't be a code. At least not a traditional one. They have people who would look for that. Whatever she sent you, Genistar's security people would have inspected

121

before it ever reached you. Every communication was monitored. Even her phone calls. Nothing would have gotten out if it said anything about what Genistar is doing. It had to be something only you two would know. Something that looked harmless enough, that nobody else could spot."

Something that looked harmless enough.

Andrea's first request, to spread her ashes, had been unexpected but not impossible to understand. It had sent me to Bikoro, where Tshala had been waiting. I thought of the video file, which had led me to the ring and the note; a note that, to Tshala's point, would seem innocent enough to anyone who did not know the origin of the rings.

My trip to Makoua was starting to make sense.

Still, nothing else in what Andrea had given me, strange as some of it was, had jumped out as a message. But I realized I hadn't really been looking for one. I decided I needed to look through the papers again. I wondered if the strange duality in the contents, where everything was clearly *from* Andrea, but not fully *of* her, may not have simply been the result of time and distance, but the opposite; she had built her code on the belief that I still knew her, well enough that I would spot the oddities she'd built into the materials.

She had trusted that we could still speak, without speaking at all.

A flood of emotions washed through me—love and loss, but above it all a sudden pride, in her faith in me, and the memory of what I liked to believe we'd been together.

We fell into silence for a few minutes in Alphonso's SUV. The dusty Toyota crawled through the heavy, chaotic tangle of cars, trucks, bikes and scooters. The normalcy of the simple houses giving way to the offices and shops of downtown, the bustle of traffic and pedestrians and the sounds of the city seemed impossible to me after what we'd just been through in Bikoro. I could still feel the tug of the bullet as it cut through my sleeve and hear the *pop pop* of the pistols and the sharper crack of Atombe's rifle. We reached an intersection controlled by one of the robotic traffic directors the city had installed to help manage the traffic flow. It was eight feet tall, probably designed to look friendly and vaguely human—but in the end had come out more like a bossy version of the Tin Man from The Wizard of Oz. Despite the retro appearance the robots seemed to work—the Kinois paid more heed to the strange devices than they did to the human police. The surveillance cameras probably helped with that. And unlike the local police, the robots didn't stop cars and shake down the drivers for money. As we waited, the robot turned on its axis and the pole that served as its right arm turned green, signaling us forward. It was another surreal moment in that surreal day, in a country where the machinery of government and the impulses of man were so maligned that a robot that looked like something from the 1950s was considered a more trustworthy authority than the police themselves.

"How was it?" Tshala asked, breaking my reverie. She'd turned in her seat so she could see my face.

It took me a minute to understand she was asking about the ceremony on Lake N'tomba. "I think it was good. I think she would have been happy with it."

"I'm glad."

She turned forward again and we lapsed back into silence.

Something worse than Ebola. I struggled to think what that could be. And started to think of Stanley Reston. The three men I'd killed had hurt Andrea and helped shatter everything we'd been. But I was starting to believe that some-how, Stanley Reston and Genistar had corrupted something else of profound importance to her: her work.

Chapter Sixteen

WE GOT BACK to the Hotel Memling in the middle of the afternoon.

"If the people from Genistar want to follow, it won't be hard for them to find out I'm staying here," I said. I thought of Thomas. "Odds are they know already."

"It's not a problem," Marco said. "This is a good location. Easy to get out if needed. And the people who run it are friends. But I'll put two people in the lobby from now on, just in case."

"Thanks."

"Don't thank me 'til you see the bill," he said with a faint smile.

"Just send it to Frank."

"What about me?" Tshala said. "I've got no place to go that's safe. I'm pretty sure I can't go back to the lab any time soon, if ever. And I could really use a shower."

"I'll get you a room here," Marco said. "And I can take you out to get some clothes and such if you like. I'll just add it to Alan's tab."

I nodded. "Whatever she needs. I have to make a call anyway. We can get together for dinner." I thought of the manila envelope with the wedding plans from Andrea. "And I need to do some reading."

I went up to my room and dialed Frank. He picked up on the second ring. "How did it go?" he said, somberly. He knew what today had been about for me, and I could tell his concern was genuine.

"That part went well."

"What part didn't?"

"We're going to get a bill for some damage to an airplane. We had a bit of trouble."

Frank's tone went from serious to worried. "In my experience, when a plane has a bit of trouble, people die."

"Not this time," I said.

"What kind of damage then?"

I took a breath. "Some bullet holes."

"Jesus Christ. You really did piss some people off last time you were there."

"This had nothing to do with what happened back then. And Marco's pretty sure that what happened the other day didn't either."

"Do I need to get you different security?"

I thought of Marco, calmly issuing instructions in the middle of the gunfight. "No."

"Well, it's over. You can come back now. And we need you. Remember the lawsuit from the Zestra deal? That's back. We need to show we can settle it before Zestra will move forward. You're going to have to get involved."

"I'll call their CEO," I said, half-heartedly.

"You can just meet with them when you get back," Frank said. "I'll set it up for beginning of next week. I've got a jet ready to get you Wednesday."

"I won't be back just yet." I said it and waited for his response. Which turned out to be about what I expected.

"Fuck's sake, Alan! What else is there to do in Africa?"

"There's something else I need to get sorted out. I'll tell you more in a day or so."

"This deal will unravel if you don't get back here."

Even though I knew he was right, I bristled. The deal that had been the high point of my career only a week ago seemed somehow irrelevant now, an abstract jumble of numbers and legal language. I told myself that was just the after-effect of my near-death experience on the runway, and the grief of saying goodbye to Andrea; that it would matter again soon. But I wasn't sure I believed that.

"Keep it going," I said anyway. "Tell them I'm on it."

He sighed. "So I should cancel the plane?"

I thought of the blood samples, and what Andrea and Tshala had gone through to get them to me.

"No, send it. I have something I need to get to Simone at Nuvostar. And it has to get there fast."

"Okay, boss," Frank said. I could hear the frustration in the last word, but I knew he'd do what I needed.

Nuvostar was one of the companies we'd invested in. It was an Israeli startup, focused on computational biology, building advanced computer models of viruses and proteins to enable much faster testing of new drugs and treatments. Simone was their chief technology officer; I'd met her at a conference in London while I was still doing aid work, and she was teaching at the Weizmann Institute near Tel Aviv. I'd recruited her to Nuvostar when I'd made my investment. At Nuvostar she'd gotten almost unlimited money for her research work, and a chance to build a world-class team to support her. She was brilliant, and still grateful to me for the opportunity I'd given her and her company. She could tell me faster than anyone else what was in those blood samples.

I decided, however, that I needed a shower before I considered anything else. As I stripped off my clothes, I noticed the tattered fabric on the sleeve of my windbreaker. It was hard to grasp that a bullet had come that close to me. And Thomas, my good friend Thomas, who'd dedicated his life to saving lives, had pointed a gun at me; nervous, even regretful, but clearly willing to pull the trigger if it had come to that.

I wondered what was worth protecting enough to drive him to do that. Andrea had known. From what Thomas had said she'd even been part of it, to a point.

I needed to know, too.

After I showered, I spread the contents of the wedding folder out on the bed again. I started with the table layout. There was Stanley Reston at the head table, with Andrea. The Genistar COO and the Chinese business interests. Then there was Kufka, the health minister, with the NGOs, including Thomas. Tshala had said the health ministry was working with Genistar on whatever their plan was; Kufka's presence at the wedding proved that.

Then there was the final column. The Chinese scientist Doctor Huang, and all the researchers.

I thought back to the video of the toast, where she'd gotten Huang's name wrong. The twang of memory buzzed in the back of my head again. I got out my computer and re-played the video. Andrea had called him 'the great geneticist Doctor Liu' the first time, and as she said that name, I saw Stanley's eyes flash, even as he kept his obligatory smile in place, sitting next to her at the head table. She'd smiled shyly as she apologized to the crowd and corrected herself, and Stanley regained his composure.

At first glance it seemed a simple mistake, But Andrea did not make such mistakes. And Stanley's reaction had not been one of embarrassment for his new wife's error; it had been a moment of clear anger and perhaps fear, even though the doctor in question had not even been there to see the slip.

What had Andrea been up to?

Doctor Huang, the great geneticist. Or Doctor Liu? I still did not know which was right. But it made sense that if Genistar had taken Andrea's work and pushed it in some other direction, they'd have needed somebody smart enough to do the pushing.

Another geneticist.

I wrote both names on a piece of paper, wondering if Marco had contacts who could look into them for me.

I thumbed through the other documents. The menu. The gifts. The Swiss chocolates. All almost Andrea, but still not quite. I still couldn't figure out what they could mean, but I had decided to trust that there was meaning in them.

Then I came to the note from the lost and found. *Return it to its original owner*, the note had read.

Andrea needed me to go to Bikoro so Tshala could meet the plane and get me the samples.

And so I had to believe she needed me to go to Makoua, too, into the heart of Ebola country, and find the strange man who'd married us.

Why, I did not know.

But did know that I would go.

Chapter Seventeen

THREE HOURS LATER, we sat sipping drinks at dinner. Tshala was to my left, wearing the kind of colorful, flowing dress common in the city. Her hair was pulled back, accentuating her emerald eyes and high cheekbones. She looked like she'd just come out of an Aspen spa, not a shootout at an airstrip in the middle of the Congo. Marco was directly across from me, his elbows on the table, sleeves rolled up to his forearms as always. Atombe was to my right, having returned from his mission to get the case to safety. He was eyeing the menu as though he hadn't eaten a week. I'd decided I needed to trust my companions, and so I'd just finished telling them my thinking on the meaning of the note and the rings.

"Andrea wanted me to go to Makoua and find Lufua," I said, concluding my story. "And I'm going to."

Marco leaned forward. "Let me get this straight. You have a ring given to you by a sorcerer who you need to take back to the place it was made. Which is deep in a territory patrolled by an army of guards all out to kill you. And all this to solve some terrible threat you don't really understand."

"Basically, yes," I said.

He sat back in his chair. "Who are you, fucking *Frodo*?"

131

Tshala burst out laughing, then covered her mouth with her hand, apologizing to me with her eyes.

I realized with a shock that I'd never heard Marco swear before. And I realized suddenly how crazy the story must sound. He went on: "And if you think I'm interested in being some sort of Aragon for you, think again."

"I sort of thought of you more as Boromir," I said, figuring there was nothing to be gained by resorting to reason until he calmed down a bit.

"You're making my point," he said. "I get that something weird and probably bad is going on up there. But I have no interest in dying in the jungle for whatever quest you're on here. Or letting anyone else die up there."

"I want to be Arwen," Tshala said, regaining her composure and ignoring his outburst. "I thought Liv Tyler was fantastic." She turned to Atombe. "And you can be Samwise Gamgee."

"Who's he?" Atombe said, trying to follow the conversation while still engrossed in the menu.

"He's a hobbit," she said brightly.

Atombe looked up, confused. "What's a hobbit?"

She rolled her eyes. "Where did you grown up, in a box?"

He dropped his eyes to the table again. Tshala, her own eyes still turned to the ceiling, did not see the look that crossed his face. It looked like embarrassment.

"Everybody's from somewhere," Marco said brusquely to her, abruptly cutting off that line of conversation. It was hard to tell, but it looked like he was protecting Atombe in some way. "Where are you from that makes you so worldly, Tshala?" he asked.

"I grew up here, in Kinshasa," she said, defiantly, reacting to his tone. "I went to university in Paris, and then Brussels."

"Ahh. Rich girl. Your parents are here. Why don't you stay with them?"

A dark look crossed her face this time. "We don't speak much anymore. My father has not appreciated my work. And I have not appreciated his, as I have grown older."

"He's with the government?" Marco asked, stiffening.

"He operates Artisanal mines. A bunch of them. Copper and Cobalt. Mostly in the east, but he has a small one north of here as well."

This time she was the one to look embarrassed. It was easy to guess why. While Artisan mining sounded quaint and homespun it was anything but. Artisanal mines were largely unregulated, unsafe for the people who worked there and destructive to the land around them. Most had been developed originally by various rebel groups during the wars. The rebels enslaved the local population to work the mines, then sold the production to multinational companies in exchange for money they could use to buy more weapons. The western world knew where the dollars were going but turned a blind eye to the human tragedy behind their diamond necklaces and compact cellphone batteries. It was said that Africa was the only place where the discovery of valuable natural resources made life *more* miserable for the people that lived there. One estimate I had seen put the value of natural resources in the Congo at $24 trillion. That was opportunity for a lot of misery.

"Why doesn't he support your work?" Atombe asked, having had a minute to recover.

"He wanted me to study geology and business. To work with him. He doesn't see the point in the aid work. He always quoted Albert Kalonji. "This is your home…""

"...Fend for yourselves," Atombe said, finishing the sentence for her. Albert Kalonji had been the leader of a secessionist state, South Kasai, five decades earlier. He'd uttered that phrase and it had become the unofficial motto for the Congolese. Some joked it was the fifteenth amendment to the DRC's constitution. It was still true 50 years later.

"You don't have to help me, but I'm going," I said, coming back to the main topic. "There's a reason she wants me to go." I realized as I said it that I still spoke of Andrea's wishes in the present tense, as though she was directing me from a condo in London, not from a packet of paper and a video she'd sent to me, for all intents and purposes, from the grave.

"I just came from there," Tshala said. "That's where the main laboratory and hospital are. Genistar built them just outside Makoua over the past year. There are soldiers everywhere. It's as Marco said. You can't just drive up there."

"I'm going," I said.

"Maybe she just wanted a second chance for me to meet you, if things didn't work out in Bikoro." Tshala said. "Maybe you don't need to go anymore now that I gave you the samples."

I thought about the video and the chance she took filming it. Especially if she was being watched as closely as Tshala and Thomas had said. "No, it was important to her that I go there and see Lufua. There's got to be something else."

"I don't do the jungle," Marco said. "I spent enough time in one of them a long time ago."

"Afraid of the snakes?" I asked, sarcastically.

His eyes suddenly got cold, and he looked at me the way he'd studied Thomas holding the gun. I realized I had crossed some unseen line. Atombe shifted uncomfortably in his seat.

"I don't do jungle," Marco said again, closing off that line of discussion, eyes hard and deadly.

"Got it," I said, hoping to take the tension out of the air. "You've done enough for me already."

"I'll go," Atombe said. Marco raised an eyebrow at him but said nothing.

"You really *are* Samwise Gamgee," Tshala said, a bit of warmth creeping into her voice.

"Maybe you can tell me about the labs," I said to Tshala. "So I know what I might be looking for."

"I'll do even better," she said. "I'll come with you. I know where the soldiers are patrolling. I can keep us out of trouble."

"You don't need to," I said.

"Andrea was my friend, not just my boss. She wasn't afraid of anything. But whatever they are doing up there had her convinced something terrible was going to happen." She took a breath and met my eyes. "I think she was willing to give her life to try and stop it. I believe you think that, too. I want to help."

"You can't just fly back to Bikoro and walk up to Makoua from there," Marco said. "They'll be watching the airstrip if they are watching the roads. Especially after today. I bet those people from Genistar were in Bikoro already doing just that."

"It's a day's drive, just to get to Bikoro," Atombe said.

"We'd have to ditch the car long before we got close," I said. "We'd have a day's hike, maybe two, to get to Makoua."

"None of you have any experience doing what you're talking about. You'd get caught before you got two kilometers," Marco said.

"I'll figure it out," I said. "There's got to be a way."

We fell into silence as our food arrived. We were all ravenous, not having eaten since the morning. We had plates of chicken and beans in spicy sauces, with plantains. I ordered a second drink and Tshala asked for another glass of wine. Marco switched to mineral water, which Atombe had been drinking all along. As the food and drinks took hold, the mood brightened again. We talked about the state of politics in the DRC. Atombe asked me about Boston and my prior years in the Congo. I told them stories of Andrea and our time together.

Near the end of the meal Atombe turned to Tshala. "You were Andrea's assistant?

"Yes," she said wistfully.

"I have a friend. She is the assistant for a businessman here in Kinshasa. She likes it very much."

There was a pause where Tshala processed his words. Then realization hit. "You think I'm a bloody *secretary*?" She said to him, green eyes blazing.

"You said you were her assistant," Atombe said, realizing something had gone terribly wrong, but struggling to make sense of her response. Marco and I locked eyes for a second and smiled, realizing what was coming.

"I'm her *research* assistant," Tshala said. "I've got a doctorate in Molecular biology and a masters in biochemical engineering. My thesis was on chromosomal drift in mice genomes, and how to use CRISPr technology to repair it. I'm not a bleeding *secretary,* you dolt." She crossed her arms and scowled at him. "I take it back. You're no Samwise Gamgee. He was a gentleman."

Atombe just stared, afraid to speak again lest he somehow unleash another tirade despite his best intentions.

"At least that means I'm not a hobbit," he said finally, in attempt to regain some sense of stature in the conversation. It was clear he'd never met a woman quite like Tshala.

It occurred to me that I hadn't either. Not since Andrea.

Chapter Eighteen

WE FINISHED THE meal. Tshala excused herself to go back to her room.

"I'll walk you," Atombe said. "I need to check on our guy in the lobby before I leave."

She shook her head. "I don't need a babysitter."

"It's my job," Atombe said helplessly.

"Let him do it," I said to her.

She sighed but nodded. She let him get his jacket. As they walked away, she put her arm through his and flashed a wicked smile. "You can be my *assistant*," I heard her say to him before they were out of earshot.

I watched them leave together. I thought about Atombe's reaction at the table when Tshala had asked about his upbringing. And the joy he showed in the help he gave to Sephora and her homes for the kids of Kinshasa.

"He was a Shegue, wasn't he?" I said.

Marco nodded.

"Are they all? The people who work for you."

"Many. But not all," Marco said. "Henry isn't, for example. I don't know if Atombe told you but Henry is still a little afraid of the Shegues, from the legends he heard as a kid. When Atombe wants to keep Henry in line he threatens to eat Henry's heart while he sleeps. It actually works."

"That's not a usual career path," I said. "Shegue to private security."

"The kids I get? By the time they reach me they've survived that life, and then made themselves into something in the homes like Sephora's, staying good kids, when the whole world's stacked against them. There's nothing I can throw at them they haven't seen." He smiled. "Except maybe Tshala, eh?"

"Your people protect them. The homes for those kids. You don't have to do that."

"These kids are innocent. Usually orphaned. Accused of sorcery and pitched onto the street. Somebody ought to look out for them."

"I figured it was your way of paying back."

"Paying back for what?" He said sharply, eyes narrowing.

"Sorry, just taking a guess. A lot of the big mining companies working in the Congo are Canadian. I figured maybe part of your business was working for them. Like Tshala said, they may not have the blood on their hands, but they're definitely not far away from it. You seem like a decent guy. I thought maybe helping the Shegues and people like Sephora was your way of evening the balance."

He relaxed into his chair. "I don't do much work for the mining companies. I may have debts to pay, but that's not one of them."

"Well, if you're helping Atombe and the kids like him from the goodness of you heart, how about the thousand like them upcountry? The Ebola outbreak alone will kill them eventually if it doesn't get stopped. Never mind whatever Andrea was really afraid of. Shouldn't somebody look out for them?"

"I don't do the jungle," Marco repeated. But this time the look in his eyes was far away, and haunted.

"Can you just help me figure out how to get up there? I'll figure out the rest."

He sipped his water. "I'm not in the business of sending my clients out to die."

"OK then, you're fired. Now will you help me?"

He laughed. "That would be the best news I've heard all day. But you didn't hire me. Your guy Frank did. And I don't think he's firing me now."

I smiled in return. "I'd miss you anyway," I said.

"Let me think about it," he said. "I still think you're insane for going up there."

"I told you. I don't have a choice. And there's one more favor I need," I said.

He sighed.

"I have a name, well two actually. The chief scientist at Genistar." I didn't tell him about Andrea's error at the toast, or my growing suspicion that it was not an error at all. I didn't want him to dismiss the request out of hand and I wasn't fully confident in my own belief that there was meaning in Andrea's apparent slip-up. "He's Chinese and I assume he's a geneticist. Do you have contacts who can look into him?"

He nodded. I gave him the names.

"Why two names?"

"That's part of the question."

I paid the bill and we parted ways. I still had time to call Simone in Israel and tell her what I needed. I knew she'd be crazy to agree, considering what I was going to ask. But Simone was Israeli. Like the Shegues, the Israelis grew up surrounded by people who wanted to kill them. They did not frighten easily.

141

Chapter Nineteen

I CALLED SIMONE from my room. I figured I owed her an explanation; a conversation centered around flying 50 samples of doctored Ebola a thousand miles to Israel wasn't something everyone would understand out of context. Not that I could think of any reasonable context for the conversation she and I were about to have.

But from what Tshala had said, we were already someplace beyond reasonable, and I had a feeling we were only beginning the trip.

Simone was as animated as ever. As soon as she heard my voice she launched right into a five-minute, pause-free stream-of-consciousness update on the progress of her work. I sometimes thought Simone had already merged her DNA with that of some amphibian, enabling her to breathe through her skin and eliminating the need for any actual intake of air. The strides she had made in gene editing were astounding. On any other day I would have been enthralled by what she was saying—and, as she spoke, I would have been calculating the impact of her work on the value of my portfolio. But I just listened, waiting for her to give me enough of an opening to jump in. Finally, I got my chance.

"That's amazing Simone," I said, not pausing for breath of my own, "And I need to tap that brilliant mind for something else, too. Something really crazy, but really important to me."

She was intrigued, which she showed by not cutting me off to interject after the first five words. Intellectual challenges were the other oxygen she breathed. That, and continuing to show me how smart she was so I'd continue to fund her ideas.

"But it's dangerous," I said. "And maybe illegal."

"Illegal in what country?" She asked. Which was actually a fair question. Who would actually be in a position to prosecute me or her if this went really wrong? Israel maybe. But she was very well connected there, as was I. Unless we got to the point where people died, we shouldn't have issues there.

Of course, that possibility was not out of the question.

"I have blood samples. A lot of them. I need you to look at them. There's a mechanism in them for altering DNA. I need to understand it."

"What's the vector?" Meaning how was the mechanism delivered to the target body.

"A virus. Or at least it's based on a virus."

"Oh." She sounded disappointed.

"The Ebola virus."

I actually got another pause out of her.

"You're joking," she said finally. "Nobody would use that."

"Somebody did. And there's more. I need to understand how it's turned on. And how it's turned off if it can be. It's different from anything you've seen before, I think." That got her both interested and concerned.

"Is it still contagious?"

"Yes, but theoretically it's harmless. Other than doing whatever it's designed to do from a genetic perspective."

"Theoretically?"

'There seems to have been some ...hiccups... in the early implementations."

"Hiccups?"

Her English was very good, but apparently that slang was not in her vocabulary. "Errors. False starts," I said.

"Errors. hmmm. Is that another word for 'deaths'?"

I knew I owed her honesty, given the risk I'd be asking her to take. "It seems that way."

"Hmmm. How will you get them here?"

"I have a private plane. I'll send it straight from Kinshasa out over the Atlantic, then across the Mediterranean up to Israel. It can land at Haifa right on the coast. They will almost never be over land."

"Until they are on the ground in my country."

"I know it sounds crazy. But I need to understand what's in these samples and how it works."

"Who gave you the samples?"

"My wife. My ex-wife."

"I thought she'd...."

I didn't make her finish the sentence. "She did. I can't explain it all right now, but she sent me here to get this. Something she was very frightened by is going on and I believe she wants me to figure out what. And I need your help to do it." I kept pressing. "Haifa is a military airport as well as commercial. There's security there." Not that there was an airport in Israel without security, but I needed to put her at ease.

"This is important?"

145

"Very important. It could be life or death for a lot of people."

"Are the samples frozen?"

"Yes."

There was silence for a minute. "Okay. Keep them that way. I still have friends up near Haifa in the Air Force. They will help. Once the samples are secure on the ground, I'll take them to my lab. We have containment facilities there."

I thanked her and hung up. I did some math in my head. The plane should be on the ground in Kinshasa by morning. The aircraft Frank had chartered was a Gulfstream G650ER. We owned a fractional share in the plane, and fortunately it had been available on short notice. The ER was for extended range, and the plane could do the trip from Kinshasa to Haifa without refueling, which was a huge advantage, both for time and for lack of worry. All I had to count on was the likelihood that the different parts of the DRC government still did not cooperate well, so the plane could get in and out of the country without the Health Ministry getting wind it was connected to me.

Done with my calls, I found myself staring at the empty space on the shelf in the sitting room where the urn had rested. I resolved again that I would find out whatever it was Andrea had so desperately wanted me to know. And while she may decide to hate me again from wherever her spirit now resided, I knew already that some more people were going to pay for however they'd hurt her.

Stanley Reston was at the top of my list of candidates. But Thomas, my good friend, my compatriot from so many years ago, was not far behind. I still pictured him with the gun pointed at me. I was sure he'd looked uncertain, even reluctant; but he'd kept his finger on the trigger. I tried and failed to resolve that image with the man I'd worked along-side in such harsh conditions, and who'd dedicated his life to the same ideals Andrea had shared.

Ideals I'd shared, too, back in that day. Ideals I thought had left me in the Congo, along with my connection to Andrea.

I thought I'd driven both away at the end of a pistol before escaping back to Boston. But perhaps, I realized, staring at the empty shelf, they'd remained behind just as I'd left them, and I was the only one who had fled.

Chapter Twenty

I WOKE EARLY the next morning. I called Marco to let him know the Gulfstream would be on the ground shortly. He said he'd send Atombe around to pick me up at 7:30 so we could retrieve the case and get it to the airport. Tshala rang my room just after I hung up with Marco. I told her I'd be heading to the airport.

"I'll come," she said.

"You don't need to," I said.

"I want to check the samples and make sure Samwise Gamgee kept them cold," she said.

"He's driving actually."

"I'll go anyway," she said.

I showered quickly. We met in the lobby. Tshala was wearing brand-new jeans and a colorful shirt, and her hair was still glistening from her own quick shower. She took up a chair near the door. I went to fetch two cups of coffee for us for the ride. Surprisingly, while there was a mix of Kinois and foreign nationals starting to populate the lobby and restaurant, I didn't see any familiar faces hanging around, or any other young men who looked to part of Marco's crew.

Atombe arrived on time to pick us up. Traffic in Kinshasa was never good but, like residents of many big cities, the Kinois were not early risers, so we made good time.

"I didn't see anyone from your team in the lobby," I said to Atombe as he drove.

He smiled. "René was there. He's another Canadian. You haven't met him. René's about your age, I think. And even whiter. And Malundama is here, too."

"I didn't see him either."

"Malundama is a woman's name," Tshala said, rolling her eyes.

"She would be happy you didn't see her," Atombe said. "Her name actually means 'hidden things.' It's a Kikongo name. She's from Matadi, south of here. Marco wanted to mix things up in case anyone was starting to recognize our faces."

I laughed. "Nice to know we're still being taken care of."

"Speaking of being taken care of," Tshala said, "Do you have a phone charger in here anywhere? I packed a little light for this trip."

Atombe tossed two cords back to her, one for iPhone, one for Samsung. "At your service," he said.

"My name means to sow or to plant," Tshala said as she plugged in her phone. "It's a Zulu name." She looked up from her work, once she was sure the phone was charging. "What's your name mean, Atombe?"

"Nothing," he said, keeping his gaze on the road ahead.

Tshala glanced over at me and rolled her eyes. "Okay, I guess it means 'grumpy,'" she said to Atombe's back, then settled in to check her texts and messages.

Atombe's friend's house turned out to be a large concrete and stucco dwelling sitting by itself on the edge of Kilembo, which was an area of parks and undeveloped jungle on the eastern side of the main city. It had been a good choice by him. Even if an accident had occurred with the samples, there was no one in the area to be threatened. The home had power, which was not a guarantee this far from the city center, and boasted modern appliances including a freezer. They were clearly a family of some means.

"I know this guy from University," Atombe said by way of explanation as we toured the house. "He and his family are away. He gave me a key and asked me to check on the property once in a while. I figured he wouldn't mind me using the freezer for a night. And I got more dry ice as well."

"You went to University?" Tshala said, sounding genuinely curious. "Where?"

"I go now, two nights a week. University of Kinshasa. I'm studying Economics and Business." He said it proudly. I bit my lip, waiting for Tshala to come up with some sharp retort for his choice of institution and embarrass him once again. The University of Kinshasa, founded by the Jesuits, had once been called the greatest university in Africa. It still offered a wide range of programs at all levels, including a medical school. During my time in the Congo worked with a number of talented doctors who'd graduated from there. But like most of the institutions in the Congo, years of mismanagement and neglect had taken their toll.

Surprisingly Tshala offered no jabs. She just nodded thoughtfully, studying Atombe from her spot in the second row of seats.

We retrieved the samples, which Tshala inspected and pronounced to be secure, and headed to N'jili airport. We got there close to 9. The plane was already waiting, engines idling. I filled out the requisite forms, slipped a hundred-dollar bill

151

into the hands of the customs officer, and brought the samples onto the plane, emptying the contents of the airplane's fridge into my duffel bag and stuffing the case into the chilled compartment to help keep it cold for the trip.

"A girl could get used to this," Tshala said, eyeing the luxurious finishings in the big jet as I worked.

"There are worse ways to get around," I said as I stood up.

Atombe watched our exchange, then suddenly pushed by me on his way out of the plane, shooting a glare at the two of us as he passed. "We need to get going," he said.

"Alrighty," I said. Tshala scowled at his back but we followed him out of the aircraft.

I explained to the pilot that Simone would meet him on the ground in Haifa to pick up a package. He didn't ask any questions. The Gulfstream was airborne by 9:30, and we were back at the hotel an hour and a half later.

Marco was in the lobby waiting for us.

"Don't you have any other clients?" I asked.

"A few. But none who require as much help as you," he said. "I'm thinking of telling Frank I need hazard pay. Or compensation for emotional distress at least."

"At least you got to meet Tshala," I said.

He smiled at her. "That has been a treat." He pulled me aside, leaving Tshala and Atombe chatting in the middle of the lobby. "Okay here's the deal," he said. "I can get you close to Makoua. Atombe has agreed to guide you from there. I'll wait with the plane for you. But we can't go until the day after tomorrow."

"That's fine," I said. "I want to get a first report on the blood samples from my friend in Israel anyway. But I thought you said we couldn't use the airstrips?"

He grinned. "It's not that kind of plane."

We rejoined the other two near the restaurant. "You all want lunch?" Marco said.

I shook my head. "I want to work out first. This trip seems like it's a little more active than I'd thought. I'm realizing how soft I've gotten over the past couple of years."

"You're going to work out here at the hotel?" Marco said. He sounded disgusted.

"It's all I've got."

He shook his head, dismissing that idea. "I'll take you to a proper gym," he said. "I brought my stuff to go there anyway." He turned to Tshala. "What about you?"

She smiled. "Atombe says he's going to check on his friend Sephora in the city. I'm going to go with him. Being shut up in this hotel all day would drive me mad."

Marco and I exchanged a look. Atombe stayed absolutely stone-faced, as if any expression he offered might cause Tshala to change her mind.

"Fair enough," I said. "I'll go put Marco through his paces. Let me get my gym stuff."

Marco rolled his eyes. "I'll wait for you. I have a feeling I'll be doing a lot of that for the next few hours." As I turned away, I saw him whispering something in Atombe's ears. The young man nodded somberly. Then Tshala and Atombe left through the front doors.

I threw my workout gear into my backpack and met Marco back downstairs. "We'll walk to the gym," he said. "It's about ten blocks. A fifteen-minute walk. Or a one-hour drive this time of day."

He retrieved a small duffel bag from the Range Rover and we headed off. I realized it was my first time really walking the city since I'd come back. The feeling of being out on the sidewalk was different from being in the back of a car, and with a sudden sense of deja vu I remembered why it was unlike any other city I'd ever been in. The roads were wide downtown, but traffic was an absolute free-for-all. Most signals and signs were ignored, with the sometimes exception of the traffic robots. Cars, trucks, bikes all competed for space. And the people. They were everywhere. Crowding the sidewalks, shoulder to shoulder. Dodging through traffic to cross the roads. Hanging on the back of the bumpers of pickup trucks or SUVs. It was chaos. But it was a kind of chaos that felt more like a celebration of some sort. A massive party of millions of people, many of whom probably did not have enough to eat, most of whom would not have electricity or running water tonight. But there was laughter and smiles amidst the honking of horns and brief arguments shouted in French, Lingala or any one of a dozen other languages. The sounds were mixed with smells—diesel fuel, cooking food, the unique odors of hot pavement and human bodies. The temperature was in the mid-80s, with the usual one hundred percent humidity, and I was sweating before we got to the first intersection.

It was an overload of every sense. I was surprised by how alive I felt, surrounded by it all. I realized with a pang how much I'd missed it. And how much it made me miss Andrea.

Marco just seemed to glide along, eyes always scanning. He seemed to move without effort but with great presence. No step was wasted. No detail overlooked.

"What did you tell Atombe before we left?" I said, as we waited for an opening to cross another jam-packed intersection.

"I told him to keep his eyes open. I don't think anyone will try anything in the city. But I told him to watch the sidewalks, not the girl."

"That'll be a tough order to follow."

"He'll do it. I'm not an expert on the whole relationship thing, but I already think the entire army couldn't lay a finger on Tshala if Atombe's anywhere nearby."

I nodded my agreement, trying to stay focused on keeping myself alive as we avoided whizzing scooters and the occasional Esprit de Mort taxicabs which, true to name, followed even fewer rules than the rest of the vehicles.

The gym was in a warehouse down a side street. It was one big room with two boxing rings, heavy bags, weights and mats scattered around the concrete floor. Inside, the smells of food and diesel exhaust were gone. The smell of sweating human beings was not. There were some old-school exercise bikes in one corner, but it was clear that this place had never heard of spin class. One of the boxing rings was active; two young men sparred, flashing punches and kicks at each other, both clearly skilled. Football, European style, was the number one spectator sport in the DRC, but martial arts was a huge favorite as well, for reasons I'd never understood. The matches got a lot of coverage on TV and in the papers, and lot of the gyms catered to the young men—and increasingly women—that wanted to participate.

We changed in the locker area, which was really just a bench and some shelves, separated from the main space by a tarpaulin draped over a cable. A row of showers lined the back wall over some drains cut into the floor; there were no curtains. There was a smaller area for women on the far side of the room. It looked equally primitive from what I could tell.

I taped my hands, put on my gloves and found an open heavy bag. I started hitting it slowly, loosening up, but picked up speed. The humidity seemed even higher in the gym than outside, if such a thing was possible, and I was quickly drenched with sweat. But it felt good to move and punch, working the tightness out of my shoulders.

"Your footwork sucks." It was Marco. He was standing a few feet away, putting on his own gloves.

"Thanks," I said, already gasping for air. He grabbed the heavy bag with a gloved hand, stopping it in place.

"Jump up in the air," he said. "And don't move after you land." I looked at him in confusion.

"Do it," he said. He did not raise his voice, but somehow there was no room for refusal in his tone.

I jumped up as he'd commanded. I landed, feet about six inches closer together than they'd been before.

"That's it. That's your stance," he said. "Don't go wider."

I started hitting the bag again. It took a minute to get used to it, but I realized my balance was better. The blows felt less satisfying because I wasn't just throwing myself into them, but I could recover more quickly, moving side to side more easily.

"Hit from your hips and shoulders, not your arms." he said, then moved off for his own workout. At one point I saw him put on headgear and climb into a ring with a much larger man, who seemed to be one of the coaches. They sparred for a good 20 minutes, snapping punches, sweeping legs, moving through a huge assortment of moves. A few of the younger men stopped what they were doing to watch. I had to admit it was quite a display. Marco's takedown of Thomas had been child's play compared to what he was doing in the ring.

We met again in the changing area once we were done. We rinsed off as best we could, but I was still sweating when we sat down to change back into street clothes. For the first time I noticed the tattoos on Marco's right bicep. I realized that despite the incessant heat and humidity, I'd never seen him in short sleeves. There were seven names inked into the skin, stacked on top of each other like a list, in plain blue ink. Six were clearly French Canadian. The seventh name seemed to be Indian.

We started to dress.

"Can I ask? The tattoos? I said.

He paused, then nodded. "Men I knew, in the military. They were in my platoon."

"They died?"

He nodded again. "Under my command."

"That's a helluva way to remember them," I said.

"They deserve to be remembered. They all counted on me to keep them alive. For most of the guys in the unit, I did. But not these guys."

"Where?"

He motioned vaguely north. "Eastern part of the DRC during the war. Somalia near the coast. A few other places in the north. The Canadian military's more active here than most people think."

"It couldn't have been your fault." It seemed stupid and gratuitous to say, but I felt I should say something.

"Maybe. But I think about them every day. What sign I missed. What training I could have given. What tactic I could have tried that might have kept them alive."

"I didn't know there were that many Indians in Canada," I said, my eyes on the final name. It was not only different in ethnicity than the others, but the workmanship seemed different too. It was clearly not done at the same time as the others.

His eyes clouded. "That one's different. He didn't sign up to be in harm's way."

"He wasn't in your unit?"

Marco shook his head slowly, looking down and pulling on a sock as he spoke. The act of dressing was an easy way to avoid eye contact, it seemed. "He was a doctor, in Detroit."

"He died on your watch, too?" I was confused and curious.

Marco spent an unnecessary extra minute putting on his other sock, apparently considering his next words with care. He seemed to come to a decision. "You trusted me. So I'll trust you," he said. He looked up and met my eyes. "I killed him," he said. "I didn't mean to or want to, but I did. He didn't deserve it. None of these guys did, but him least of all."

"What happened?" I knew I was pressing my luck, but he seemed open to talking, at least a little.

"When I was close to getting discharged from the military I started to get recruited by a big company. A Canadian firm. They wanted me to run security, working directly for the CEO. I figured working on the civilian side would be less dirty than crawling around the jungles of Africa. Turns out the opposite was true. It was just a different kind of dirt. One that's harder to wash off."

I decided to take another chance. "And that's why you're here, running a security operation in the Congo, and not hanging at a bar in Toronto?"

He nodded. "I got caught up in something bigger than just corporate intrigue. It turned into something bad in a dozen different ways. I tipped the Canadian government off to somebody who was handing some very important secrets over to some very bad people. They were able to stop the transfer. They were grateful. So was your government. The Americans agreed not to extradite me. My friends in

158

the Canadian intelligence agency got me a pass out of the country. I do a lot of work for them here now. When I'm not baby-sitting knuckleheads like you."

"The doctor. He was part of that?"

"No. He was just trying to save a little kid's life." He smiled wistfully. "Which he did, in the end."

"That doesn't sound like the you that I know," I said.

"It's not the me I know either," he said. "At least not the one I want to know. I think about that man every day, too."

I could see the regret in his eyes. And I thought of those three men kneeling in the dusty street.

"I wonder if that's how you know what you really believe in," I said. "You decide what you're willing to kill for."

He shook his head. The look in his eyes changed, growing more resolute. "Nah. You want know what you really believe in? Figure out what you're willing to die for."

He put on his shoes, stood up, and blew out a long breath. "Okay, enough blabbering. Let's go back to the hotel and see if Atombe's practicing his frisking techniques on Tshala."

"I think she'd be running that operation," I said.

We retraced our route and were back at the hotel in a half hour. Atombe and Tshala were not there but Marco checked in with them by phone. Atombe assured him everything was okay. Marco and I ordered beers in the bar and waited for them to return. The pair of them rolled in a half hour later, and we got lunch. Atombe tore into his food, as usual. Tshala picked at hers quietly. The day seemed to have made her more thoughtful, too.

"How's Sephora?" I asked Atombe.

"She's good. The generators were delivered today. She said to thank you. And to tell you she was thinking of her friend Andrea."

"What did you think?" I said to Tshala.

"Sephora is incredible," she said. "The kids were amazing, too. So polite. I grew up in Kinshasa. I always saw them on the streets. The Shegues. But I'd never thought much about them. They were just part of Kinshasa to me."

As heartless as her words sounded, I had to admit I knew what she meant. I couldn't count the number of homeless people I'd avoided on the streets of Boston or San Francisco, in a hurry to get to a meeting or a dinner. "Those kids can turn out to be pretty special," I said, speaking to her, but loud enough for Atombe to overhear. He pretended not to notice and stabbed another piece of pork. She nodded. "They can be." Then her voice brightened, and I could hear some of the sass return. "The boys seem to worship Atombe. I guess it's hard to blame them. They are only children, and don't know better." She eyed him as she said it, a twinkle in her eye. He glanced up and put on a mock scowl. "The girls could use a role model for themselves," he said. "I just can't think of anyone worthy enough for the job." Tshala stuck her tongue out at him and then returned to her own plate of food.

Apparently it had been a very educational trip.

Chapter Twenty-One

I WAS BACK in my room after lunch thinking through the next steps to unraveling whatever mystery Andrea had left for me. I'd done the math in my head a dozen times. A 10-hour flight to Haifa. A day for Simone to do any sort of useful analysis of the samples. It would be the following night before I got any news from her. At least with luck it would happen before we set out for Makoua.

Marco had asked for clothing sizes from Tshala and me, pointing out that we'd need better clothing if we were going to hike through the jungle. He was right: I'd packed for a week mostly to be spent in Kinshasa; Tshala hadn't packed a thing except the blood samples. She'd rolled her eyes at his request but gave him the information. I gave him my sizes as well.

"Looks like you could use another trip to the gym," he'd said with a grin, when I'd rattled off my waist measurement.

Henry dropped off a package to me around 3 that afternoon. I tried on the calf-high boots, the heavy cotton shirt and the tan pants, which were lightweight but rip-resistant, with deep pockets and a wider belt loop. Everything fit well. There was a rain jacket, flashlight, compass and water bottle in a small backpack as well. I wasn't sure how much use those would be, since I thought we would be in and out in a single day. But I was learning to trust Marco on those sorts of things.

I spent the rest of the afternoon reading up on the Zestra deal. I had to force myself through the pages of details on financing, terms and conditions, and stock payouts. But Frank's words rang in my ears; a lot of people were depending on me to help get the Zestra deal over the finish line—it would literally be life-changing for some of them. As I read through the information the dollar figures started to be mind-numbing. Zestra would pay a billion dollars for a business that had yet to make any money. My firm would make over $200 million, five times our investment, in only two years. Twenty percent of that would go to me personally. Once the deal closed, two computers would trade a few bits of information, and $40 million would appear in my bank account. At least, I told myself, the work the company was doing was valuable. Simone's ideas alone, if commercialized, would mean more gene therapies making it to market faster. More people would be saved from debilitating illnesses.

At least the kind of illnesses that afflicted the rich world.

But I thought of the lunacy of it all. Simone, the genius behind the work, would certainly see her effort rewarded; she'd make a million dollars off her stock options. And she'd be positioned to continue her work with the nearly unlimited funding Zestra could bring to bear. But I, simply for knowing how to attract money and spot a promising talent like her, would make twenty times that much. There was a dark side to the deal; everyone who was not in research or development would have to be let go. But that was not unusual; Zestra already had all the finance and business people they needed. Nobody would starve—those who got laid off would get severance and we'd pay out for the stock options they'd earned, but they'd all be on the outside looking in when the deal closed, and they'd be looking for new employment. It was cold-blooded. But that's the way the business world worked.

Fend for yourselves. I guess that mantra walked the streets in the Western world, too—just in a better suit of clothing.

Marco had asked us to stay in the hotel for safety. He sent word that he and Atombe were tied up with another client so Tshala and I were alone for dinner. Two of Marco's team were in the hotel, he said, but I did not spot them.

"Nice as it is to have a proper shower, I'm getting sick of this place already," Tshala said when we sat down to eat. "I can only imagine how you feel."

"I think I have the menu memorized, I said. "But at least the bartender knows what I like to drink."

"Drinks. That's a good idea," she said. "It's hard to get a good martini in the jungle."

True to her word she ordered a vodka martini, and I got my usual scotch. The glasses were empty before the meal arrived, so we ordered another round. The alcohol warmed my blood, and I felt neck muscles I hadn't realized were tight start to relax. Tshala grew more animated, talking about her university experience, and her work with Andrea. Her green eyes darted and flashed as she spoke. She not only had Andrea's eyes, she had some of her mannerisms and choices of words, picked up no doubt from all the time they'd spent together. She spoke with admiration about Andrea, lauding her intelligence and her determination. I was proud in a way that Andrea had had a big impact on her both as friend and colleague. I found myself living vicariously through her stories, remembering the same kind of effect Andrea had had on me. The impact of her words, coupled with the location and the alcohol, peeled away the last three years even more than the past few days already had. I could see Andrea. I could hear her. I could *feel* her, as though she was in the room with us.

I suddenly realized Tshala had stopped speaking and was studying me.

"I'm sorry," I said. "I was just lost in thought."

She nodded. "I can imagine. Being back here. You miss her."

I nodded in return.

She took a breath. "I can tell you still care about her."

"More than I even thought."

"So why did you never come back?"

"Andrea didn't tell you?"

"She told me what those men did in Makoua. And what you did. But you two splitting up for good? That part I've never understood."

I took her through the whole story. The insane pressures and stress of trying to do our jobs in the middle of a war, the civilians ignored at best and used as pawns and slaves at worst. The bribes that needed to be paid to get supplies into the clinics. In this morass of suffering, a village near Makou had had an outbreak of cholera; the local official had stopped Andrea and her driver, refusing to allow a shipment of medicine to the village. Her satellite phone had failed; I'd been in Kinshasa, unable to reach her.

She'd offered money, and they said she'd need to go with them, alone, to their offices, to negotiate. She knew the risks that came with that proposal and she'd refused their demand for a day, until four more of her patients died. Six more were very sick and would die within another day, so she eventually agreed to go with him.

He'd betrayed her twice: first when he brought her to a building where two of his friends also waited and locked the door behind them; and again when, the next day, he still refused to allow the shipment, unless a cash bribe was paid as well.

I told Tshala how I'd found out what happened the following day, when I made it back to the village and saw the bruises on her face and body. And how I'd tracked the official and his friends down to that shabby metal building on the road north of Makoua. How I'd forced him to make a call to release the shipment, the gun barrel grinding a dime-sized circle in his skin as I'd jammed it into the back of his neck, then how I'd lined the three up in the road and killed them, one after another.

I told her I'd left them in the jungle by the side of the road for the animals to eat.

"Do you regret it?"

"A little. The animals deserved better food than that."

She raised an eyebrow, but just waited patiently.

"Okay. I regret a lot of what happened, but no, not that part. I was so angry, so frustrated. What I regret was that I hadn't been there when she needed me. It was my job to keep her out of that sort of danger—her and everyone else on the team. I failed her."

I wiped away a tear as I spoke, still hardly able to relive those events, feeling myself start to break apart a little, the way I had shattered so completely over those final two days in the Congo and for so many months afterwards. Tshala sat still, waiting for me to go on with the story. "But she wouldn't see me after," I said, the hurt and disbelief still in my voice. "Wouldn't even talk to me. She was angry at me. Or ashamed of me. It didn't matter. So I left."

"She wasn't ashamed of you," Tshala said quietly. "She was ashamed of herself. For what she felt she let happen."

"No. Andrea didn't see the body that way," I said, shaking my head. "You know that. She was a scientist. To her it was a machine. A vehicle. Something to be fixed, healed. But not to be ashamed of."

She fiddled with her martini glass, gathering her thoughts. "I think I get it now. Some of the things she said to me over the last couple of years—I didn't have the context then." She took a breath. "You want to know what I think?"

"Yes." I drained half my scotch, not at all sure if that was true.

"I think she didn't wait for you to get back from Kinshasa because she wanted to show you that she could take care of things herself. I think she wanted to make you proud. And yes, because she was so damn impatient that she never wanted to wait for anyone on anything." She laughed, wiping away a tear of her own. "But when *that* happened, she felt she let you both down, as well as all the people still suffering in that village. I also think in some way she felt betrayed by the country itself; that the land she'd worked so hard to help could do that to her; that she could be just another victim of the conditions here, not a savior of it. It was the worst humiliation possible. When I met her, a few months later, she was still angry. And more focused on her work than ever."

I shook my head. "It wasn't her fault. She just tried to do what she always did by making things better."

"She told me about her childhood. About what happened to her."

"She'd tried to put all that behind her," I said. "She had some tough days, but she'd come to grips with it."

"I don't think anybody ever puts something like that behind them," Tshala said. "Maybe she buried it. Maybe the whole thing about the body just being a machine. Maybe she convinced herself of that idea because it made it easier to think about what had happened to her. If the body was just a vessel, nothing sacred, then it was easier for her to think nothing important had been taken from her. But when she saw your reaction, she couldn't pretend any more that that was true. So, she couldn't face you."

"That's not it. She was furious at me for what I did."

"That's the thing, Alan. I think part of her was glad you did it. And that was the worst part of all for her, because it made her think she wasn't any better than those men, taking satisfaction in knowing how they died. That she was just another monster. It was her betraying everything she thought was true about herself."

My mind reeled. "That can't be true."

Tshala shrugged. "Maybe it's not. But I spent a lot of time with her. She talked about you. She *missed* you. She just thought you were better off away from her, so you didn't have to keep re-living what had happened." She met my eyes. "Maybe it's not true. But I believe it is. I think that's why she threw herself even harder into the work. She wanted to end all the suffering with one big swoop. What the situation here does—the diseases and the hold they have on the people; the opportunities the chaos here gives bad people like those men—what it all did to her, and did to you, and does to so many people? She wanted to end all that, once and for all."

The conviction in her voice shook me to my core, and the past few years reeled through my mind. Three years spent running from Andrea, first in burning anguish, then in cold denial. And finally in numb acceptance. All because of a belief that might be completely wrong.

"But then it started to get out of control. I think she realized all the consequences of what she was building. As maniacal as she'd become about the work, she knew she had to pull back. And she did."

"Then why wouldn't she reach out to me?" I said, my voice tight.

"Why didn't *you* ever reach out to *her*?"

I was silent, wondering that same thing myself. It all seemed so stupid now. Now that I could no longer do anything to fix it.

The waiter appeared. Tshala ordered another drink for me. Hers was still half-full. "I had a professor once," she said. "He taught psychology and philosophy. He used this metaphor. He said we all live alone in deep holes that we dig with our fears. Those holes get deeper over time, through our pain and loneliness. We shout to each other from the bottom of these holes, trying to make contact with others. Sometimes people shout back. We create pictures of those people from what we hear. But we never truly see anyone else, because we're stuck too deep in our own holes." She sipped her drink and those bright green eyes locked onto mine. "That's what I think happened to you two. I really believe you saw each other better than any two people I've ever met. I hope someday somebody gets to know me half as well as you knew her. But after that happened, you were just shouting to each other from your holes. You couldn't see the pain she was in. And it never occurred to her that you might be missing her, too. She didn't hate you. She just didn't think she deserved to be missed by you."

I felt the tears stinging my eyes. "I never thought I deserved to be missed by her either," I said. "And now it's too late."

Tshala shook her head. "No. Now she needs you more than ever. We need to figure out what Genistar is doing and stop it. That's what she trusted you to do. She needs you to do it."

I smiled. "I think she needs *us* to do it."

Chapter Twenty-Two

THE NEXT DAY was quiet. Tshala and I hung around the hotel. She bought a bathing suit in the hotel's gift shop, and spent time lounging in the pool. I traded emails with Frank and Kara, trying to help advance the discussions with Zestra as best I could. Around two I got a call from Kara. She asked how everything was going, and how the ceremony had been for Andrea. The questions were polite, but I could hear the worry in her voice.

"What's wrong?" I finally asked.

"People are killing themselves to get the work done. But they are asking where you are. They like Frank and trust him, but they need you."

"I know it's tough—" I started to say.

"It's more than tough," she said, cutting me off. "It's getting really shaky. You need to get back here."

"Not quite yet," I said. "I have one more thing to do."

There was silence for a moment. I could picture her scowl. "Frank is calling an all-hands meeting tomorrow, to settle everyone down. It would be great if you called into it."

"I can't," I said, thinking of Makoua. "I'll be tied up."

"With what?" she asked. "You did the ashes. What's left?" She sounded scared and angry, but I knew at that moment there was nothing I could do about it.

"I'll explain more when I get back. I made a promise to somebody."

"You made promises here, too," she said.

"I keep my promises," I said sharply. I felt my own anger rising, mostly defensive anger. Kara was right—I knew people in Boston would not understand. But I knew I had to find out what was happening at Genistar. And I had to get to Makoua to do it.

Kara heard the rise in my tone, and she softened hers. "We just need you back here. Frank's going to need you back here. I'm just saying,"

"I know. I'm sorry. A few days. Then I'll be on my way back."

"There was a story on the news this morning," she said, a different kind of worry in her voice. "About the Ebola outbreak in the Congo. That's not where you are, is it?"

"No." Technically it was not a lie. It wasn't the part I would be in for almost 36 hours.

"It seems really awful," she said.

You don't know the half of it, I thought. I said aloud, "There are a lot of smart people tackling it. They'll get it under control."

"That's not what the woman on the news said."

I made a mental note to check the news once we were done. She listed the other calls I'd gotten and some emails she needed my thoughts on so she could respond on my behalf, then hung up.

I went to my news feed and found a story in the *Washington Post*. Sure enough, the head of the CDC had just

172

confirmed that the Ebola outbreak in the eastern part of the country might not be containable. His pronouncement came just as the U.S. government had started pulling American experts from the outbreak area, citing the risk of violence from local fighting.

Kara was right. That was very scary. Genistar was failing to get their mess under control. And a lot of people could die because of it.

Marco stopped in, as usual, around dinner time. "I figured it out," I said, when Tshala and I met him in the bar. "You only show up at mealtime."

He smiled, but it was a quick, distracted smile. "Something you learn in the army. Never pass up food or sleep." He looked thoughtful.

"What's up?" I said, feeling a bit of *deja vu* from my discussion with Kara a few hours earlier.

"This company, Genistar. They're locked down tight," he said.

"That's what Tshala said. They watch everybody."

"No, I mean online." He leaned forward on the small round table. "I have a few other skills I've developed over the past few years," he said. "And when I worked for that Canadian company, I ran cybersecurity, not just physical security. I know how companies protect their networks. And so I know where the weaknesses usually are. Plus," he smiled again, "I have a few special tools I got from some friends in the intelligence community. There are not many networks I can't break into. But Genistar is like a house of mirrors. Every time I thought I'd gotten in I hit another dead end or another line of defense. I've never seen anything like it, commercial or government, short of the military stuff."

"They have a lot of intellectual property to protect," I said.

"I get it. But so do a lot of other companies. Nobody's got security like this. It must have cost a fortune."

"Why were you even looking?"

His face got darker. "I was thinking about what you said yesterday. And I don't know if you saw the news this morning?"

I nodded.

He continued. "I figured maybe I could get a better sense of what they were up to. Maybe save you a trip to Makoua."

"You're still worried about me?" I grinned. "I think you're starting to like me."

"I just worry Frank won't pay me if you die. But yeah, I'd rather you not have to go up there. Any of you."

I held up my phone, which still displayed the *Washington Post* story. "This had to get stopped," I said. "The U.S. is bailing out on the crisis. The Ministry of Health here seems to be part of what's causing it. Near as I can tell the only ones who can figure it out are us. Andrea wants me to go to Makoua. There's something there I need to see, or something to learn. I don't know what it is, but it's there."

He considered that. "I get it. But I'd still like to get a look inside their company. He looked at Tshala. "This killswitch you talked about. Maybe they're close to figuring it out. Maybe there's something that can help you."

"You can't get in from the outside, but what about from the inside?" Tshala said. "My laptop may still be in my room in the dorm. I might still be able to get onto the network. Would that help?"

"That's too risky," Marco said.

"That's not what I asked," Tshala said. She locked eyes with Marco. "Would it help?"

He met her gaze for minute, until it was clear she was not backing down. "Yes. If I could get some of my tools onto their system from inside their firewalls, I'd have better access."

"Then tell me how to do it," she said. "The dorms are mostly deserted during the day. Everyone's at the labs. But the dorms are wired for network access, too."

"Dorms?" I said.

"Yeah. They built a whole complex there. About a quarter mile outside the town. Dorms, Labs. A cafeteria. Power. Air conditioning. It's their own little city. There's even a pub of sorts. If you like local beer and bad wine."

"If you get caught," Marco said. "It could be a death sentence."

She got a hard look on her face, her green eyes darkened. She took a breath. "It's okay. I already have one of those," she said quietly. We both just stared, trying to make sense of what she'd said.

"Did you ever wonder why they still trusted me even though I worked with Andrea?" she asked.

"It had crossed my mind," Marco said.

"I'm sick. I have rare form of cancer. Almost nobody gets what I have, so there's no specialized drugs for it. No protocols. But Genistar has a trial drug that they were giving me. To beat back my cancer. It's what keeps me in remission. They told me that if I didn't stay in line, they'd stop the treatments."

I was too stunned to speak. Tshala was so full of life. Energy. She was so much of Andrea. The thought that she could be dying was incomprehensible.

175

She lifted her shoulders in a fatalistic shrug. "But it's not a commercial drug yet. So the only people who have it are in Genistar. And I don't think they're going to be in a mood to give me any more."

"You don't look sick," Marco said.

"I don't feel sick. Not yet. But it's just a matter of time before I start to notice it. A few months after that?" She shrugged. "I told you. Andrea was willing to give her life to stop whatever they're doing up there. I decided I'm willing to give mine, too."

"That's why Andrea didn't tell you what she was afraid of or what she knew," I said. "If Genistar thought they couldn't trust you, they might stop giving you the medicine."

She nodded. "I think they used my sickness to threaten Andrea too, to keep her from talking. I was their hostage."

"Still, that's no reason to go back there," Marco said. "You don't need to have your time cut short if you get caught up there. There's got to be other medications."

"There aren't," she said. "And I want to do this. I need to do this. For Andrea."

Marco was silent for a minute. "Okay," he said. "I'll load up a USB drive. All you will need to do is put it in your laptop while it's on the network. It will do the rest."

"Thank you," she said. Then she took a breath. "And one more thing."

We both waited.

"Don't tell Atombe, okay?"

Chapter Twenty-Three

I GOT A text from Simone just after dinner. *Will call you at ten tonight your time*, it read. Another one came in a minute later. *Andrea was right.* Then nothing. We were leaving the hotel at 3 a.m., but I needed to know what she'd found. I called Tshala and told her to meet me a few minutes before 10 p.m. I wanted her to hear whatever Simone said. It would likely make more sense to her than it would to me.

Tshala arrived and we sat in the common room. She was wearing lounge pants and a sweatshirt, still looking very much like the grad student she'd been only a few years earlier. The picture of health and vitality. "Thanks for coming. I know you'd rather be sleeping," I said. I tried to sound upbeat, but her revelations at dinner still had me reeling.

She shrugged. "I don't think I'd be sleeping much tonight."

"Me neither."

My phone buzzed, and I saw Simone's name. I nearly jumped. But it was a text. Not a phone call. *Need 10 more minutes,* it said. *One more test to complete.*

I told Tshala about the delay. She saw the manila envelope on the coffee table. She glanced at me for permission and I nodded. She started browsing through the contents, stacking the pages carefully on the coffee table as she skimmed them. "I miss her," she said.

"There had to be another way," I said. I realized as I said it that I wasn't just referring to the cryptic clues in the wedding plans, but to Andrea's final decision, too.

"I keep thinking about that. But she was never alone. All her communications were watched. She was basically a prisoner in the lab we're visiting tomorrow. She'd figured that Stanley's only soft spot was the wedding. She convinced him she was so thrilled to marry him that she was throwing herself into the planning of it." She put down the papers. There were tears in her eyes.

"But to kill herself? Just to get my attention?"

"I think there's more than that. Whatever is happening. Whatever Genistar is doing. I think she felt it was her fault. That she'd put it in motion."

"Still, she'd have kept fighting."

"I think she felt she was out of options."

"She took a terrible chance, trusting me," I said.

Tshala shook her head. "I think she knew you wouldn't let her down. Either way, she had no choice." She took a breath. "If she hadn't done what she did at the end, if she'd just slipped you a note somehow saying she needed your help, would you be here right now?"

I'd asked myself that question myself, and the answer was a pain I'd carry in some way forever. I just shook my head, unable to voice that truth.

"She could have told *you*," I said.

"No. As I said, they trusted me. They thought they had all the leverage on me they needed. But even with that, communications between the two of us were watched. Everybody was watched. Anything she told me they'd have known about.

Even in code. They were looking at every piece of paper. It was brilliant, actually, what she did. No codebreaker in the world would see anything in what she gave you."

"I work with the best talent in Bioscience," I said, changing the subject. "I know you say there's nothing that could help you. But I'll put every resource I have on it. There's got to be a way. I mean it."

She smiled, her eyes shining. "I know you do. Let's figure this out first. Then we can worry about me."

My phone buzzed. Simone again. This time a call. I put it on speaker and put the phone on the coffee table.

I introduced the two women to each other. "Oh my God. I've read your work," Tshala said breathlessly, once I gave her Simone's full name. "It's brilliant."

Simone's voice immediately perked up. "We'll have to meet sometime, after this," she said. "If there is any 'after this.'"

"What are you talking about?" I asked. "How bad can this be?"

"It's one hundred percent genius. And two hundred percent terrifying," Simone said. "I've never seen anything like it. I looked at the pathology of the samples and broke down the mechanisms. I haven't had much time, but I built a quick model I could run simulations on. I'll need to fine tune it, but what I saw already has me in awe. And looking to move to Antarctica."

"So what have you found so far?"

"The samples have the same vector. And yes, it's Ebola. Modified in a number of ways, but Ebola for sure. But you said on the phone the other day they were trying to deliver a genetic protection from tuberculosis?"

"Yes," Tshala cut in. "That was our original focus."

"Well, some of the samples seem designed to do that. But I found five different modifications in the samples so far. Five different bits of DNA that different virus samples were designed to modify. This thing is a programmable machine. What did you call it—a platform? That's the right word for it. It seems whoever made this can easily reprogram it to target different subsets of DNA almost at will. They can modify any part of the genome they want."

"That was the goal," Tshala said. "To make it easier to do gene therapies on our patients. The *ex vivo* treatments are too expensive and won't scale."

"Ex vivo?" I asked.

"That's when we take the cells out of the patient's body. We modify them in a lab setting and re-inject them into the patient. We wanted *in vivo* treatments- just introducing the virus into the patient and modifying the cells inside the person. Imagine if we could just scratch someone's arm with a pen loaded with the vector. The virus would infect the body and do the rest. That's not perfect because we'd still need to get the medicine to the patient, but it'd be far more scalable and easier to administer in the field. Then Andrea stumbled across a strain that was effective but still contagious. She started playing with the idea that we could go one step further, and create a cure that would self-propagate, and protect entire populations. The last obstacle to widespread cure would be eliminated. That's why we started working on the failsafe, as a backup in case something went wrong with that strain. But then Andrea suddenly backed off that research entirely. Something scared her. That's when Stanley took over and pushed us to the side."

"The failsafe part must not have worked," I said. "The Ebola outbreak in the DRC. They caused it. The people who are doing this. They screwed up."

There was a silence for a moment on the phone.

"Simone?"

She spoke again, and there was a cold fury in her voice. "Whoever engineered this didn't stop there. They created another modification to the virus."

"It's still contagious," I guessed, thinking of the outbreak happening to the north of us.

"Worse. It's not just contagious. It's aerosol."

Tshala gasped.

"What does that mean?" I said.

"It can spread through the air," Tshala said. "One of the things that keeps Ebola from being even more dangerous is that it can only be spread via contact with fluids. They made it *more* contagious. Not less."

"Why would they do that?"

Tshala gathered herself. "As I said, Andrea played with that idea, too. Out of frustration. From her aid work. You've felt it. It's hard to deliver any medicine or do any treatment in this region. Bureaucracy gets in the way. Corruption gets in the way. Lack of infrastructure gets in the way. Heck, right now the Ebola outbreak in the east is largely unchecked because of the rebels operating in the area. Andrea joked that if we just made the medicine contagious enough, it could spread itself. We wouldn't have to doing a thing. Think about it—a contagious virus that actually protects people from disease. We'd have turned the enemy against itself, so to speak. But that's when Andrea backed off."

"She might have had second thoughts, but somebody decided the risks were worth it," Simone said.

"That must have been what Andrea was afraid of," I said.

"I think she was afraid of more than that," Simone said, cutting back into the discussion.

"What's worse than that?"

"These viruses are modifying the germline."

"Nobody would do that," Tshala said. "Not even Stanley,"

"They did," Simone said. "They targeted the germline cells."

"What's the difference?" I asked.

Tshala stood up, pacing the room like a teacher in front of a class, which I'm sure she'd been in her graduate school days. "There are two basic kinds of DNA modification. One, called Somatic modification, targets cells in the body, usually specific cells that were causing an illness or condition, such as cancer. Those techniques modifying specific cells could create new cells in the body with that same modification, but it would not be passed on to children born of that person. This is the commonly-accepted approach to genetic therapy. It's what the companies you invest with are doing."

She gathered herself, as though she needed to steel her nerves to consider the second approach. "Germline modifications are different. Any modification that changes the germline would be passed on to future generations. It's not just re-engineering specific cells in the body. It is re-engineering people themselves. No one does that kind of therapy and the research associated with it for the obvious ethical reasons attached."

"Not quite no one." Simone's voice was thin over the phone speaker, but I could hear the anger in it. "A Chinese doctor did. About six months ago."

"Oh, I'd forgotten about that," Tshala said. "A Doctor Liu. He edited the genome of six unborn children, without the parent's consent. He said he was protecting them from AIDS. Those edits will be passed down to their children, too. There was a huge uproar about it."

Doctor Liu. The hairs on my neck stood up when Tshala said the name. It was what Andrea had accidentally called Genistar's new chief science officer.

"He lost his post at the university in Shenzen. I think he's pretty much disgraced," Simone said. "I'd heard he's disappeared, probably into Chinese prison."

"Do you know if he had any connection to Doctor Huang at Genistar?" I asked Tshala.

She shook her head. "Doctor Huang came from Beijing University. I don't know if they ever worked together."

I still didn't believe it could a coincidence. I made a mental note to push Marco to see if his friends had found any connection between Doctor Liu and Doctor Huang.

While that piece still didn't fit together in my mind, the rest did. Genistar seemed to have perfected that second approach, targeting the germline. And if their platform was delivered by a virus as contagious as their version of Ebola it meant they could engineer wholesale modifications of entire populations, without the consent or even the knowledge of the people being targeted.

"The virus seems to stay dormant in the body, like the cold sore virus," Simone said. That means it not only can modify sperm cells over time but would target any embryo. So, both men and women are affected.

Would stopping that have been enough for Andrea to die for? I wondered.

Either way we were getting ready to fly into the heart of a region where that virus was already on the loose. Suddenly Antarctica was looking pretty good to me, too.

"There's one more thing I didn't understand," Simone said.

"There's more?"

"I tried to work the technique myself. To insert a different modification. But the virus particles I tried it on just died."

"They were designed to do that," Tshala said. "We didn't want just anyone with a little skill to be able to leverage the vector. So, we build a sort of chemical lock. There is a specific chemical that has to be present in the environment when the modification is done, or the virus dies. It's something that doesn't occur in nature. No one but us would have it. Without it, any attempted changes to the virus particles causes them to just shut down. We would use different compounds for different batches. Sort of like changing the locks in your door. We were working on another failsafe, too. Another molecule that would shut down the virus even in people already exposed to it, in case somehow it did get out of hand. We called it the killswitch. I told Alan, that's what Andrea was focused on at the end. But she hadn't got that one to work right when they split us apart."

"Too bad. That would have been handy," Simone said, dryly.

"So, what's next?" I asked.

"I'm going to keep looking at this thing," Simone said. "Maybe I can figure out the killswitch as you call it. Or some other way to shut it down. And I'm going to just to admire it. The science is amazing, even if the use case is terrifying. What are you going to do?"

"We're going to see a witch doctor," I said.

I could almost feel Simone shrug on the other end of the phone. "That's as good an idea as anything I can think of," she said. "Good luck to us both."

Chapter Twenty-Four

WE GATHERED IN my room at 2 in the morning. With my new clothes and backpack, and the butterflies roiling my stomach, I felt like a kid getting ready for the first day at a new school.

Marco passed a USB drive to Tshala. "All you need to do is put this in the laptop while you're logged into the network. But don't forget to take it out after you're done. I don't want them figuring out what's on this thing." She nodded and put it in her pants pocket. He also handed each of us a map of the area with the town of Makoua circled, and the areas where Tshala had said the labs and dorms were located drawn on the map with a red marker. He'd added the compass headings to use to get from the a nearby lake to those locations, and the return headings as well. He made us repeat them back to him. Tshala looked at her compass with a combination of curiosity and contempt, as though he'd handed her a sextant and spyglass and suggested she find her way around with those.

"I don't need this thing. I have my phone," she said. "It has GPS."

Marco growled. "Cellphones stay here. They're no use up there. No charging stations in the jungle anyway."

He led us down the stairs and out through the deserted kitchen. He was more serious than usual, his instructions clear and precise, but with no banter or wasted words. "If there's anybody watching from the outside, I don't want to make it any easier for them," he said as we slipped out the back door. A Volkswagen van was idling in the alley behind the hotel. The exterior of the van was a mass of dents and rust marks—unremarkable on the streets of Kinshasa. Atombe waved to us from behind the wheel as Marco slid the side door open. The inside was surprisingly clean and plush, with firm leather seats and the quiet sigh of air conditioning. "Sometimes we have clients who need to get around without a lot of attention," Marco said, when he saw my surprised look. "They want to be unnoticed, but not uncomfortable."

I saw Atombe glance back at Tshala. He smiled brightly. She managed a smile back. I felt my heart break for them both. At that moment he could see nothing but a bright, endless future. I was sure he was starting to imagine Tshala in that future, with no idea of the disease that was no doubt already starting to expand its foothold in her body. And for her, carrying that terrible secret, trying to enjoy her time with him before the truth became too obvious to hide.

We sped through the sleeping city, the tall buildings and shopping malls giving way to low storefronts and fenced-in homes, and then to the densely-packed concrete houses that ringed the city. Once we left the downtown area power became spotty, then non-existent, and the only lights were our headlights. There were few road signs, but Atombe drove confidently. We worked our way south east for nearly an hour, the roads themselves going from the multi-lane boulevards in the Gombe district to narrow pavement, then finally to rough dirt tracks. Fortunately it still had not rained much yet, even though that season was approaching. The roads were rutted, but hard and dry.

"Where's the plane?" I said, finally. "There are no airstrips out here."

"Don't need an airstrip," Marco said. I dropped back into silence, not sure what to make of that response.

We left the populated areas and entered the rainforest, the bottom of the van barely clearing the deeper cuts in the uneven road. After a few minutes we came to a space that opened onto a lake, its shape outlined by the light from the quarter moon shining off the still water. A pontoon plane was tied to a small dock directly in front of us.

"We'll use this to drop into the lake near Makoua," Marco said. "From there it's a half-hour hike to the lab and the dorms."

"The field hospital where they're treating the Ebola victims is near the town, a few minutes past that," Tshala added.

"Who's flying?" I said, looking around.

"Me," a voice said from my left.

Alphonso stepped out of the shadows.

"This is yours?" I pointed to the pontoon plane.

"My regular ride's in the shop," he said. "Got some holes in it. But yes. This is mine. There's more water than runways in the Congo. It comes in handy." He turned to Marco. "About time you got here. I was getting lonely."

"We're actually a few minutes ahead of schedule," Marco said.

I checked my watch. The simple steel watch Andrea had given me. Its hands glowed confidently, positioned at just before 3:30 a.m.

"We're flying in the dark?" Tshala said doubtfully.

"Yes," Marco said. "We'll land at first light. That will give Alphonso enough visibility to put us down, but still be dark enough where it's still unlikely anybody up there will spot us. We'll hide the plane and I'll watch it with Alphonso while you guys do your thing."

"Won't they hear us land?" I asked.

Alphonso smiled. "Let me worry about that," he said.

Based on the way he smiled, I decided I'd keep worrying about it, too.

We put our backpacks in the plane. Alphonso wandered off for a final cigarette, and then we all climbed aboard. There were two seats up front for pilot and co-pilot, then a bench seat that would have been comfortable for two but was more than cramped for Tshala, Atombe and me. Tshala sat in the middle.

The takeoff was smooth, but still nerve-wracking in the pitch dark. As the plane picked up speed across the water, my imagination conjured trees, rock formations, boats and any number of other objects in our path that could end our trip before we even got airborne. I barely noticed Tshala's fingernails digging into my forearm as we raced forward into the blackness. I had a feeling Atombe was getting the same treatment on her other side. In the dim light from the cockpit dashboard I could see Marco checking the time on his watch. He might as well have been on the 5:00 commuter train into New York City, for all the concern he seemed to show about our headlong rush towards an invisible shore somewhere ahead.

I could feel my fellow passengers exhale once we were airborne and above any possible threat from even the tallest trees.

"How could you see?" I asked Alphonso, as he settled into our cruising altitude and turned the plane towards what I assumed to be north.

"I couldn't," he said. "I just count. If I reach twenty before we are airborne, then I know I have two more seconds left."

"What are the final two second for?"

"To apologize to my passengers."

"Don't let him fool you," Marco said. "He's done this a dozen times. Look on the bright side. At least nobody was shooting at us this time."

The drone of the engine lulled everyone into silence. Outside my window the dim light of the downtown area of Kinshasa was dropping out of sight behind me, leaving nothing but pitch black below. It was astonishing to think that millions of people lived there, this close to the city, without light or power. The night was clear, and I could see stars scattered above. I thought about my late-night plane trips back into Boston or into San Francisco. The ground on those trips was awash with light of every kind for as far as the eye could see, streaming from streetlights, office towers, parking lots. houses, headlights. The light soaked the ground and radiated into the sky, washing away the stars. If you lived in those developed parts of the world, you never really knew what true darkness was; a darkness so thick you felt you could feel it on your skin, so physical that it seemed to flow around you as you moved. Here, that darkness was a way of life for most people.

About 20 minutes into the flight, Alphonso turned the plane to the east. We started a long, lazy turn. For a minute I thought Marco or Alphonso had aborted the trip.

"What's up?" I asked.

"We're a little ahead of schedule," Marco said. "We'll circle here for a few minutes, while we're still out of earshot of Makoua. Then we'll make our approach. I don't mind taking off in the dark, but even Alphonso can't land in it."

"Sure I can," Alphonso said from the pilot's seat, sounding a bit hurt.

I hoped he wasn't insulted enough to insist on proving his point.

We continued with our endless turn to the left for about 10 minutes. When we made the fourth full turn, I could start to see a thin line of silver glowing on the eastern horizon, a hair's-width of light against the blackness above and below.

"Perfect," Marco said. "Let's do it."

Alphonso pointed the plane north again, checking a hand-held GPS against the map Marco had unfolded. I realized we might be landing on the lake with a bit of light, but we basically had to find it in the dark—a black spot of water against a featureless tree canopy that ran for hundreds of miles in all directions.

Alphonso made a few minor course corrections as we moved north, but generally he and Marco had been on the nose with their navigation. I was on the right side of the plane so I could watch the thin strip of light fatten in the east. It was still pitch black below, to my eyes, but Alphonso and Marco seemed confident.

Marco started counting down the time when we were two minutes out. Marco slowed the plane as much as possible, reducing the engine noise to a gentle thrum. He and Alphonso traded information in short bursts that grew even shorter as the plane dropped lower in the sky.

"Two minutes to destination," Marco said.

"Eight hundred feet altitude."

"One minute."

"Six hundred feet."

"Thirty seconds."

"Five hundred feet," Alphonso said. "Cutting engine."

Before I had time to even process his last words, he flipped a switch and the engine noise stopped. Tshala gasped. The only remaining sound was the rush of air over the wings and through the now-still propeller.

"Fifteen seconds," Marco said, as though nothing unusual had just happened.

I could start to see movement below; the treetops flashing by below the plane. They felt so close I kept waiting for the pontoons to catch one and spin us into the jungle in a ball of fire. But the plane continued its smooth descent.

"You're there," Marco said to Alphonso.

"Got it," Alphonso said. I saw the treetops disappear into a different blackness. It took a second to realize that we were over water. For what seemed like an eternity Alphonso kept the plane airborne, then we all lurched forward in our seats as the pontoons caught the lake surface. We slowed quickly, and then settled into a gentle drift.

"Took you long enough to put it down," Marco said.

"I wanted to be sure we got near the far shore," Alphonso said. "You want to row this thing in from the middle of the lake?"

"Good point," Marco said. He opened his door and told me to do the same. "There are paddles strapped to the pontoon struts," Marco said. "We'll need those."

I stepped out onto the pontoon on my side of the plane and, in the growing light, spotted the paddles. I untied them from the pontoons. Tshala climbed out on my side, too. Marco and Atombe moved to the far side. Pilots, apparently, were not required to paddle.

"Pull hard, you two," Marco said to Tshala and me. "I don't want to just go in a circle all day."

Tshala's eyes flashed as I handed her a paddle. We braced ourselves against the fuselage and began to stroke in unison. The plane moved more easily than I'd expected, and in a few minutes the shoreline ahead started to separate itself from the grayness behind. "Over there," Marco said as we got closer, pointing to a small cove cut into the bank. We angled the plane in that direction and it slowly drifted in against the finger of ground that jutted out slightly into the water.

We climbed out onto dry land. The jungle was coming to life as the sun rose. Birds called to each other from the canopy, and there were quiet rustlings on the ground. Atombe tossed our packs onto the ground from the passenger compartment then jumped out as well. As we distributed our gear, Marco and Alphonso covered the plane with a huge square of green netting that had been stored in the aft compartment. The camouflage would not survive close inspection but it made the plane surprisingly hard to spot to anyone not looking for its outline.

"Remember the compass headings," Marco said. "And if you see trouble just come back. We can find a different way if we need to." He was clearly worried and seemed to be torn between his concerns for us and whatever memory the jungle brought forth for him.

"Keep your wits about you. And listen to Atombe," Marco said, by way of final instruction.

We tightened our backpacks. Atombe checked his GPS and took the lead, and the three of us set out into the jungle.

Chapter Twenty-Five

THE HIKING WAS difficult, but not impossible. The thick tree canopy kept the undergrowth to a minimum. We had to climb several hills, and the sound of Tshala and I breathing hard became a constant backbeat to our footsteps. There were some small streams leading down to the lake, but they were shallow and easy to cross. Atombe stopped a few times to check our direction and location.

A half hour into the trip, we stopped to rest and drink water. "I'm going to come in a bit south of the camp and town, Atombe said. "We'll intersect the road and then use that to work our way back. That way we can't miss it."

It was only 6:30. Tshala said the dorms didn't empty out until around 8, and I doubted Lufua would be in his shop before then, so time was not a problem.

"How are you feeling?" Atombe said to Tshala.

"Fine," she said quickly. She shot a suspicious, inquiring glance at me. I shook my head, letting her know his question had been an innocent one, and that we'd kept our promise to her about her illness.

"I certainly didn't go to school for this though," she said, more brightly.

"I did," Atombe said.

"You were in the army?" She said it like an accusation. The army in the DRC didn't have the best reputation for professionalism. Or integrity.

"No," he laughed. "That would be too easy. Remember René? You saw him once in the lobby. He was Marco's sergeant in the service. Marco insists on jungle training for all of us, even though we mostly work in the city. But René does the training."

"Why won't Marco go into the jungle?" Tshala asked.

"I don't know," Atombe said. "I've never seen him afraid of anything. But he gets strange whenever it even gets mentioned. René doesn't even ask him to go. And René won't say why either."

We put the packs back on and continued our march. In another 10 minutes, Atombe held out his hand, motioning us to stop.

"The road is just ahead," he said. "We need to look out for patrols now."

We retreated a bit back into the jungle then turned north. We tried to stay as quiet as possible but I found I mostly blundered along, snapping dry sticks under my feet, catching my pack on vines and branches. A simple crack of wood sounded like a thunderclap, but we moved without incident towards the lab compound.

I could see the brighter light of the cleared land ahead while we were still 50 yards short of it. Atombe motioned us to a stop again. We drank more water and I tried to wipe the sweat and bug spray from my eyes. Atombe looked as fresh as when we'd met at the hotel four hours earlier. I was once again reminded of how soft I'd gotten in my years in Boston.

"You stay here. I'll go take look," he said. Tshala's face showed a moment of panic at the thought of Atombe leaving us, but she nodded. He left his pack, taking a pair of binoculars and a GoPro camera, and slipped off silently into the bush. Tshala and I stayed put. He returned five minutes later.

"There are some guards wandering about but no clear method to their patrol," he said. "There are a couple of blind spots we can use to reach the dorms." He hit "Play" on the camera and handed it to Tshala. "Watch this and see if it's what you expect."

She studied the viewfinder as it replayed the video he'd taken. She nodded. "Looks just the same as when I left. The guards are on a different schedule than everyone else, so they're not changing shifts when most people are filing into the lab or going back to the dorms. The next guard shift will start at noon."

"Good to know," Atombe said. "You should look, too," he said to me, holding out the small camera.

I shook my head. "I don't need to go in there," I said. "I'm going to head up to the town and be there when Lufua shows up."

"We should stick together," Tshala said.

"You don't need me," I said. "And if we do both things at the same time, we can be out of here in half the time. Plus, if Lufua decides to be an early riser today I don't want to miss him."

Atombe scowled.

"I know the town," I said to him. "You don't need to help me there. I'm just going to see him and then hightail it back here."

He thought about it and nodded. I figured speed was an advantage, and he knew it, too; the longer we were skulking around the area, the more likely a patrol would blunder into us, no matter how sloppy they were. "Be careful," he said.

"If I'm not here in ninety minutes just head back to the plane," I said. "I don't know when my guy will show, but I'm hoping it'll be sooner rather than later."

Atombe nodded. I put my pack back on and turned back east, heading toward the road. That way, I'd run directly into the town, and avoid any patrols on the road.

It took me 20 minutes, and one or two panicked moments when I thought I'd gotten turned around, but then I saw the outline of some low buildings through the foliage. Makoua was really just a collection of six or seven concrete buildings along the road, with mud houses scattered around them. One of the buildings facing the road was a clinic run by Doctors Without Borders. Andrea had spent a year with the organization before I'd met her. We'd spent another year together there, with me running the field operations for what was called the Bikoro Health Region and her running the medical care. Another building was a small bar, serving local beer and grilled meats. And a third was the shop and church run by Lufua. Many locals turned to him for medical care before reaching out to the doctors down the road. That was common in the villages where Western care was still viewed with suspicion and belief in the power of magic and sorcery was strong. It was a huge source of frustration for the clinic doctors, who often only saw patients when they were on their last legs, only coming to the clinic after all local remedies had failed.

Lufua provided potions for various illnesses and fashioned jewelry that he claimed was imbued with magical powers. That's where Andrea had seen the rings. He'd claimed to use human tissue as part of his magic. Andrea had never fully believed that detail, but she'd like the story of it.

He also performed exorcisms. I wondered how many kids he'd pronounced as possessed, sentencing many of them to a life on the streets of Kinshasa or Lubumbashi, or the other big cities of the Congo.

I wondered if Atombe had been one of those kids.

I worked my way around the back side of the village. His shop was on the opposite side of the street. I found a spot where I could stay under cover, but still see the front of his building.

I saw him twenty minutes later. He opened the door to his shop from the inside. I realized the building was also where he lived. He was wearing a black suit, as always. He was more stooped than I remember, and just as thin. He swept the doorstep with a grass broom, and went back inside, leaving the door open behind him as the day began to warm.

I waited to the count of 10, looking up and down the street. It was still early, and there was no one in sight. I took a deep breath, stood up and simply walked out of the jungle and into the morning sunlight. I felt like there were a million eyes on me but I just looked straight ahead. I crossed the open space without breathing and stepped into his shop. I closed the door behind me.

He was standing at the counter that served as his storefront. Behind him was a shelf crowded with jars and talismans. To my left was a door that led to a large open room with a dirt floor where the religious services were held. Where Andrea and I had exchanged our vows, and those rings.

He looked up as I entered. There was a moment of shock, then he just nodded.

I stared at him, not sure exactly what to say. He saved me the trouble.

"Ahh, you did return," he said solemnly in French. "She said you would."

Once again, my mind raced. Andrea must have known for weeks what she was intending to do, in order to put this piece of her plan in place. I thought of her walking the street I had just crossed, or standing in this very building, only a few weeks earlier, planning her death. And leaving the clues she'd had to pray I would find and follow.

"You look older," he said eyeing me critically.

"So do you," I said.

He smiled. "I have cures for many things. Time is not one of them."

I took the ring out of my pocket. Andrea's ring. "I'm supposed to give this to you, I think."

"Yes," he said. "But I need both of them."

I hadn't considered that. I looked at the ring on my finger. I hesitated, thinking of one more connection to Andrea, one of my most prized possessions, being lost to this strange journey.

"Don't worry," he said, as if reading my thoughts. "I have something in return for you."

I put both rings in the palm of my right hand. They were heavy. And cool to the touch, despite the heat and time next to my body. I held them out to him. He studied them without touching them.

"Very strong magic in those rings," he said. "I warned you about that." He shook his head sadly. "You and your wife, you did not believe me. Perhaps you do now."

I wondered how much he knew of what had happened to Andrea and me since we'd taken those rings. Or of what had happened to her more recently. He took the rings, placing them on the counter, then turned and rummaged in a drawer. He lifted out a necklace: a wavy, cone-shaped metal ornament on a leather cord. "This is for you," he said. "She left it for you."

I took the necklace with a shaking hand. Now that I could study it up close, I realized it was a unicorn's horn, made of steel. The leather cord ran through a small ring on the back of the horn, set a bit down from the top.

"For long life, she said to tell you," he said.

I choked back tears, and put the necklace over my head, tucking the ornament into my shirt.

"When did she give this to you?"

"Maybe two weeks ago? She said she was about to leave for the United States."

"Is there magic in this one?" I asked.

He shrugged. "I did not make it, so I do not know. She just asked me to give it to you when you came. But all things given with love have some magic in them, I think."

"Was there anything else?" I said, confused. "A letter? Some documents?"

He shook his head. "This was it. It was all she could leave. Men from the camp came and searched my shop after she left, looking for such things. But they showed no interest in this."

He said it as though such searches were commonplace, but the words struck me in the gut. Andrea knew she was being watched and followed. I felt the anger and outrage growing again, thinking of how she spent her final months under the thumb of Stanley Reston and Genistar. I took a breath, getting my thoughts back under control. "Do I owe you money?" It seemed like a strange question ask, after such a strange conversation. He waved a hand dismissively. "The

199

rings are all the compensation I need. I was wrong to sell them to you. I am glad to have them back."

"I don't think the rings caused my trouble," I said. "I think I did that all by myself."

He smiled. "We always think that, don't we?"

I thanked him and turned to leave.

"*Attendez*," he said, stopping me in my tracks. "I am wrong. There *was* one other thing." He rummaged through the drawer and took out a small, square scrap of wrinkled paper. "She left this, too." He handed it to me.

On the frayed piece of paper was the word 'Hi.' Written in Andrea's curlicue handwriting. There was a crude smiley face—just two dots and a curve—after the word.

I read it and felt the whole world tilt for a moment. It seemed all the years, and even the space between us, across whatever boundary death created, fell away for a moment. I could feel her in the room, that most simple and casual of expressions in her note breaking down any sense of time and space. We'd written a thousand notes just like that to each other over the years, left on bulletin boards, in tents, on cots after one of us had to catch a flight or vehicle to some other part of the country. She'd written this one knowing what she'd intended to do, yet I could still feel her joy and optimism in that single word. I wiped tears from my eyes.

Lufua gave me a moment to compose myself, as if he'd known the impact the note would have. Then he moved around the counter to the front door and opened it. He looked left and right, then waved me forward. "The street is clear now, but there are always soldiers about. Be careful," he said.

I stepped outside, and he shut the door behind me. The sun was now well above the treeline, and I blinked a few times in the bright light. Then I walked quickly across the dirt track and back into the bush. I found my pack and started to make my way back towards the lab and dorms where Atombe and Tshala were. I fingered the pointed ornament on the leather strap. It was lighter than I expected, given its composition. I wondered where she'd gotten it, and why she'd choose to make that her final gift to me—and why it mattered so much. Unicorns had never been part of our world together. Too frivolous for either of us. In fact, she'd spoken of them derisively. When somebody proposed a solution too difficult to implement, or suggested a project that was beyond our resources, she'd tell them to stop chasing unicorns.

I felt like that was what I was doing now. I'd made it to Makoua and found Lufua. And I was no closer to figuring out how to do what Andrea wanted than I had been when we got on the plane that morning. I hoped Tshala and Atombe had had better luck.

Retracing my steps proved easy. In 20 minutes, I was back near the dorms where I'd left my companions. I was at the back corner of one of the dorm buildings. There were three of them, side by side, connected at the far end by a wider structure. They were 50 yards long each, single story structures of concrete with metal roofs. I could hear generators whirring in the distance, providing power both to the dorms and the labs. As Tshala had predicted, the dorms seemed deserted now that the workday had begun. The occasional pair of camouflage-clad soldiers, rifles held loosely in their hands, wandered by without any sense of urgency or vigilance. I decided Atombe and Tshala been not been detected.

I saw one such patrol come around the middle building from my right side. And as I watched, I saw Atombe and

Tshala step out of the third building on the far left. The door they'd exited was almost half way up the structure, so the middle building blocked the view between them and the patrol. The two were dangerously exposed in the open space between the buildings, as they walked quickly but casually towards the treeline. My heart started to race. The soldiers would come around the back of the middle building just as Atombe and Tshala cleared that same building from the opposite direction. They'd run right into each other. I tried frantically to think of a way to signal them. There was no time to try a satellite call. Atombe and Tshala continued to move quickly, without running. The two soldiers sauntered along, wasting no energy, but without altering their course. Both groups were cutting the angle down between them with every step, less and less of the building blocking their view from each other. I realized I had to act.

I took a deep breath, took off my backpack, unzipped my fly, and stepped out into the daylight, walking straight towards the soldiers.

Chapter Twenty-Six

THE TWO SOLDIERS stopped and stared at me in surprise as I walked towards them. They didn't even raise their weapons.

"Sorry, I couldn't wait," I said in French, making a show of zipping up my fly. "Too much coffee at breakfast." I tried to move casually. I kept walking past them, forcing them to turn around to keep their eyes on me, putting their backs to the rear of the building where Tshala and Atombe would appear.

"I need to get to the lab though," I said, picking up my pace. "Keep up the good work."

The two had recovered from their surprise, and while they didn't look hostile, they were still studying me closely.

"Your ID," one of them said. "Where is your ID?"

Of course, I thought. This was a company operation and highly secure. There would be ID badges. I fumbled at my pockets. "I must have left it in my room," I said. As I spoke, I saw Atombe and Tshala appear from behind the building. They froze when they saw me facing the guards. *Run,* I thought to myself, trying to look relaxed but annoyed at the guard's request. I sucked in a breath when Tshala actually take a step towards me, but Atombe pulled her back. I watched them disappear into the jungle just as the second guard put a radio to his mouth. I couldn't hear what he said.

"I can just go back and get it," I said. "No need to bother you."

"I don't recognize you," the one with the radio said. Now there was hostility.

"I just got in, from London," I said.

"Nobody has landed in days," he said.

I considered my options. I could try and make a run for it, counting on surprise and their poor training to give me a chance of making it to the jungle without getting mowed down by gunfire. But that would just bring more patrols our way and risk everyone else getting caught. Or I could just keep trying to bluff my way out of my mess, even though that seemed increasingly unlikely.

"I'm sure it's just a paperwork thing," I said. "I really do need to get to the lab. Do you want me to tell Stanley Reston that you made me late for his meeting?" I turned around without waiting for an answer, figuring I'd start walking until they either shouted to stop or shot me in the back. Instead as I turned, I came face to face with three more men. Two were soldiers in fatigues, with rifles pointed at my chest. The third man was Caucasian, and at least a decade older than the other two. While the first two looked like children playing army, he had the indisputable air of a professional. He looked at me with a raised eyebrow. "I'm pretty sure it's not a paperwork problem," he said. "But we'll figure out exactly what your problem is, don't you worry."

"Check the perimeter and the buildings," he said to the others. "Get some help. See if there are others."

I prayed I'd given Atombe and Tshala enough time to put some distance between themselves and the camp, and that they hadn't stayed put to see what happened to me.

One of the soldiers pulled out a zip tie and secured my hands behind my back. The two of them marched me along roughly, the officer speaking into his radio as we walked. They led me away from the dorms and up a wide path. We came to another cleared space in the jungle and a larger building that looked like it could have come from any office park in the states, with its glass windows and flat roof. It was nearly a hundred yards long. Air conditioning units hummed on the roof, working hard to control the temperatures within.

The soldiers led me around the back to a double door. The officer radioed again and the door opened from the inside, operated by another soldier. The two holding me pushed me inside and down a short corridor. The one who had opened the door unlocked another door and they shoved me through it. The room I found myself in was windowless and empty except for a few plastic chairs. The soldiers pushed me down into one of the chairs and then left the room. I heard the door lock behind them.

I slumped in the rickety chair, racked by panic and futility, the plastic tie cutting into my wrists. Whatever laws existing in the DRC applied even less out here than they did in Kinshasa. I couldn't imagine I would get out of that room alive. But, just like in the SUV after I'd been pulled from the restaurant, my worry about my own fate was overwhelmed by a sense of failure. I still didn't know exactly what Andrea had sent me up there to do, but I was certain I'd just lost any chance of ever figuring it out.

I sat that way for what seemed like an eternity but was probably no more than a half an hour, feeling more helpless and foolish with every minute. Andrea had given her life to set me on this course. And I'd failed her miserably. I started to wish she'd trusted someone else instead. Someone better able to live up to what she'd so desperately needed. I don't think I had ever felt lower in my entire life.

That's when the door opened, and Stanley Reston stepped through it.

Chapter Twenty-Seven

TECHNICALLY SPEAKING, IT wasn't Stanley who stepped in when the door opened. It was that same white man I'd seen outside. He had a shaved head which made his age harder to place, but I figured late thirties. He sported biceps that looked as big as my legs, and had a curled wire leading from inside his shirt to an earpiece in his right ear. He might as well have had a sweatshirt with "Head of Security" written across it. He took up a position across from me, arms crossed. Then Stanley entered.

In hindsight, I should have expected I'd see Stanley. It was his operation, and it made sense he'd want to see who the Caucasian intruder was, since clearly I was not just some local who'd wandered into the wrong place. But I hadn't really made that connection beforehand.

From the look on his face when he entered it was clear he hadn't seen a meeting with me coming either. He stopped short two feet into the room, trying to get his head around my presence in his building. I could almost see the same process going through his mind; in hindsight it made great sense that I'd be the trespasser, given everything that had happened in the past few days. But the idea that he and I could come face-to-face here, in a place where Andrea's memory was so fresh, was almost beyond comprehension.

But there we were.

"How did you get here?" The security guy said.

I didn't answer. I just looked at Stanley. I could see him work through a range of emotions in a matter of heartbeats: surprise, confusion, understanding. He calculated for a second and must have come to the conclusion from my presence in his lab that I had at least some idea what had driven Andrea to her death.

"I didn't push her," he said. Of all the things I thought he might say, that one was not even on the list. I was taken aback for a moment. It seemed important to him that I believed that. But my anger was building, too.

"Not physically," I said.

"We're doing amazing work here," he said. "It was her work."

"Killing people? That's not her work."

He set his jaw, getting some of his confidence back. "No, killing people was not her work. You should know that better than anyone. But for us, at least, any deaths are an accident. A bit of hubris, I admit. We thought we were ready. We weren't. But we learned from it. Get better, going forward. What you did, that was no accident."

"Going forward into what?"

"Fulfilling her dream. Ending the scourges of a dozen diseases on this continent. And around the world. Imagine a population resistant to malaria. To Tuberculosis. Children who don't die or wind up crippled from measles or orphaned by AIDS."

"That's a nice dream. But it won't end there. You can't predict all the consequences of what you are doing. Go visit the field hospital down the hill. You're already seeing the risks. You have no right to do what you're planning. You can't change who these people are without their permission. Even to save their lives, if that's really possible."

He shook his head. "The body is just a machine, right? Their bodies aren't who these people are. We're just going to make theirs a little... better. You have to agree Andrea believed that, at least."

I thought of what Tshala had told me about Andrea's shame. "No, she didn't think that. Not really."

He smiled, a smug, condescending smile. He was over his shock and back to being himself. "Maybe in the end I knew her a little better than you," he said.

"You don't know her at all. But you do know the ethics on this. It's why no responsible country allows germline research on people."

He sighed and continued. "I do know the ethics. But malaria doesn't give a damn about ethics. Measles doesn't. Neither do the people dying from these diseases. Once people see what we can do, then they'll understand. Your friend Thomas came around. He knows the heartache. The frustration of trying to help millions of people, one at a time. Spitting in the ocean. Spitting in a universe of oceans."

"Who gets to decide what changes get made to people?" I said, nearly shouting. "Is it *you*? Sure, you don't like malaria. But what about blue eyes? Freckles? Short people? Who gets to decide what 'better' means?"

Stanley seemed bored by the question. He was clearly still lost in the science, and the vision he had of himself as a savior of some kind. "We'll figure that out. That's the way it always works. The science comes first, then people figure out how to manage it."

"That doesn't work here," I said. "These changes are permanent. You're changing *people* for God's sake. That has to be thought through. This isn't a new dating app."

He shifted his weight, growing impatient. "How did she tell you? How did you know to even come here?"

"Maybe in the end I knew her a little bit better than you," I said.

Anger flashed in his eyes then disappeared. "Hard to imagine. You left each other," he said.

I thought of the video, and the folder, and the trust she'd shown in me, and the feeling I'd had that she was somehow near me every single day since I'd come to Africa. "No, we never really did," I said.

"She was my wife when she died," he said, almost as though that was his trump card or trophy.

"She was mine first."

He smiled. "Not in any court that mattered."

I glared at him but didn't speak. I realized Andrea had to have told him; our marriage had been a local ceremony, with a few friends as witnesses and Lufua presiding. And no paperwork. Andrea had said we'd do a legal ceremony once we got back to the States, but that the vows and rings were enough promise for her. The distinction had stopped mattering to me; in my mind, we'd been married. But it meant she wouldn't have had to file for a divorce in order to marry Stanley. In the eyes of the DRC government or the Western world, I could not prove we'd been married at all.

His smile became a thin line across his narrow face. He turned to his security guy. "Put him in the quarantine room."

"There's somebody in there," the man said. I finally placed his accent; he was Belgian.

"I know that," Stanley snapped back at him. "Once he's incapacitated, take him down to the field hospital. Let him die there. If he disappears without a trace, people will come looking. If he dies in the field hospital, he's just another victim of Ebola. And cut the ties on his wrists. I don't want the marks raising anyone's suspicion." He made a point of looking at me. "Once they get his body."

Stanley kept his eyes on me. "You'll be a hero. Another rich Westerner who died trying to help fight the Ebola virus. Andrea would have been proud. And don't worry—the strain in that room is especially... fierce. It's one we've actually retired. The infection rate was astounding, but we couldn't control the lytic phase. It was too destructive. It'll be over for you in a matter of a day."

"What if there were others with him?" security guy said.

"Did you find anyone else?"

The man shook his head. I felt some relief. Atombe and Tshala had gotten away. "There's still Tshala," the man said. "We haven't seen her in three days. And those samples are still missing."

Stanley shrugged. "She won't be a problem for much longer. She has her own issues." He looked at me for a moment, as if there was something more he wanted to say. But then he just turned and stalked out of the room.

Chapter Twenty-Eight

THE BELGIAN TALKED into his earpiece and two soldiers
showed up. He pushed me out of the room and into the hallway, one hand on the back of my neck, thick fingers digging
into my muscles so hard I saw spots. He guided me down a
corridor that looked like every corridor in every research facility I'd ever visited—no decorations of any sort except signs
articulating safety procedures or pointing the way to various
labs and administrative offices. The surfaces were all hard and
smooth. Easy to clean, difficult for things to grow on.

We went through a set of double doors that required
a code on a keypad. There was an identical set of doors in
front of us. The Belgian had his two men watch me while he
disappeared through a side door. He came out a few minutes
later, covered head to foot in biohazard gear. He nodded to
his men and one of them punched in a code to open the
second set of doors. He pushed me through that door, but
his men did not follow. I thought about trying to knock him
down with my shoulder and make a run for it somehow. But
his grip on my neck was too tight, and his other hand was
now on my elbow, twisting it in a way that meant I could not
turn without excruciating pain. We were in a large square
space with two doors on either side. Next to each door was

a viewing window. He steered me over to the closest door, and jammed me up against the glass, holding me there long enough to enter a code into that lock as well. He pushed the door open and shoved me inside, slamming the door behind me. As he shoved me, I felt a tug on my wrists. He'd cut the band with a knife even as he'd pushed me in. I landed on the floor, hitting my forehead on the tile as my numb hands failed to stop my momentum.

I stood up. The room had four things in it. A portable toilet on wheels, in the far corner. By the smell in the room, it had been used at least once. A sink, mounted to the wall near the toilet. A gurney, against the far wall. And a body, lying on the gurney. It was a man. His breath was coming in rasps. His nose was running. As I studied him, he began coughing—raw, guttural coughs. With one final cough he spit up a strand of bloody mucous that began to run down the side of his face, shining against his black skin. He did not seem to know I was there.

He was obviously deep into an Ebola infection. Simone's words came back to me. It was aerosol now. Meaning his every breath, every cough was spewing virus particles into the air. There was no way I could escape them in that sealed room. And that had been Stanley's point. I'd contract Ebola, and they could say I wandered into camp, already sick, and that despite their best efforts they couldn't save me. I'd be on the news for a day, as a wealthy Westerner and former aid worker, but that would be it. The government wouldn't investigate. The foreign nationals had all been pushed out of this area by government security under the guise of the danger of infection. Tshala and Marco could say what they wanted to, but no one would listen, at least not fast enough to get in the way of Stanley's plan.

The man coughed again. I thought about covering my face with my shirt, but it was probably already too late. The room had to be full of the virus by now.

I kicked at the door and pounded at the glass. Neither one even vibrated. This room was designed to keep people in—even people who wanted desperately to get out. I debated lowering the man to the floor and using his bed as a battering ram, but I knew that would be a waste of time as well.

I tried to get the attention of my cellmate, to find out how long he'd been there. And how long he'd been sick. He stirred restlessly, but he did not speak. I knew enough about Ebola to know what was happening inside him. Virus particles were entering his cells, using their own DNA to hijack the cell's operation, turning it into a factory to produce more virus particles. Once they'd multiplied by the thousands the cell walls would lyse, or burst, spilling the virus particles out to find more cells. It was an exponential spread, and Ebola was very good at hiding from the human immune system, which is why it could spread so fast and kill so effectively. And why Stanley and his team had wanted to harness it for their own purposes.

I also realized what Stanley's problem had been. If the virus spread uncontrollably it would kill the host in a matter of days, or less. They had to control the destructive reproductive cycle, the lytic process, so that enough of the virus spread to alter the cells they targeted, but not so much that they rendered the host fatally ill. They'd failed at that, which is why the virus was still spreading like wildfire. And the killswitch they'd designed for that situation hadn't worked. But if they could get that part of the equation under control, they'd have the perfect mechanism. One able to alter the

DNA of huge populations, in any way they wanted, simply by releasing it into the air. Infection would do the rest.

Turning the enemy against itself, Tshala had said.

Or creating a whole new enemy; a combination of man's ambition and nature's ferocity that would be almost impossible to stop.

I tried the sink. It worked. I decided not to drink from it.

I sat on the floor, wondering how long it would take before I'd feel the first symptoms. Headaches usually came first, and a cough. Then muscle aches and terrible cramps, as the virus started spreading, eating away at organs and muscle tissue. Often the face would start to droop as the underlying tissue was dissolved away. Bleeding from the eyes, nose and everywhere else would start at some point.

Then death.

I checked the time on my watch. They'd frisked me outside, taking the hand-held GPS I'd stuck in my pants pocket. But they'd left the watch and my necklace. My gifts from Andrea. Despite the circumstances I almost laughed. Had Stanley known the origin of those two items I'm sure he'd have taken them too, out of jealousy or spite.

A masked and goggled face appeared in the window for a moment at noon sharp, then disappeared. And again at 2. Two-hour intervals.

The man on the gurney still coughed, but he moved less. At 4 p.m., just after the guard did his two-hour check, I felt the sharp pain in the back of my head.

It was starting.

I shifted my spot on the floor. In the silence, my head started pounding, I couldn't avoid the realization that Stanley had been right about one thing. I had thought I knew better than Andrea what she'd wanted. What I thought she *should* have wanted. I thought about my own arrogance, pouring money into companies who were trying to do, in smaller ways, what Stanley was close to achieving here. I'd been happy to let them play God in their own ways, for my cut of the profits. I'd given up my ideals. Or at least buried them, to help ease the separation from Andrea. To convince myself that what I was doing still mattered somehow.

And now I'd failed her.

I wondered what she'd do, in my situation. Would she give in to despair? Anger? It seemed from what Theresa had said that Andrea may have given herself over to those darker feelings after we'd split up; that she'd been willing to cut corners and take risks. But she'd come back to herself, in the end. She hadn't lost her humanity, even if she'd run away from it for a bit.

I couldn't blame her for that. I'd run away from mine as well.

And in the end, I realized, her worst crime was trying to heal the whole world at once, not just one person at a time.

With that thought, I knew what Andrea would do, if she were in my place.

I got up. I went over to the gurney. I ripped off a corner of the sheet at the foot of the bed. I wet it in the sink, and I used it to wipe the spittle and blood off the man's face. He sighed as I did it, not in pain but in relief, as the cool water soothed his skin.

I ripped another piece of the sheet and soaked it in the sink. This time I dripped some water into his mouth, wetting his cracked lips. To my shock, his eyes opened.

"What's your name?" I asked.

He made a noise but couldn't form the word.

"I'm Alan," I said. "I'll help you as best I can." I wet the strip of cloth again and wiped his forehead. He closed his eyes, but his breathing seemed a little more even.

He was going to die. So was I. But I figured I could ease his suffering, at least a little, even knowing in the end it would not change his fate.

I was sure that's what Andrea would have done.

My headache got worse and spread further down my neck. The first cough surprised me when it came. It was quick and sharp.

I wet the cloth and this time I left it on the man's forehead, hoping the cool water might ease the throbbing in his head, which had to be far worse than mine. Then I went and sat down.

The guard appeared again at 6. But this time another face appeared at the window for a brief moment as well, also covered in a hood and mask. Both faces disappeared, but through the thick glass I could hear voices. One was shouting, his anger clear even into the sealed room. The other was arguing back but in a more reasoned tone. I couldn't make out the words. But the one shouting sounded like Thomas.

I thought about getting up, rushing the glass, pounding on it and calling him every foul name I could think of. But the voices grew faint and then faded to silence before I could muster the willpower to climb to my feet. I got the sense the argument had continued even as the men had left the containment area.

I realized I hoped it had been Thomas. That he'd at least had the courage to come see first-hand what kind of people his new friends really were.

My shoulders and arms ached, and I was starting to get cramps. I decided to wind the watch. I wasn't sure it needed it, but it felt good to do something with it, to care for the thing Andrea had given me. The watch was so perfectly her. Efficient, simple, perfect in doing its job.

I thought again of the necklace. It seemed so frivolous. The unicorn horn. It was fitting, I decided, through the haze of pain in my head. Chasing unicorns. The unachievable task. Like getting out of this room. Like succeeding in my quest for Andrea and stopping Stanley from his own insane quest.

Like perfecting the killswitch.

Damn.

That would be perfectly like Andrea.

I pulled off the necklace and studied the unicorn horn. It had seemed odd to me to that the ring holding the leather cord to the horn was on the back, not the top where it would hang more easily. My eyes had some trouble focusing. Then I saw it. A fine line around the circumference of the ornament, an eighth of an inch from the top. I checked the time. There would be no guard for almost another two hours. I grabbed the very top of the horn with one hand, holding the other part tight in my other hand. I realized my hands were shaking. The muscle tissues were starting to be attacked by the virus. I focused hard on my hands and twisted them in opposite directions. The top of the horn came off with a faint pop. I turned the horn upside down over my palm.

A small glass vial fell out into my hand. I stared at it as if it was not real. It was closed with a rubber stopper. It held barely an eye dropper's worth of liquid, gold in color like light maple syrup.

The killswitch. It made sense now. Any notes—anything obvious—would have been found when Lufua's shop was searched. She had to count on the likelihood that neither

Lufua nor the Genistar guards would see anything remarkable in the necklace itself. Another huge chance for her to take, but what choice would she have had?

I held the vial up to the light. If it worked, I could stop the Ebola that was building its terrible momentum inside my body. Then I could figure out a way to get out of this room. I realized I was crying, both from relief and from a feeling of pride for Andrea. She'd found a way to overcome everything.

I got ready to undo the stopper when the man on the gurney coughed again.

I walked over to him. His breathing was shallower but still steady. I got the sense that while the airborne contagion route caused the virus to take hold almost instantly, the final stages of the illness proceeded only a bit faster than normal.

Put another way, the man lying in front of me was very sick. But maybe not yet too sick.

If the container held just one dose, then I know I'd be sentencing both of us to death. But I had to give him a chance. We'd live or die together. Maybe I couldn't save the world. But I'd know I did my best to save this one man, in this one moment.

And that, I realized, was all Andrea had ever tried to do.

I undid the stopper. I poured half the contents into his open mouth in a series of drops, letting them fall one at a time onto his tongue. He coughed a bit, but I saw his throat work as he swallowed the serum. I started to tip the vial back up, taking a breath to down the rest of the serum myself.

Maybe it was the bitterness of the liquid. Maybe the water and damp cloth had revived him a bit, but whatever the reason, that's when he finally, unexpectedly, decided to move.

He swung his left arm up, waving it over his face to push away whatever was causing the taste in his mouth. His wrist struck my hand, knocking the vial out of my grasp and upwards. The rest of the liquid spilled out over the back of my hand as it flew and then the glass container struck the floor with a high-pitched ping, skittering across the tile. I searched for it frantically finally finding it near the side wall.

It was unbroken.

And empty.

I put the stopper back in the glass vial with a shaking hand, reassembled the ornament and put the necklace back on. I sat back down, looking at the wet slick on the back of my hand where the serum had splashed, and more tears flowed down my face. I wanted to be angry at the man—I'd tried to save his life and in return he'd cost me mine. But I knew it wasn't his fault. I turned my anger towards Thomas for betraying me. And Stanley for the insane risks he was willing to take, and for the cold sneer when he'd told his men to put me in this room. I felt helpless again. Only a few minutes earlier I'd thought I'd live, and maybe find a way out of this room. Now I was sitting on the floor, wondering what the next few hours would be like before my body finally collapsed in upon itself, its contents as much virus as human.

Lost in my anger and frustration, it was a few minutes before I realized my headache had faded to a dull throb. It was a few more minutes after that before I felt the pain ease in my gut. Then I heard the man on the gurney moan. I got up to check on him. His breathing was far deeper and more relaxed. Twenty minutes after that he opened his eyes. They were still red-rimmed where the vessels had been burst open by the virus, but they were clear and focused.

I wet the cloth and squeezed some water into his mouth. He swallowed eagerly.

"Where am I?" he said in French.

I laughed out loud, a giddy, almost hysterical sound. The serum had worked on him. And somehow it seemed to be working on me, too, even just through the contact on my skin. "You're in quarantine. The virus is stopped. And we're going to get out."

He thought for a minute. "Yes. I was working in the field hospital. My mask ripped. And then they brought me here. But the virus. They had no cure."

"Apparently I have one," I said. "Or at least I did. Can you get up?"

He nodded. I helped him swing his legs over the side of the gurney. He was unsteady, but after getting his balance he took a few halting steps.

"You're going to be weak for a while. And you might have some other symptoms. Your organs were under a lot of stress. But you should recover."

I asked him his name. "Wilson," he said. "How did you do this?"

"Wasn't me," I said. "And we can talk later." I checked my watch. It was 7:30. The next guard visit would be in half an hour. I thought quickly. The worker at the labs had started filing in around 8:30. But Tshala had said the next security shift would start at noon. That hopefully meant a noon-to-8 shift for security. There should be a new guard on the next rotation, making his first rounds at 8:00. That might do the trick.

I explained to Wilson that they would never let me go alive. And that they'd assume he knew too much now, too, for reasons I'd share later. We had to escape. He nodded enthusiastically. Apparently, his loyalty to his employers had diminished when they left him in the quarantine room to die.

I told him my plan. He hesitated when I outlined the first step. But I told him it was essential.

At ten of eight I stood in front of him and closed my eyes.

"Now," I said.

"You sure?"

"Just do it," I snapped. "Before I change my mind."

"Okay," he said. Then he hit me as hard as he could, right on the nose. He was weak, but still stronger than I'd expected. I stumbled backwards but stayed on my feet. I felt the warm blood trickle down my chin.

"Good," I said, through a swelling, bleeding nose. "I wouldn't want to have to do that twice."

He got back on the gurney, facing away from the door. I smeared some of the blood on the corners of my eyes, leaving the rest on my chin, and took up a fetal position near the sink, facing the door, making sure I would still be visible to anyone looking through the viewing panel.

I calmed my breathing, keeping it as shallow as I could. My eyes were slits, open barely enough to see the door.

I'd counted to 200 when I saw a bit of motion in the window. Then nothing happened for what seemed to be forever. Finally, when I'd almost given up hope, the door swung open. Two figures entered, both in biohazard suits. They pushed an empty gurney. I realized they'd had to go back for the second gurney, but the ruse had worked. They'd seen me on the floor, blood streaming out of my nose and eyes. That would look to them like late-stage Ebola. Not having seen me earlier, they'd assume I was near death, which meant Wilson was probably already dead. As I'd hoped, they'd come to bring us down to the field hospital, following orders.

I'd told Wilson what to do when they entered. Right on cue, he moaned and started thrashing on the gurney. Both the guards moved over to him, surprised by the fact he was not dead. I rolled to my feet. I hit the first figure before he even turned, driving him towards the far wall and slamming his head into the tiled surface. He dropped to the floor without a sound. I turned on the second figure who was backing away in shock. The two had expected to be retrieving corpses, or people who may as well be, and the bizarre sight of one the bodies rising from the floor to attack was providing the surprise I'd needed. I snapped out a left jab, then a right uppercut, knocking the second man backwards. Two more blows to side of his head and I had him reeling, but he refused to go down. I rushed him, grabbing him around the waist and driving him into the far wall, then spun him to the side. He fell hard, his head banging off the edge of the sink far too hard for the material of his hazmat hood to cushion the force. This time he lay motionless.

"Quick now," I said to Wilson. We stripped the biohazard suits off the two men and put them on ourselves. Wilson worked slowly, his muscles uncooperative, but with my help we were both dressed in a few minutes. Then we lift the bodies onto the gurneys. We covered them head to toe with the sheets but left them in the room. Hopefully anyone looking for a while would assume the two bodies—the ones they thought were mine and Wilson's—had been prepped for removal but left in the room for some reason. I grabbed the ID badges, giving one to Wilson and keeping one for myself. Both the men were locals, but with the biohazard gear and goggles covering all exposed skin, the face on the badge was irrelevant.

"Here we go," I said. I retraced the path we'd followed when the guards had brought me in. I counted on the doors only being locked from the outside not the inside—a common setup in labs in case the building had to be evacuated quickly.

I was right. We moved through the first set of double doors, then to the second. We were through them in a matter of seconds. We jogged down the hallway. My heart was pounding. Halfway down was a sign marked "Sortie." We stepped through the door under the sign and into the twilight. We'd come out on the back side of the building, near the generators and a long row of propane tanks which fed them, and the bulk of the machinery gave us a bit of cover. We stripped off the biohazard suits, stuffing them against the side of the building and out of sight. The edge of the cleared space around the lab was 100 feet away, well-lit in the fading light by the lab's windows and by spotlights on the corners and over the doors. It seemed like miles. We took off toward it. Wilson sort of hopped along, his muscles still weak and atrophied by the virus, but he knew the stakes and found a way to keep moving as best he could. We reached the jungle and crashed in 10 feet deep before stopping. I turned to look back. There was no one in sight and no sign of alarm.

Chapter Twenty-Nine

ONCE INTO THE bush, the last rays of sunlight were blocked by foliage. A dim wash of manmade light bled into the edge of the jungle from the lab building, just enough to keep our surroundings from being pitch-black. We huddled where we were for a minute, until our breathing slowed.

"Can you keep moving?" I asked Wilson.

"Is there a choice?

"No."

"I didn't think so."

"Do you know which way the dorms are?"

He pointed towards the right, his arm barely visible in the shadows.

"Then that's the way we're going."

We worked our way in that direction, moving slowly to cut down on noise and to use our hands to feel the route ahead. I didn't know how much time we had before the guards would be found, but I figured it couldn't be too long. We needed to get to my pack, which I hoped was still where I left it on the far end of the dorms. I couldn't imagine Marco and the others had hung around this long, but I decided the best plan was to try and get back to the lake, hoping the patrols that would soon come after us would mostly focus on the road and the route to Bikoro, figuring that's the direction I'd head.

I checked my watch. It was 8:15. It took another 20 minutes to make it around the far end of the dorms. Twice we had to lie flat while patrols passed by, but they stayed in the cleared areas, and were easily spotted in the lights from the building.

"Wait here," I said to Wilson when we were opposite the middle of the dorm complex. I tried to picture the way the dorms had looked when I dropped the pack and started walking towards the soldiers. I kept moving along the edge of the jungle. When I felt I was at that same angle, I started feeling around for the pack. It took longer than I'd thought it would, and I started to despair, thinking that maybe Atombe had taken the pack with him. But then my hand touched a nylon strap. I felt at least one level of stress wash out of my shoulders. With the pack we had a compass—and a chance to find our way back to the lake. What we'd do after that I had no idea. But Marco had called that the rally point, and from there at least I could figure out a better plan.

I retrieved the compass, the water bottle and the small flashlight from the pack, then strapped it on my back. I found Wilson where I'd left him.

I drained half the bottle, realizing I hadn't had anything since early that morning. "Drink," I said, holding out the plastic bottle to Wilson. He swallowed the other half greedily.

"That way," I said, pointing in the direction the glowing needle of the compass showed.

It was even slower going as we moved away from the buildings, with me propping Wilson up as we walked and giving him short breaks to rest. I didn't dare use the flashlight yet, so we blundered our way along, making far more of a racket than I would have liked.

We were 10 minutes into our escape when I heard alarms sounding behind us. The guards we'd locked in the room had clearly been found. I prayed it would take a few minutes to organize the search, and I tried to pick up speed, pulling Wilson along, daring a few flicks of the flashlight beam to spot the best path forward.

We made it another 20 minutes before I heard shouts in the jungle, still well behind us. At least one patrol seemed to be on our trail, or maybe just assigned to fan out in this direction. There seemed to be five or six voices spread out over 100 yards or so.

"We need to go faster," I said to Wilson.

"I don't think I can," he said. "Just leave me. I'll hide until I'm stronger."

I put his arm over my shoulder. "That's not a choice either," I said.

We pushed forward that way for another 15 minutes. I checked the compass heading a few times, shocked at how easy it was to veer off course almost immediately in the darkness. Once, I walked us directly into a tree trunk. I cursed in shock and pain as my forehead slammed into the unyielding wood. Wilson just grunted, but I knew the blow had to feel like a car crash in his weakened state.

The shouts behind us were getting closer. Our pursuers didn't seem to have any trouble following our trail, even in the pitch black. I kept us moving, still using the flashlight a bit, but hooding the beam with my hand. Soon enough, the light would be a beacon to the men behind us, but for now it let us move a little faster. I hoped that the patrol would eventually assume, if they didn't find us, that we'd gone in a different direction and they could give up the chase.

I heard more yells behind us, but this time they sounded more fearful, and confused. Someone shouted out what seemed to be orders, although I could not make out the words.

I hoped that meant they'd lost the trail, and I urged Wilson forward even harder. In a few minutes I pulled him back and down. Ahead, through a final line of trees, I could see a shimmer of moonlight and open sky.

We'd reached the lake.

We were a few hundred yards down from where the plane had been hidden. I guided Wilson in that direction. I figured once we got close to the where the plane had been, we could move away from the water and hunker down in the bush. Hopefully, the soldiers would just pass us by in the dark.

We were halfway to the spit of land when out of no-where, a hand closed over my mouth, and another one drove me to the ground. I felt, more than saw, Wilson dive at my attacker, but he was knocked backwards like he'd hit a brick wall. I tried to roll over to get at least a little purchase to tear the hand away.

"Jesus, quit moving. It's Marco." He hissed the words, and it took a second for them to register. I held up a hand to Wilson, so he didn't try another rush. Marco took his hand off my mouth. "I didn't want you to shout," he said by way of explanation, but not apology.

"There are men following us," I said.

"There were. They aren't anymore," he said. He didn't elaborate.

I climbed to my knees. "How did you find us?"

"I was tracking a herd of elephants, but you two drowned them out," he said.

"I thought we were being quiet."

"I could have heard you from Kinshasa. Who's this?" he asked.

"His name is Wilson. He was locked up with me."

"Okay," Marco said. He turned to my companion. "Hey, Wilson?"

"Yes?"

"If you don't do exactly what I say to do, I'll break both your legs and leave you here, got it?"

"Got it," Wilson said.

"Those guys were right on us," I said. "They could track as well as you can."

Marco held up the small GPS unit the security team had taken from me. "They were just retracing your route from this morning."

He led us to the end of the lake, then back away from it again, into the jungle. About 100 yards in, he stopped. "We'll lay up here for a while." He opened his own pack and took out some energy bars and another bottle of water. Wilson and I downed them immediately.

We got as comfortable as we could on the damp ground. Insects buzzed around us and, absent any noise from us, I could hear rustles and chirps in the bush around us. Even at night the jungle was active. In a few minutes I heard a gentle snoring from Wilson. I knew how exhausted he must have been. The killswitch had worked remarkably quickly, but it couldn't undo whatever damage had already been done to his body. Only time would do that.

"What happened?" Marco asked. I told him about seeing Lufua, and then seeing the patrol closing on Atombe and

Tshala. I explained my diversion and attempted bluff with the guards.

"That took guts," he said.

"Not really. I saw them in trouble and I just didn't see any other options."

"That's generally how it works," he said.

"Why are you still here" I said.

"I figured if you did get away somehow, you'd head this way," he said. "I sent the other three off, so the plane didn't get found. I waited here. If you didn't show by morning I was going to head down to the labs and try and find you."

"I got the killswitch," I said. "Andrea got it to work."

"How do you know it works?"

"I'm alive." I told him about being locked in the room with Wilson and figuring out Andrea's cleverness with the necklace.

"It's amazing you figured that out," he said.

"It's amazing she knew I would."

"You sure you're not contagious?"

"Yes. The serum knocked the virus out in a matter of minutes. It's remarkable. Wilson would never have lasted this long if it wasn't."

"Get some rest," he said. "When that patrol doesn't report in they'll send more men. It may get a little sporty here before we're done."

We sat quietly for a few minutes, but I knew there was no way sleep was an option.

"Atombe and Tshala made it out okay?" I said, keeping my voice low.

"Yes. They got the software installed no problem. She said her access had been cancelled but she knew Andrea's password, and it still worked. I guess they didn't count on your ex-wife coming back from the grave to help stop them."

I thought of the clues, and the vial. He was right in more ways than he realized.

"I can see if the software is working, once we get back to Kinshasa." He said it without a hint of doubt, like we were just waiting for the next shuttle bus to get us back to the city.

"I thought you didn't do jungles," I said.

"I don't. Not anymore."

"Why?"

"Jesus, you're relentless." I couldn't see him, but I heard him shift his position slightly. He was silent for another minute. "Okay, you want to know?" he said, finally. "It was a jungle a lot like this, actually. Night. My squad had taken up a holding position to provide cover for a larger team that was going into a nearby village at dawn. The larger team's mission was to grab the leader of the militants there, and bring him back, along with whatever intel they could scoop up. We were lying low in the bush when a band of the rebels walked right through our position. They set up camp right next to us. We just sat tight but in the middle of the night a few of their soldiers left camp to take a piss. They stumbled right into two of my guys. The rebels dragged them back into their camp. The rest of my guys wanted to go get them, but I said no. If we'd started a firefight we'd have alerted the village and the mission would have been a failure before it even started. So we stayed put." I could hear him shift his position again, and pictured him, in the dark, with that distant stare I'd seen on his face when he'd spoken about the names on his bicep. He continued, still speaking in a murmur that barely reached my ears. "Once I heard the gunfire from the village at dawn we swept into the militant's camp. We wiped them out. But my guys were already dead. Their throats slit. They were tortured. But they never revealed our position. The mission in the village was a success. I told my commander as soon as we got back to base that I wasn't going to re-enlist. He tried to talk me out of it. Said I'd done the right thing, putting the mission first. But three months later I was out, and working for a Canadian defense contractor, thinking I was on Easy Street."

"So that was the last time you put the mission first?" I asked.

"No. The doctor. In Detroit. That was the last time. Old habits die hard."

"Yeah, they do," I said. Then we lapsed into silence.

Despite my expectations, I dozed off. I was roused by Marco's voice talking quietly into a satellite phone. I checked my watch. It was 4 a.m. He put away the phone. "Wait here," he said. He disappeared into the darkness without a sound. I woke up Wilson and told him to get ready. Marco reappeared a few minutes later holding a large duffel bag. "Time to move," he said, fully back into his command mode. Marco led us to the west, towards the far side of the lake. "There's a patrol working its way up the east side," he said in a hushed voice. "But they don't have your GPS now, so they don't know exactly where to look for us."

I realized I'd never asked him how my GPS had wound up back in his possession. And I decided I didn't really care.

A few minutes before dawn, we had made our way about halfway up the far side of the lake. We stopped at an open spot on the shoreline. The lake was easily 400 yards across at this point, but I could see flashlight beams probing through the jungle on the far side. Marco checked his watch. "Okay, let's do this." He opened the duffel bag and dragged out a large rectangular shape and some foldable paddles. He unfolded the paddles and handed them to me. "I had Alphonso leave the emergency raft from the plane. We're going to paddle out into the middle of the lake. Alphonso will pick us up there."

"Are you crazy?" I hissed. "The patrol will see us for sure."

"People don't see what they aren't looking for. Or don't expect," Marco said. "Their eyes are on the jungle. They won't notice us. At least not right away."

He pulled a tab and the raft inflated automatically. He pushed it out into the water and we climbed in. Marco and I paddled slowly out toward the center of the lake, with Wilson sitting in the middle of the raft on the floor. There was a hint of light creeping into in the sky but the moon had set. Marco was right—the flashlights stayed pointed along the bank or inland, their operators never expecting that their quarry would be floating in the middle of the lake only a few hundred yards away.

When were nearly in the center of the lake Marco told me to stop paddling. He took out the sat phone. "We're in position," he said into the phone. "But there's a patrol on the eastern shore. You're going to have to come in hot."

"Roger that," A voice said on the phone. "ETA one minute."

I heard the drone of the plane engine 30 seconds after that. In the darkness it was impossible to tell from which direction the sound was coming. The men searching for us must have heard it, too, because the flashlight beams suddenly started pointing out and up over the water. The fingers of light passed over us a few times, but the men were looking into the sky for a plane, not onto the water.

The plane came in from the far end, low and fast, appearing over the treetops at the very last second before reaching the lake. I heard shouts from the far bank. Then gunshots. Alphonso kept his speed up. He seemed to spot us when he was 20 feet over the water. He turned slightly towards us then dropped the plane down onto the lake.

"Paddle now—*hard*," Marco said. We started rowing as fast as we could toward the plane even as Alphonso kept heading towards us, moving fast, the pontoons kicking up sprays of water. The passenger doors on both sides opened. From a door on the far side I saw a gun barrel poke out and immediately start pouring fire towards the distant bank.

We closed the distance with the plane. I started to see columns of water shoot into the air near the raft, kicked up by bullets hitting the surface. "They spotted us," Marco said. "Just keep paddling."

Fifty feet away from us, Alphonso pegged the rudder to the side, spinning the plane around like a fishtailing car. The propeller looked close enough to cut our raft into pieces as it swung by in front of us, then I felt the backwash from the whirling blades. Alphonso cut power to a minimum, letting the plane coast to a near-stop. The shooter in the plane moved to the opposite door and started firing towards the shore again.

I heard a *thwack* and then a steady hissing. A bullet had passed through the raft near the bow. We began to lose air quickly. "Faster!" Marco urged. I put everything I had into pulling the paddle through the water. The raft bumped up against the plane's pontoon seconds later. Hands reached out and pulled Wilson in, then me. Marco rolled into the plane just as the raft started to sink under the water. Alphonso immediately accelerated the engine, racing down the lake. We lifted off the surface, just clearing the treetops at the far end of the lake.

We all untangled ourselves in the back. Marco's partner René was the man with the gun, and the one who had pulled us in. He climbed back into the co-pilot's seat. "Everybody okay?" Alphonso shouted. We all responded in the affirmative.

In a matter of a minute, we were nearly a thousand feet high, the lake more than a mile behind us.

"You know, I'm really getting tired of doing that," Alphonso yelled to Marco over the roar of the engine, which was still at full throttle as we climbed away from the dangers behind.

"Me, too," Marco yelled back.

"Welcome back, Mr. Wright." Alphonso said. "You owe me a raft now, too."

"I owe you a lot more than that," I said, my heart finally slowing after the exertion and the stress.

"Who's that?" Alphonso said, motioning towards Wilson, once we were a few minutes into the flight.

"His name is Wilson. He worked for Genistar."

"Isn't that where that girl Tshala worked?"

"Yeah," I said.

"Thank you," Wilson said to the group at large. "I know you didn't have to take me with you."

"Don't feel bad. He's apparently starting a collection," Alphonso said. "He picks one of you folks up every place he goes."

Once we'd caught our breath, I asked Wilson about his background.

"They hired me to help in the field hospital," he said. "They paid very well. Plus a place to sleep, and food. My family is in Lubumbashi. I came to work here for the money.

I wanted to move my family to Kinshasa. To get away from the Ebola. And the soldiers."

"Is epidemic getting better? Are they getting it under control?"

He shook his head. "That is what I don't understand. That doesn't seem to matter to the doctors here. They give people injections and take many measurements. They say they are giving the people a vaccine. But I don't think they are. The people get sick anyway. But they don't seem to care whether people get better or not. They just seem to want the data."

The hospital wasn't really a hospital at all, I realized. It was just an extension of the lab, where they could trial the different strains of the virus and see whether their modifications were working. Whether the people lived or died didn't matter—their outcomes were all just valid data points for the research.

I fingered the necklace with the now-empty vial hidden back inside. I'd saved Wilson, and somehow myself. But now we had none of the serum left to save anyone else.

I hoped Simone was having better luck.

Chapter Thirty

WE LANDED BACK at the lake near Kinshasa just as the sun was climbing fully into the sky. Atombe was waiting there, leaning up against the Land Rover. He wrapped his arms around me, a broad smile on his face. "I wasn't sure we'd get you back," he said.

"I wasn't sure either," I said, laughing. The stress of the adventure was finally draining out of me, and I felt almost euphoric.

"I saw what you did," he said, more seriously. "We would have walked right into that patrol."

"I wasn't trying be a hero," I said. "I actually thought I could bluff my way out of it."

Atombe drove us back to the hotel. Tshala was in the lobby. She dashed forward and hugged me as well. I brought Wilson to my room and we each showered. I loaned him some clothes which fit him reasonably well. I ignored the messages on my phone from Frank and Kara for the moment, too burned out from the last 24 hours to wrap my head around the nuances of a business deal.

We reconvened downstairs. Marco had gotten us a table outside, away from the rest of the breakfast crowd. I filled everyone in on what had happened while we ate. "So, the killswitch worked," I said. "But we used it all."

"Give me the vial," Tshala said. I took off the necklace and handed it to her, showing her how the hidden compartment worked, and taking out the glass vial.

She held the vial up to the light. "There's plenty of residue in here. I need a chemistry lab."

"I think we just escaped from the closest one," I said.

Atombe shook his head. "There's one at the University. I'm not an expert but it seemed pretty well-equipped when I was there. It might have what you need."

"What were you doing in the chemistry lab?" Tshala said. "I thought you were a business major?"

"I am. I dated a girl in the Chemistry department for a while. I visited her there a few…evenings."

Tshala shot him a look that would have slain half of Kinshasa. He pretended not to notice it but I could see the satisfaction in his eyes at her reaction. Tshala turned back to the business at hand. "There's residue in the vial. I'd been working with Andrea on the killswitch for a while. If I can figure out what her final modifications were, I may be able to reproduce it."

My spirits lifted. Maybe I hadn't failed Andrea after all.

I looked at Wilson. "How do you feel?"

He nodded "I feel okay. Weak, but way better than I have any right to. I should be dead now."

"Is there anything else you can tell us about what they were doing at that lab? What they plan to do next?"

He thought. "I don't know what they were going to do. But whatever it was, I think it's soon. Some of the doctors who came to the field hospital to run tests said they were glad they only had a few more days of that kind of work. They said the trials were complete and that the agents were ready for deployment."

"I need to get back to my office," Marco said. "I want to see if the software Tshala dowloaded did the trick. Hopefully, I can find out more about what trials they're talking about. And what it is they might be deploying."

"Do you want to stay here?" I asked Wilson.

"My family is in Lubumbashi. I want to get back to see them. They have no idea what happened to me."

"I'll get Alphonso to fly you," Marco said.

I went back the room. My clothes from the trip to Makoua were still on the floor. I rummaged through the pockets until I found the scrap of paper. I looked at Andrea's handwriting again. I had an urge to carry the note with me, to have some evidence of her close by. Instead, I put it in my suitcase. I had lost enough connections to her on this trip already. I was not about to lose that one. I turned the shower on as hot as I could stand it and soaked for nearly half an hour, trying again to wash the fatigue and stress out of my body. I finished and got dressed. I checked my watch. It was only 11 a.m. I figured I needed to give Simone a few more hours before I started quizzing her for more information. And I had run out of ways to avoid calling Frank.

He answered on the second ring, simply muttering "Hold on" into the phone. There was some noise in the background than he came back on the line. "I was in the war room," he said, referring to the conference room that had been converted to command central for the merger project. "Where the hell have you been, Alan? We figured the jungle had swallowed you."

"It pretty much did," I said. I took him through the trip to Makoua, and my eventual escape with Wilson. "Jesus," was all he said. I knew he was trying to make sense of it all.

"I don't know what Genistar's doing here, but it's not good," I said. "They're taking some huge risks at the very least. And I get the sense it's not just recklessness. They're breaking every convention there is in genetic engineering."

"That's not hard to do," Frank said. "We're still figuring out the boundaries of this stuff ourselves."

"That's just it. They don't seem to see any boundaries."

"You need to tell the government."

"The health ministry is working with them. The government won't act. At least not fast enough to make a difference. Neither will the WHO—they're counting on Genistar to get the outbreak under control. It would be weeks before we could convince them to investigate their best partner."

"How would they distribute it?"

"Good question," Frank said.

There were not a lot of ways to spread the virus quickly in the Congo. There was little air travel throughout the country, and the road networks were all but non-existent. Trying to use the river traffic would be too slow and unpredictable. Stanley had to have a way to get the virus out into the most rural parts of the country, where the people most at risk were located. I couldn't think of an easy way for him to do that. But he must have found one.

"What are you going to do?" Frank asked.

That was the question I'd been asking myself all morning. "I've asked Simone to try and figure out what it is they're creating. That might tell me how they plan to use it. And Marco's seeing if he can hack into their systems and learn something that way."

242

"How'd you even know where to look?"

"Andrea knew. She was being watched. Her whole wedding to Stanley was staged to leave clues for me. Things only I'd understand."

"Jesus," he said. "Even…?"

"Yeah. Whatever they're doing here, it was enough for her to die to try and stop."

"I take it you're not coming back any time soon then," he said.

"I need to figure this out."

"If you don't start showing your face, the Zestra people will get cold feet. Their executives have already been asking where you are."

"I need a few more days. I have a sense this will be over one way or another by then."

He paused. "Okay. I'll make it work here. I'll tell them you caught some sort of bug in the jungle and that you're laid up for a few days."

"One thing, Frank?" I wanted to handle this part gently.

"Sure."

"I got the sense from Kara that things were rough back there. That people are sort of freaking out."

He laughed. "Everyone's busy, and they're confused by your absence. But no, it's all going okay. Kara's the one freaking out. But not because of the deal. She's just worried about you."

I thought of that quarantine room, sitting hopeless on the cold floor, feeling my body start to react to the onslaught of Ebola, knowing the horror of what my final hours would be like. I shivered, despite the two hot showers and warmth of the hotel room. "Tell her I'm doing fine," I said.

We ended the call. I picked up the manila envelope bulging with the wedding documents. I knew there was something I was missing. Something else Andrea had been trying to tell me. It was playing at the edge of my mind, but I couldn't bring it into focus. I lay down on the bed, trying to calm my roiling thoughts and create enough space for that thin thread of insight come to me.

And immediately fell asleep.

Chapter Thirty-One

I WOKE UP disoriented, thrashing at the air, an alarm buzzing nearby. I'd been dreaming of a locked room, the oxygen slowly being sucked out of it as I gasped for breath. The walls had been glass and people had been gathered around the outside of the room. They were sipping drinks, entertaining themselves by watching me struggle to live. Most of the people had been the faceless people of dreams. But I knew Stanley had been there. And Thomas. But Thomas had looked angry, shouting at the others, his words kept from me by the thick glass between us. The others ignored him, chatting and laughing as my life ebbed out of me.

I'd had another dream, too, still echoing on the edges of my memory. Of walking through Makoua with Andrea. The air in the dream was warm and moist, but the breeze had been comforting. We'd held hands, and I'd watched the sunlight stream through her hair, igniting her red highlights into rivers of fire against the darker brown. Her green eyes had met mine as we walked, but she did not speak. I had been filled with a bliss I'd not known in years, holding her hand in mine. I could feel the land around us, healthy, happy, clean. Somehow, in the dream, I knew her vision had been realized.

Africa was free from the ravages of the diseases that killed millions every year. She was at peace.

I realized I was lying on top of the bed covers where I'd sprawled after my call with Frank. Afternoon sunlight still streamed in through the thin curtains. I found the clock on the bedside table. It was 4:00, I'd slept for three hours. I realized the alarm had been my phone chirping at me from the foot of the bed where I'd left it when I'd flopped down.

I checked the screen. It had been Simone. I hit "Call Back" as I rubbed the sleep out of my eyes.

She answered immediately. "Alan, this thing is ten years ahead of anything I've ever seen," she said, breathless. "They have built an incredible platform using the Ebola virus as the foundation. It can be easily configured to deliver almost any sort of genetic modification they want. I found seven different modifications in the samples you sent me. And the locking mechanism is very strong. I can't find any combination of chemicals that enables me to make changes of my own."

"Isn't that just a matter of time?" I asked.

"There's not that much time in the world," she said. "There's almost an infinite number of molecules that could do the trick. To get the right combination of three out of that number? It's not practical."

"I thought you'd said there were five modifications."

"I found two more in the most recent samples. But those seem to be flawed."

"How so?"

"They target PTH and Aldosterone. Those modifications wouldn't help people—they'd actually be fatal."

"Are you sure? Lots of drugs try and regulate Aldosterone production." I knew managing that hormone was important for controlling high blood pressure. There was huge money in any treatment for that condition. I wasn't familiar with the other hormone though. "What's PTH?"

"It regulates calcium levels. Without it, your muscles stop working. You'd die quickly when your diaphragm started spasming."

"They both sound worth regulating."

"Yes, but the modifications I found don't help regulate production of these hormones. They turn it off entirely. Without Aldosterone to regulate sodium levels a person would be dead in a week. A lack of PTH would have the same result."

"Maybe they're still working on those," I said.

"Yes, but to include them in potentially contagious samples at this point? To me that means they're testing them somehow. And if those things got loose in the wild it could be catastrophic. A generation born without the ability to produce those hormones? They'd either need an artificial source for their whole lives or they'd be dead in a matter of days. That's not ending a nightmare. It's creating a new one."

"Great, another nightmare for Africa to fight," I said.

"I'll keep studying these," she said. "Tell Tshala the science is incredible." She said it with a mix of awe and fear, the way I imagined other scientists had reacted decades earlier when they'd seen the first blueprints for the atom bomb.

I thanked her and disconnected.

I still couldn't get my mind around the sheer recklessness of Genistar in testing those kinds of modifications in such an uncontrolled way. But there was one thought that kept nagging at me, spurred on by the image of Andrea in the dream. Even if there were risks involved in the work Genistar was doing the payoff could have been everything she'd dreamed of. Genistar's work could actually make some of the worst diseases in the Congo manageable for the next generation. And maybe, with more time, just a memory for the generations after that.

Without a massive infrastructure buildout or billions of dollars in aid money, without even having to end the violence and stabilize the political situation, they'd have achieved an incredible goal. Sure, Andrea would have fought to slow the process down, to reduce the risks, even to get public buy-in for the effort. She would not tolerate their recklessness. But I could not imagine she would die to stop the work.

There had to be something else.

My phone buzzed again. I looked at the number and took a deep breath before answering.

"Hi, Dad," I said.

"How'd it go?" He was never much for small talk.

"It went fine. I'm back in Kinshasa now." I decided to skip the part about the blood samples and the gunfire. He'd just see them as more evidence of my insanity for coming back to the Congo.

"The Zestra people are starting to wonder what's up with you." My father was also one of the biggest investors in my venture fund. The Zestra deal would make him far more money than it made me.

"Frank told me. But they must know why I'm here."

"Yes. But you've gotten that done, right?" Leave it to him, I thought, to treat my final goodbye to Andrea like some annoying task that just had to be checked off the list. It occurred to me that that was probably no accident; he and Andrea had argued over almost every dinner table they'd been at together. She was about people; he was about profits. Those two ideals seldom mixed well.

"So why aren't you on your way back?"

"I've got something else to do here."

"Saving the world again? I thought you were past that."

I thought of whatever fear had led Andrea to the actions she'd taken. Something far worse than Ebola, Tshala thought. And my own nagging belief that I was still missing something that was right in front of me.

"I've got a few details to wrap up," I said.

"Come on, Alan, your investors are getting nervous, too. They want to know you're a hundred percent committed to getting this deal done. They don't like this uncertainty." His reputation and network had helped attract other investors to my fund also, which meant many of them were his colleagues or friends. That was a detail he seldom let me forget. It was true; I'd just returned from Africa, with few contacts of my own left, I wouldn't have been able to start my business without his help. I'm not sure I would have even considered doing it at all but for his urging; a return to the world of finance could not have been a bigger change from the life I'd led with Andrea. In the end, that was exactly why I'd done it.

"I've made your buddies a bunch of money already," I said. "They can wait a few more days on this one."

"They all know about Zestra. They want it done now."

I was familiar with their impatience, and their arrogance. Running a venture fund required making a deal with the devil. You were investing money that generally was not yours; the investors felt their money meant they owned a small piece of you. Or sometimes a not-so-small piece.

"I could just scrap the Zestra deal and focus on things here. That would take care of the uncertainty." I said it nonchalantly, assuming he'd get the point. The venture capital world was a two-way street, I'd learned finally; it was the

249

investor's money, but I managed the fund, and the success of deals such as Zestra hinged on me.

There was another minute of silence. The idea of me having leverage over my father was one he still had a hard time accepting, even though he knew the reality of the Zestra relationship as well as I did.

I liked to think he respected me for pushing back like that. But I knew the reality of our relationship, too.

"I'll tell them you'll be a few days," he said. "But you need to get your ass back here."

"Thanks, Dad."

Chapter Thirty-Two

I MET TSHALA in the lobby around 6. Marco was there, as usual. And Atombe.

I asked Tshala about the serum. "The lab at the university is actually quite good," she said. "I set up a few tests that will take a few hours to run. We'll go back later tonight, and I'll know for sure if I have the result."

Marco started to head toward the restaurant. I stayed put. "I can't eat here again," I said. "I think I know the menu better than the chef. And they could really use an update on the drink list."

"I know it's a pain," Marco said. "But I know nobody will try anything here. We can protect you better this way."

"I'm with Alan," Tshala said. "I want to go out. I want to have a proper glass of wine. And I want to go dancing."

Marco and Atombe both looked horrified at her third request, although I suspect it was for different reasons.

"It's risky," Marco said.

"I didn't ask," Tshala said, setting her jaw. I was already beginning to know that look. She would not be denied.

"Let's just play it safe," Atombe said. "There will be plenty of time for dancing in the future."

I saw the shadow cross Tshala's face. Marco must have seen it, too. She was insistent because she was thinking there may not be a future that included dancing for her. He met my eyes for a minute. I nodded silently. He thought for a moment, then pushed his chair back from the table. "You know what?" he said. "We can make it work," he said. "Give me ten minutes to make a few calls." Atombe stared as though Marco had just peeled off a human mask to reveal some sort of alien creature underneath.

It seemed to me the reverse had occurred.

Tshala shouted with joy and went back up to her room to change. I wasn't planning on any dancing, so I stayed dressed in my loafers, tan slacks and polo shirt—the standard uniform for expat businessmen in any country in the world near the equator.

Tshala made it back downstairs in record time. She was wearing a shorter, snugger dress—definitely more club attire than anything she'd put on before. I was amazed at how much shopping she'd gotten done in her one day in Kinshasa.

"You ready for some moves?" she said to Atombe, shimmying her way across the lobby, arms raised high. He rolled his eyes, but never really took them off her.

I couldn't say I blamed him.

Marco was back a few minutes after that. "Saddle up," he said. "We've got a plan."

The Range Rovers were out front already. René was driving the first car, with Henry in the passenger seat. Marco motioned Atombe and Tshala into that one. He and I then piled into the second car. A man I had not met before was in the driver's seat, with a young woman next to him. I wondered if she was Malundama, but the two were all business, and made no effort to introduce themselves. It was clear Marco had called in reinforcements to make sure we could be safe out in the town.

As we crawled along in the usual street chaos, I filled Marco in on my conversation with Simone. I didn't tell him yet about my worry that I was missing something important.

He just nodded, taking in the information as though it were a military briefing. Which I guess it sort of was.

"The malware injection worked. I got into their network," he said, once I was done. "I've started with the email system. That's usually the easiest to hack in any company since every-body needs access to it. I also I found the servers where they keep the trial results. I'll have more work to do when I get back, but it's a good start."

We arrived at the restaurant in about half an hour even though it was less than a mile from the hotel. Marco had chosen Restaurant de Vins, in the Bella River Hotel. Marco, Tshala, Atombe and I were ushered to a table on the bal-cony, where we could see the Brazzaville bridge spanning the Congo River, connecting the two capital cities. I ordered the seared salmon. Tshala went for the chicken. Marco and Atombe ordered the beef filet. The wine list was one of the bigger in the city. We ordered cocktails to start and I selected a bottle of French red for dinner. The evening was almost cool by Congo standards, and the rain was still holding off. The lights of Brazzaville shined in the distance, barely a mile away.

Service in the Congo is legendary for being slow and sometimes surly, but our staff was attentive and smiling. The restaurant was still fairly quiet. It was a surreal feeling, having the sort of meal I'd had a thousand times before in the finest restaurants in the wealthiest cities in the world, but now only a day away from being curled up on the floor, waiting for my organs to turn to mush and my heart to finally give out as the Ebola virus destroyed my body. The bullets kicking up sprays of water as we'd paddled for the plane seemed almost a quaint afterthought compared to my time in that room. And I knew even as I sat in that restaurant that only a few hours north, hundreds of people were suffering the very fate I'd avoided. Except for them there was no hope of salvation. Even worse, Genistar's vaccine seemed to be a fraud from what Wilson had said. Just another part of the protocol to test their strains of Ebola and to try and get the killswitch to work. But they hadn't made it work. Only Andrea had.

"I think we have enough evidence now to take it to the WHO or to Interpol," Tshala said. "They can shut down Genistar's work in Makoua until there are better controls in place."

"The WHO won't move fast enough," I said. "You were right. They're counting on Genistar's money and people. They won't want to hear that it might be all a fraud. They'll just say they'll study the situation."

"What about the Ebola outbreak?" Marco asked.

"If we can reproduce the killswitch, which shouldn't be that hard, we can use that for the people already affected by the engineered strains," Tshala said. "In the east we'll need to help using traditional methods. Quarantine, proper care of the bodies. Restricting movement of people as much as possible."

I thought of the dream, and the vision of Andrea and I walking through a Congo where those challenge no longer mattered.

"What if they're right?" I said. "What if Genistar can pull this off, and perfect the virus so it is truly benign? They could arm the next generation of people in this country to be resistant to Ebola. And Measles. Malaria. Who knows what else? What if they're one step away from success and we're the ones who stop them?"

They all stared at me.

"I know it sounds crazy. I'm just saying," I looked at Tshala. "That's what Andrea was working for. That's what you were working for, correct?"

Tshala shook her head. "Not to start engineering people without their knowledge. We weren't trying to play God."

I struggled with the words, trying to hammer my conflicting thoughts into coherent sentences. "It just doesn't feel right to me that she would have died to stop that dream. Yes, she would have fought their tactics and pushed for more control. She would have consulted with ethicists, and other doctor and scientists. But she wouldn't have done what she did. She wouldn't have been *that* afraid."

"What are you saying?" Tshala said.

I shrugged. "I don't know for sure. I just know I'm missing something. I think we could get the lab here shut down. the work would continue in a safer way. But I don't think that's all Andrea was worried about."

"You've done everything she could have wanted," Marco said. "We figured out what's happening in Makoua. You will probably have the killswitch." He smiled across the table. "We even got Tshala."

I shook myself out of my funk and raised my glass, matching his smile. "Yes, the best part of all." We clinked glasses just as our food arrived. The rest of the meal was more light-hearted.

We shared creme brûlée and ice cream after dinner, and I ordered glasses of Port wine for the table. "Okay, now dancing," Tshala said. "Then back to work."

Marco's guys brought the car around and we were back on the road. The next stop was the New Savannah Bar. The bar, which called itself a disco, was a series of connected rooms with low ceilings and various colored stage lights and speakers mounted in all the corners. The decor was modern and simple. The bar was painted black and the chairs were black and silver. All in all, the place looked like a W Hotel lobby on a bad batch of LSD. It was a Thursday night and only 10 p.m., but the bar was pretty busy with people from a variety of nationalities, and the dance floor was already halfway full, Western music throbbing through all the speakers. There was a table waiting for us along the side in a back room that was quieter than the main floor. Tshala dragged Atombe straight onto the dance floor. Marco and I took up seats at the table and ordered beers. René joined us, too. The rest of Marco's team fanned out through the night club, covering all the key vantage points.

"Looks like you brought an army tonight," I said to Marco, clinking glasses. "Frank will fall over when he sees the bill for this one."

"This one's on the house," Marco said. "We all earned it." He didn't say it, but I guessed he was thinking about Tshala, and how many nights of dancing she might have left.

"I finally heard back from my friends," Marco continued. "The doctor you wanted me to look into? Huang? It's an odd case."

"How so?"

"He's got a pedigree a mile long on paper; taught at Beijing University, published a whole bunch of papers."

"What's the odd part?"

"The people who have been studying the region for a long time, and who have contacts there, say they'd never even heard of him, until he got the Genistar role. All the papers look legit, but if you look back in time into the websites they're published on, none of them appeared until six months ago; even the ones dated a few years back don't show up on the older versions of the site."

"So, he was below the radar?"

"Could be," Marco said. "But to my contacts, who are very good at this stuff, it's like he didn't really exist until six months ago, then he suddenly popped out of nowhere."

"A recluse?" I asked.

"Or a cover," René said.

Marco nodded. "That's what my contacts think. Another odd thing; there's not a picture of him anywhere. Not even on the university website. My friends say that for all intents, he just appeared in the world about a month after your other guy disappears. I'm thinking your two doctors are the same person."

I thought about that. Would Stanley have been desperate enough to take on a discredited Chinese geneticist to keep his work going after Andrea started resisting? It was hard to imagine; his company would come under huge criticism from every ethical scientist in the field. But it made perfect sense. Andrea had stopped helping. Stanley would have been desperate to get another geneticist who had those same skills. Maybe it was a risk he'd taken. But why the Chinese government would go to great lengths to give him a new identity only to then let him apply his talents for a Western company? That didn't make sense to me.

As I turned this over in my mind, Marco and René told stories about their various exploits in Africa. René was different from Marco in almost every way. He had broad shoulders, slower movements, a constant good-natured scowl on his face. While Marco was all grace and speed, René seemed more brute force. He drained half his beer with a single tip of the glass. But his eyes were bright, and he had an infectious laugh. I knew Marco and René were leaving out a lot of their most clandestine work, but they talked about life in the Canadian military, and the trouble making any sense of the strife in the eastern part of the country.

René tilted his glass and drained the rest of his beer. "Well maybe the Chinese will sort it out. They've got enough money invested into this country to care. And God knows, *they* know how to control a population."

I ordered another round. To my surprise, Marco did not beg off the second drink as he usually did. We clinked glasses again watching the crowd of young people on the dance floor and the older businessmen and women at the tables, all mixing happily.

René leaned over to me. "So, you got to see Marco in a fight, eh?"

"He's something," I said. "Never seems to lose his cool."

"I swear time stops for him," René said, putting down his beer and freeing up his hands. "The rest of us are like this." He jabbed a series of quick punches in the air and ducked his head by way of explanation, bobbing and weaving as much as his sitting position would allow, "...and Marco here, he just sees this," René did the same series of moves in exaggerated slow motion, mouthing a silent "Loooook ouuuut," at the same slow rate. I choked back my laughter. Marco just watched him, neither amused nor annoyed. Clearly it was a routine he'd seen René perform before. "He's a freak when it comes to that. He knows what's going to happen in a fight before it happens. Saved my life more times than I can count."

"And mine more than once already," I said, raising my glass to him.

A few minutes later, Tshala and Atombe made their way back to the table, both shining with sweat from the dance floor. I thought they were done for the night but instead she reached out a hand and grabbed mine, pulling me to my feet. "Andrea always said you were a good dancer, Mr. Wright. Let's see what you've got."

I tried to protest, both for decorum's sake and because I was still stiff from my romps through the jungle and manic paddling in the raft, but she refused to hear my objections, and led me to the dance floor. I recognized the song blaring through the speakers from various bars in Boston.

We danced. I did my best to keep up with her. She moved effortlessly, joyously, losing herself in the music. The rest of the crowd on the dance floor, a mix of skin colors, nationalities, languages, ages, all did the same. It was infectious. There was none of the pretension I was used to seeing in the clubs at home, where the patrons eyed each other to check out wardrobes, watches, automobiles, keeping score to see who was outdoing who in the money they spent, or the money they made. There were flamboyant clothes and bright jewelry all around me as we danced, but it seemed to be part of the celebration, worn for the enjoyment of the onlookers, not the vanity of the wearer. Once again, I felt as though I was slipping back in time, re-living a dozen different nights with Andrea, dancing in clubs in the cities such as Kinshasa with throbbing sound systems, or in metal huts in the countryside moving to the thin beat of a single battery-powered radio. I smiled at Tshala and she returned a smile bright enough to shame the strobe lights bathing the dance floor. It seemed for this one moment she was not thinking of her own illness or the uncertain future ahead for her.

I was glad to give her that moment of joy. I wondered if she had any idea that she was doing the same for me.

We clapped at the end of the song and threaded our way back to the table. Atombe had ordered two bottles of water and handed one to Tshala, which she accepted with a flirty smile. Then he flicked an icy glance in my direction. I just shrugged, thinking he was annoyed I'd extended the evening when there was work to be done. We finished our drinks and Marco nodded to René. He made a gesture to someone I couldn't see. We paid up and by the time we got to the door, the cars were outside. Marco and I headed towards the hotel while the other car turned left to head to the university. The drive back to the hotel was only a half mile, but traffic was still heavy. Marco dropped me off. "Atombe has tonight's shift once they get back from the university," he said with a smile. "But I added an extra man here, in case Atombe gets otherwise occupied."

"You always know what's going to happen," I said, mimicking René. I said goodnight and made my way to bed, totally exhausted, a little drunk and relatively content.

Chapter Thirty-Three

CONTROL A POPULATION.

Shit.

I sat up in the bed, the only light in the room a soft haze from the night light in the bathroom. I tried to push aside the thought that had dragged me awake, but the realization that had somehow come together in my sleep made too much sense.

I turned on my laptop. When it booted up, I opened my browser and typed in the first name, "Doctor Liu." Sure enough, a page of listings popped up related to the news announcement six months earlier. I remembered it. He had broken new ground, and created a global controversy, when he announced he'd altered the embryos of six couples during fertility treatments. The first of the babies had been born—with an immunity to HIV he'd edited into the six unborn children. When the storm of protest erupted, Doctor Liu took leave from his university, Southern University of Science and Technology in Shenzhen. He had defended the work, saying his goal was to show that humans could be safely modified to prevent any number of diseases or hereditary conditions. Before the announcement, he'd been speaking or blogging on a regular basis, promoting his belief that the ability to modify human DNA for future generations wasn't just possible, but was a moral imperative. After the firestorm he was completely gone from the digital world.

I typed in "China modifying humans" and got a series of stories on a Chinese initiative I'd read about before called the "Social credit system." Chinese cities were already rolling out social scoring of citizens. Those citizens with good—meaning state-approved—behavior got rewards. Good behaviors could include donating blood or doing volunteer work. It certainly did not include criticizing the government in any way. Those who misbehaved were punished and barred from certain rights and luxuries. China had already kept over 11 million people from booking flights and prevented another four million from taking rail trips. Other services on the list that could be denied to low-scoring citizens included high-speed internet, access to the best schools for their children, and even the ability to own pets.

Then I decided it was time to follow my final hunch. I keyed in Doctor Liu's name and "social credit system."

The search returned one listing, an article from two years back that listed him as one of the scientists advocating for such a system in China. In the article he talked about how new technologies could make the system even more effective, even foolproof.

I could guess what technologies he meant. As René had said, the Chinese were very good at controlling a population. And not afraid to use methods the rest of the world would frown at. I thought about what Simone had said, about the virus samples that would edit out the ability for people to produce certain hormones. That kind of deficiency would make a person, or a population, completely dependent for life on whoever could supply them with those hormones.

So far, as I understood it, the social credit system the Chinese government was rolling out used rewards and punishments such as airline travel or education to control behavior; I could only imagine how much more effective it would be if the reward was literally life or death. How many people would speak out against the government if only the government could provide the treatment they or their families needed to stay alive?

I lay awake in the dark, trying to find a different fact pattern that made more sense than what I was imagining, because it was hard to get myself even to believe the insane theory rattling around my brain. But as Andrea would have said, the theory needs to fit the evidence, not the other way around. This theory did fit the evidence. And preventing *that* theory from becoming a reality was definitely something she would have been willing to die for.

And if I was right, it meant Tshala's success in reproducing the killswitch was even more crucial. That compound wouldn't just be the only thing standing in the way of Genistar's plan to start modifying human beings. It would be the only thing in the way of a path to start enslaving them.

A few minutes later, I heard my phone buzz again. This time it was a text from Atombe saying *She did it*. He must have still been at the lab with Tshala. But that meant Tshala had figured out how to reproduce the compound for the killswitch.

Apparently sleep was not on the agenda for anyone that night. But what Tshala had re-created might be the key to any of us ever getting a good night's sleep again.

Chapter Thirty-Four

I HAD JUST fallen asleep again, around 5:30, when my eyes shot open. I fought my way to consciousness, realizing someone was pounding on the hallway door. I dragged on a pair of pants as I stumbled towards the noise. Part of me was wondering what I could use as a weapon in case Marco had been wrong about our safety in the hotel. I looked through the peephole, trying to keep my body to the side of the doorway to avoid any gunshots through the wood. I was relieved to see Marco's face peering back at me, stretched and warped by the fisheye lens in the door. He pounded again, more urgently, shaking the door hard enough to make me take half a step back. Clearly, he didn't care who else on the floor he disturbed with the racket. I opened the door a crack.

"We need to go," he said through the narrow opening. "The national police are on their way here for you."

I opened the door and let him in. "I thought you said we were safe here."

"That was before you got the whole country turned against us. I got a heads up from a friend on the force. They're going to arrest you and Tshala. You for trespassing at the lab. Her for theft. Get your stuff. You have ten minutes."

"What about Tshala?"

265

"She's already packing. Atombe's helping her." He managed a grin at that development, despite the situation. "We've got the van downstairs behind the hotel. You need to move, now."

"On it," I said. I hadn't brought much with me, and I'd given one set of clothes to Wilson. I stuffed the rest in my suitcase. I packed my laptop and cables and made sure the manila envelope was safe in my bag. I took the stairs down the three flights to the lobby. Tshala was there, in a sweatshirt and lounge pants. Atombe was with her. He had a cold, dangerous look in his eye I hadn't seen before. We piled into the van while Henry kept watch at the end of the alley. René was behind the wheel. "Here we go, boys and girls," he said. He dropped the van into gear and tore out of the alley, slowing just long enough at the end of the alley for Henry to climb in. The traffic was light and René pushed the van at a near reckless pace, tossing us around in our seats as he swerved around the small trucks and buses that were out this early. When we were a half-mile away from the hotel, he made a series of sudden turns, looping back around the block, slowing and then picking up speed again, checking his mirrors. "We're clean," he said finally. "No tails." Then he settled into a more inconspicuous pace.

"Where's Marco?" I asked.

"He'll stay at the hotel to chat with the police," René said.

"Isn't that risky for him?" Tshala asked.

René smiled. "Nah. They police would take you if they found you, but they won't mess with him. The Canadian government has made clear to the authorities here that they want him left alone. Plus, he contributes a lot to the local authorities, shall we say. The local guys will make sure he doesn't get hassled by the national police."

266

"Where are we going?" I asked.

"My friend's house, where we kept the samples," Atombe said. "He and his family are abroad. Nobody will know to look for you there."

"It's a good spot," René added. "Not much around it, so we'll know if anybody's coming."

"Somebody in the government sure wants you guys," René said.

"I told you, the health ministry is working with Genistar," Tshala said. "They must have complained enough to get the police to act."

"I was getting pretty sick of that place anyway," I said.

I checked my phone, which I hadn't done since Marco had assaulted my door. There were some notes from Frank about the deal. And a text from Simone that simply said, 'I know why you are alive.' It was early for her, too, but she was apparently part of the late-night crew that prior evening. I called her.

We skipped the pleasantries. "Tshala had sent me the formula for the compound you found," she said. "I was able to cobble a small amount together. I tested it on the samples. It's a hundred percent effective."

"But I never even took it."

"That's the magic part. You know what Batrachotoxin is?"

"No, Simone." I wasn't in the mood for a quiz.

"It's found on frogs. One touch would give you enough poison to kill ten people, maybe more. That's what this thing is like. Even a bit on your skin is enough to start to trigger the reaction."

"How'd it work so fast?"

"Magic part number two. It not only shuts the virus down, it triggers the cells the virus has infected to start making more of the compound. It actually turns the cells themselves against the virus, so it cleans it out in short order. It's remarkable. And it's stable. It'll stay potent in the air or on your skin for hours. For a biologist Andrea was a pretty good chemist."

"One thing though. It won't work on natural Ebola," Simone cautioned. "The Genistar versions are designed to be susceptible to it."

"Got it."

"Where are you?" She asked suddenly, hearing the blaring of horns around us as we moved through the city. I told her how we'd been chased out of our hotel.

"This is serious, isn't it?" she said.

"Yes."

I went to hang up, but she stopped me. "There's one more thing," she said. "Ari told the team yesterday that we're laying off half of the workforce. People are really upset. Is it true?"

I'd forgotten that that was part of the deal with Zestra, to cut costs before we did the deal. That sort of decision seemed so far away from me now, and so miserly. I knew the office in Israel. They were all friends with each other. Some of them would call me a friend too, and many had reached out to me after Andrea's death. I suddenly wondered what they'd think of me now. "It's true," I said. "I'm sorry."

"That sucks," she said, and disconnected.

I realized she was right.

We got to the house in an hour and unloaded the little bit of stuff we'd brought. Atombe showed me to a bedroom I could use. The bedroom walls were covered with posters of pop singers and martial arts stars. It was clearly the room of a teenager. But it was clean and comfortable. Marco arrived an hour later. I was sitting on the back veranda by then, looking out into the undeveloped jungle behind the house. Marco came out and sat with me. His mouth was set in a thin line.

"No issues with the police?" I asked.

"I just played the dunce. Stayed in the lobby and told them I was waiting for you both to come down so I could drive you to breakfast. I acted as shocked as they were when they checked your rooms and you were gone. My local buddies used that as proof I couldn't have been involved. The national police were annoyed, but they couldn't be bothered to do anything about it."

He was holding a bottle of water and sipped at it absently, scowling a bit as he swallowed. He started peeling a banana.

"No sleep makes you crabby?" I asked.

"I'm going back to Makoua," he said.

It took me a minute for his words to sink in. "Did you find something on their computer systems?"

"Yes. But not everything I need. There are some files I couldn't get to even with my software in place. It would take me another few days at least, maybe never, without some information I can't get here."

My pulse quickened, not just because the coffee was starting to kick in. "What did you find out?"

"I got into Stanley Reston's email account. They're planning to distribute the virus three days from today. They think they've got all the problems licked; that they've made it contagious but not fatal. And that they can demonstrate their ability to do this thing safely, on a huge scale."

"We can't let that happen," I said.

"At dinner I got the sense you might be coming around to his plan," Marco said, studying me closely.

I shook my head. "Don't get me wrong, I believe in the power of genetic engineering. Our genetic code is the most incredible, beautiful construct I've ever seen. Think about it. All life—everything that walks, crawls, swims, flies—all the trees, bugs, flowers—all of it created from a code with four letters." I pointed at the half-eaten banana in his hand. "Thirty percent of your DNA is the same as that banana. Seventy percent is the same as a sea sponge. Ninety-nine percent is the same as a chimpanzee. It's the most powerful programming language in the world. But sometimes it doesn't work right, and that can have terrible consequences for people. And sometimes there are genes that can make us better, healthier if we could just incorporate them. But we only understand a fraction of this language. If we mess it up, it could be devastating for all mankind."

Marco smiled, but it was a joyless smile.

"What?"

"I was thinking of the irony. Computer viruses got their name from the biological kind. A way to hack into a computer and alter its programming. What Genistar is launching is a biological version of that same thing. A programming virus that can hack people."

"Yes. And we know what viruses can do to computers. Imagine that happening to the human race. Except we can't just reboot people." I stirred my coffee. "The funny thing is, this might be an inevitable next step. This might be what genes had in mind all along."

He looked at me quizzically. "Genes can't think."

"No. But there's a school of thought that says all of behavior, for all creatures, is simply designed to enable genes to propagate. No living creature is immortal. But genes are. That's why you share most of your genetic code with a sponge—those genes have been around since almost the beginning of biological time. Maybe genes create people and then people create genetic engineering just to help improve the ability of genes to reproduce in new ways." It was my turn to smile grimly. "We think we're the top of the biological chain. But we're not. We're just the transport mechanism. We live for seventy, eighty years. Genes basically live forever. Heck, a lot of scientists say that's why parents will die for their children—just to ensure the genes are passed on into the future. Our genes are the only thing that lives beyond us."

Marco shook his head. "No, they're not." He leaned forward in his chair and locked his eyes onto mine. "Ideas do, too. Values do. People don't just die for their children. They die for their friends. They die for the things they believe in."

I thought of the tattoos I'd seen at the gym. "The names on your arm. Those are men who died for ideas. For their friends."

He nodded. "Your Andrea. I'm thinking she did, too."

"So, what are you saying?"

"I'm saying I'm going back to Makoua. I need direct access to the computer servers there."

"Did the emails say how they're going to release the virus? Or where?"

He grimaced again. "Not directly. All I could tell is that they're working to produce it in quantity. Then they'll release it back into the population in Africa."

"When?"

"Next Tuesday."

Three days. "How will they do it?"

271

"I don't know. None of the emails said."

I thought for a minute.

"I need to go with you."

"No offense, but you'll only slow me down."

"I need to talk to Thomas."

Marco rolled his eyes. "Your buddy? Hasn't he betrayed you enough already?"

I told him about the shouting I'd heard when Thomas looked in the quarantine room. "I know it's an outside shot. But I think he's finally figured out that Stanley is out of control. I think he can tell us how Genistar is going to release it. He's the only one who can."

Marco sighed. "I'll find him and ask him."

"He won't talk to you. It has to be me."

"You might have just been hearing things in that room. It might not have been him."

"It was him," I said, with more conviction than I felt.

"There's one other thing," Marco seemed more worried now. And a little bemused. "I told you, I used to run computer security for a big company. When I was in Genistar's networks, I saw some telltale signs."

"Of what?"

He took a breath. "Somebody else was in there, too. Somebody who'd gotten way deeper into their systems than I had time to do. They got all the way in, I think."

"What does 'all the way in' mean?"

"The chemical codes? The ones Simone told you couldn't be broken. I think they got those. Plus, all the other research. If they got what I think they did, they can reproduce everything Genistar is doing."

I felt a chill despite the warm air.

"Who could have done it?"

"Hard to say. Russia maybe. China? It was somebody sophisticated, but beyond that, it's impossible to say." He shrugged. "Welcome to the digital world."

That was bad news. It meant even if we could stop Genistar, somebody else might be able to pick up where they left off. But that was a problem for another day. I knew there was potentially even worse news than that. "Was there any hint of another plan?" I asked.

"I didn't see any."

I told him about my fear; that the Chinese had been willing to place Doctor Liu into Genistar under a new identity, in order for him to perfect his research, and to give him a laboratory in which to test the work; that laboratory being the population of the DRC.

To my surprise, he didn't push back on my theory or dismiss it. He just nodded thoughtfully.

"It fits," he said. "That's a classic Chinese cyberattack strategy. Get somebody on the inside of the company you're interested in, then use their access or their knowledge to hack into the computer systems and lift everything you need. They do it through joint partnerships with Western firms all the time. Stanley Reston may not even fully realize what they're really doing. They'll fund his research and help him make a ton of money, but they'll keep siphoning off the work and using it for their own purposes."

"He has to know," I said. "I just think he's decided not to care." I let him take a bite of his banana, before I asked him the question I'd been considering: "Do you think they'd do the rest of it? Actually modify their population in that way?"

He nodded. "The leadership in China wakes up every day terrified that half a billion people in their countryside will revolt against the increasingly rich folks in the cities.

273

Even though they've made huge strides in reducing poverty, their entire approach to government is still built around preventing that sort of rebellion from happening. And old habits die hard. So yes, I think they'd at least like to have the option."

"Even if we stop Genistar, we don't stop that," I said.

He fell into thought again. "Maybe we can," he said. "But that's just one more reason we need to get to Makoua."

I was relieved he'd switched to "we."

"How do we do it?" I asked. "We can't fly there again."

He grinned. "This time we drive."

"How are we going do to that?"

"Tshala needs to talk to her father."

Chapter Thirty-Five

TSHALA WAS GETTING sick, faster than she'd expected.

Marco and I had gone back inside the house to meet the others. She sat at the kitchen table. She was pale, and I noticed her hand shook a bit.

Atombe noticed it, too, although he did not know the reason. He asked her if she was okay.

She managed a smile. "Yes, just a little rattled from this morning. And from not much sleep last night." She looked briefly at the floor to hide a shy smile. It was clear their lack of sleep wasn't just because of the trip to the university.

"We need your help," Marco said. Tshala nodded for him to go on. "Your dad runs a mine north of Kinshasa, right?" She nodded again. "A small one. Most of his operations are in the east and south."

"We need one of his trucks. A cargo truck. Something with a company logo on it."

"Okay," she said slowly, trying to make sense of the request.

"And some dynamite."

Her eyes went wide.

"Alan and I are going back to Makoua," he said. "There's some stuff I need from their computer I can't get from here."

275

"Dynamite?" I asked. He hadn't mentioned that on the veranda.

He looked around the room "We all agree Genistar has to be stopped, right?" We all nodded. "Then we're going to put that lab out of operation."

"If you just blow it up, it could spread the virus over a wide area," I said.

"We won't just blow it up," he said. "We'll incinerate any trace of it."

"What about the people who work there?"

"Nobody will die," he said. "We can empty the lab before we blow it."

"What, you're going to just ask them all to leave?"

Marco smiled. "Trust me, they'll be very happy to oblige."

"I'll call my father," Tshala said.

"I thought you two weren't close?" Atombe said to her.

"We're not. But I think I know how to get him to cooperate."

Marco, Atombe and René moved outside to walk the perimeter and talk about how to secure the house. I was left at the table with Tshala.

"How bad is it?" I asked gently.

"I'm okay," she said. "I've missed two treatments now. I'll be better with some rest."

"Can I get you anything?"

She sniffled and shook her head, fighting back a tear. She'd pulled her legs up under her sweatshirt and was hugging her knees. She looked small and infinitely fragile. "I'm going to tell Atombe tonight," she said. "He should know, so he doesn't get too... involved. I just wanted a few days, you know. Where it could just be... normal."

I fought back tears of my own. And felt more anger well up at Stanley and Genistar for using her treatment to keep her hostage, and now for their willingness to let her die simply because of her loyalty to a friend. "You both deserve that. And a lot more," I said.

"Thanks," she said. She unfolded herself from the sweatshirt and stood. She was barefoot. I hadn't realized before how short she was. Her fierce personality and drive had made her seem inches taller in my mind's eye. But her green eyes were still bright and shining a bit from the tears she refused to spill for herself. "I'll call my dad," she said. "Then I'm going to lie down."

I watched her go, and thought about what a brutal, unfair world it still was. And how nothing we could do to Genistar would change that for her.

I decided to unpack and lay down for a bit as well. The closet was stuffed with a seemingly infinite number of variations of dark jeans and colorful shirts. As I started to take stock of my own clothing I had a moment of panic, thinking I'd left the note from Andrea at the hotel. But I found it tucked in my suitcase, safe and sound. I held the thin, fraying scrap of paper, which felt as fragile in my hands as Tshala had looked in the kitchen, and I lost myself in the simple word scrawled on it. A greeting from Andrea, left to me across time and death. Like Tshala, Andrea had known she was going to die soon. But she, too, somehow found a way to take some joy and even a bit of whimsy in the moment.

My anger burned more brightly for her. And for Tshala. Marco had promised that no one would die in Makoua. But I hadn't.

Chapter Thirty-Six

AT NOON THE next day I was lying under a rough tarpaulin in the back of a two-ton truck, soaked with sweat and inhaling the smell of moldy canvas and other men's bodies. Every ache I'd picked up over the past few days was magnified by the pounding of the stiff suspension on a rutted dirt track that was considered a major highway in the interior of the Congo.

Marco was lying next to me. Between us and the back of the truck were crates of mining tools, and two boxes marked "*explosifs*" with the image of a bomb blast stenciled above it. The word might have been French but the message was pretty clear in any language. The idea was that the heavy crates and those images would discourage any soldiers from wanting to look too closely into the rest of the contents of the truck. Although with every bone-jarring trip through a pothole or over a rock, I felt the boxes of dynamite shift, and I debated the wisdom of that strategy.

Henry and another of Marco's men, also young and African, sat on the crates at the end of the truck bed, dressed in dirty work pants and shirts. The two had been coached to looked as bored and disinterested as possible, no matter who stopped the vehicle.

René was in the driver's seat, wearing a shirt with the logo for the mining company Tshala's father owned. The same logo was on the side of the truck. The hope was that this all-too-familiar sight in the Congo—a white foreman driving the truck, with a couple of local workers relegated to the back—wouldn't draw much attention from any roadblocks we encountered as we got close to the lab and Makoua. Suffering under the tarpaulin, I did manage a smile to myself at the thought that, for once at least, the local men did not have the most uncomfortable spots in the vehicle.

Tshala had talked to her father the previous day, and after an argument about her lack of respect for her parents, he'd agreed to give her what she'd wanted, starting with the truck we now rode in.

"How'd you do that?" Marco had asked her once she'd relayed her success to the rest of us.

"He's got no love for the health ministry," she said. "They work too closely with the Red Cross and the other aid groups that complain about working conditions at his mines. Plus, I told him that if we don't stop this virus from spreading, he won't be able to get workers anymore and he'd be forced to shut down his operations." She shook her head in disgust. "That was all he needed to hear."

Earlier in the morning Alphonso had flown us up to a small airstrip that served the mine. The foreman there had the truck ready, including the work clothes and the explosives. "You know how to use this stuff?" he'd asked René, pointing to the boxes of dynamite. René had smiled and patted him on the arm. "I think I can manage." René had packed a bag of his own special gear as well—a dozen wireless triggers he'd rigged the night before, with parts purchased at a couple of hardware stores in Kinshasa. He'd also brought several lengths of flexible tubing and some wrenches. The foreman's eyes went wide as René laid out his gear to inventory it. "Just some stuff I like to keep handy," René had said brightly, repacking the gear in his duffel bag.

I'd asked what the wrenches were for. Once he told me, I was sorry I had asked. But I'd understood better how Marco could be sure than none of the virus would escape into the open air.

Now, four hours later, that bag of supplies was digging into my ribs as we hit an especially deep rut. I started to think René was steering to hit the rough spots on the dirt road, rather than avoid them.

After another half hour in the truck, I felt it decelerate and come to a stop. There was a conversation in French at the driver's door. I could picture René explaining to the soldiers that he was on his way from the mine up north down to the airstrip at Bikoro, to move the tools and supplies to one of the mines on the eastern border of the country.

The conversation went on for a few minutes. René's impatient growl came through in any language, and he had the sort of hard-nosed look that fit perfectly for a mine foreman, where most of the laborers were not there by choice. Waiting for the soldiers to finish their questions, I realized the intermittent breeze caused by our movement had been the only thing keeping my uncomfortable position under the tarp from becoming unbearable. Now unbearable was all I had left.

I heard voices in the back of the truck as another soldier chatted up Henry.

Just when I'd gone from fearing I'd pass out from lack of oxygen to hoping I would just to end the misery, we started moving again.

Twenty minutes later, we stopped again. "All out," René shouted, pounding on the side of the vehicle. Marco and I flung the tarp back and I gasped at the fresh air. Marco rolled out of the truck and surveyed the road in both directions, getting a sense of his surroundings. His shirt was wet with sweat but otherwise he looked like he just climbed out of a chaise lounge. I found a bottle of water in the cab and drank it down without a break.

"Makoua is just up the road," René said. "The lab is ten minutes thataway," he added, jabbing a finger toward the jungle on the right side of the road. He opened the bag with his timers and other tools in it, and put all that gear, plus 10 pre-wrapped sets of dynamite from the explosive boxes, into a large backpack. Each set had three sticks of dynamite, bound together with duct tape. He saw me looking at the makeshift bombs. "Duct tape, good for everything, eh?" he said. He noticed my forced smile. "Ahh, don't worry," he said, as he started to move the backpack to the side of the road. "This is nothing. Try jumping out of a plane with a bunch of this stuff on your back."

As he dropped the backpack in the dirt he turned back to me and added with a grin, "At night."

"Only to have me have to cut you down from a tree after I reached the ground, eh?" Marco growled. I noticed his Canadian accent was stronger when he was focused, as he was now, and his eyes moved constantly, always watchful, never nervous.

"That part was unavoidable," René said, winking at me.

Marco opened another bag and pulled out three biohazard suits. Those had been far too easy to find in Kinshasa. The plan was for Henry and his partner to stay with the truck pulled to the side of the road, spreading out the jack and

282

spare tire as though they'd gotten a flat, a commonplace occurrence on the bad roads. If the soldiers at the checkpoint had remembered René, they'd just say he'd wandered up to Makoua to see if he could get a beer while they fixed the truck, and that they were to pick him up when they came through town. Even if the soldiers had questions, which would be doubtful, it would take them a while to sort it all out.

We stuffed the suits into our backpacks. We were ready to go when Marco turned to me and handed me a pistol; a Sig Saur nine-millimeter.

"Only use it if you need to," he said. "We're not here to kill people."

I didn't respond. And I didn't tell him about my anger from the prior day, which was still running strong.

Marco, René and I began our hike to the lab. The terrain was flatter near the road, and we made good time. René's estimate proved good, and 10 minutes later we were in the jungle, looking out onto the path that led from the dorms to the labs. It was a bit before one in the afternoon, so the path was mostly deserted, the day workers all back at the, eating lunch in the cafeteria. We were counting on them heading back into the lab after the lunch break ended.

Marco went through the plan one more time as we waited, quizzing us about key parts to make sure there were no misunderstandings.

We got our break a few minutes later when a small group of people came up the path, heading back to the labs, chatting and laughing.

"Here we go," Marco said. He put on the coveralls of the biohazard suit, but had the hood back, and kept off the gloves and mask. He'd used the ID badge that I'd lifted from the guards in the quarantine room as a model and fashioned an ID for himself. The magnetic strip on his wouldn't open any doors, but he wasn't expecting to need that. He had a computer backpack slung over one shoulder.

He waited for the group to get 10 yards past us then he stepped onto the path, pulling out his cellphone. He strode up the path as if he owned the complex, head halfway down in the pose of somebody deep into a phone call. He got close to the group in front of him but not so close they felt the need to turn around and see who was behind them. As he walked, René and I moved as well, taking up a location on the edge of the jungle where we could see the lab door, and could walk out into the open space without having to step onto the path.

My heart started pounding as Marco approach the lab entrance. One guard stood leaning against the post that held up the portico over the doorway, casually eyeing the people heading into the lab. Marco closed the last bit of distance between himself and the group in front of him just as the first person in the group swiped their badge to open the door. The rest of the workers showed their badges to the guard and swiped them over the magnetic strip as they entered. Marco held his badge up quickly, phone still glued to his ear and sort of waved it near the card reader. The guard seemed to make a move towards him, since the green OK light wouldn't have lit up at Marco's badge. Marco snapped an impatient glare at young man, pointing at his phone, daring the guard to interrupt his call. The guard stopped moving, and Marco continued moving into the building.

"These are not the droids you're looking for," René whispered in the bushes next to me. I almost laughed out loud.

"That man could fake his way into a kangaroo's pouch," René said. We ducked down as another group of workers came by. Once they were safely past, we put on our own hazmat suits.

We only had to wait a few minutes in the stuffy suits before a dozen sirens started wailing in unison, the high-pitched noise echoing off the jungle and back into the clearing. A flock of birds exploded out of the canopy at the sound, curling overhead a few times before picking a direction to escape the howling. René checked his watch and nodded; Marco had achieved his first objective, locating and pulling one of the breach alarms mounted on the wall throughout the lab area.

The people still on the path froze, then turned away from the lab building, moving quickly to return to the dorms. A few seconds later the lab doors flew open and people began streaming out, moving quickly down the path. We pulled on our masks, hoods and gloves and stepped out into the open space, moving quickly towards the lab. René had his backpack over his shoulder.

"Keep moving," René shouted to the people leaving the lab. "Go to your rally spots in the dorms." The stream of wide-eyed people leaving the building already looked intent on moving as fast as possible without pushing down the people in front of them, although there was a more than a little jostling—every one of the workers knew what was in those labs and they all wanted to be as far away as possible in case the alarm was not a drill.

We made it to the doors and René pushed his way in. The guard had moved away from the building, pulling a mask out of a deep pocket on his cargo pants. He made no attempt to stop René from entering. I didn't blame him for thinking nobody who had a choice would enter a lab where a containment breach alarm had just been pulled. In fact, we'd been counting on that response. I saw René disappear into the building, working his way upstream against the thinning flow of people as the lab grew empty. Tshala had told us the protocol set into motion when the alarm sounded. The workers were supposed to go back to the dorms, which would be sealed and flooded with filtered air to create positive pressure flowing outward, keeping any contaminated air from entering the building. The guards were supposed to move well away from the lab toward the edge of the jungle and don their masks, but not abandon their posts. They seemed to be doing that in practice, but the reality, of course, was that those young, lightly-trained men would be thinking more about their own safety than anything happening around them, unless something obvious like gunfire broke out.

The biohazard team would then suit up and respond to the danger, keeping the building empty until they'd remediated the problem and given the all-clear. They'd be dressed just as the three of us were now. Tshala had also given us a better sense of the layout of the building so Marco and René knew where to go, since they'd only have a few minutes before the real response team showed up.

I stayed near the pathway, scanning all the faces as they exited the buildings and hustled past me towards the safety of the dorm. I needed to find Thomas, but part of my mind was hoping I'd also spot Stanley or his Belgian head of security. I could feel the pistol snug in my belt. I could unzip the biohazard suit and have it in my hand in a matter of seconds. I wondered if I'd really use it, if the chance presented itself.

I didn't get the opportunity to find out. The flow of people had slowed to a trickle when I spotted Thomas. He was moving more slowly than many of the others, almost as if he didn't care that much whether whatever was running free in the lab found its way to him or not. I kept motioning the remaining people towards the path but sidled in Thomas' direction to intercept him.

He reached me, his head still down.

"Thomas!" My voice was a hiss through my mask.

He stopped short and looked up, as though he'd heard a ghost. Which, considering where I was the last time he'd seen me, wasn't that far off.

I said his name again and this time it registered. He looked at me in shock. "Bloody hell," was all he could manage.

"I need your help," I said. "And then we need to get out of here."

He was still staring at me, trying to get his head around my impossible presence standing in the middle of the lab grounds. The guard on our side of the building started to move towards us, clearly curious about our odd interaction.

"It's too late," Thomas said.

I wasn't sure whether he meant too late for me to trust him, or too late for him to be of any use to me, but either way his blank stare and wooden tone were making me nervous. The guard moved closer, his hands closing around the stock of his AK-47.

"I know what Andrea was afraid of," I said. "We can still stop it."

At her name, Thomas seemed to come out of his trance. I kept talking. "And there's something a lot worse than that going on. *I need your help.*"

I could see his mind working quickly. He glanced at the approaching guard and then back to me. Then he seemed to reach some sort of decision. He turned and waved the soldier over to us. My face froze, but my hand went to the zipper of my suit, ready to lower it enough to reach the pistol.

Then Thomas barked at the young soldier. "I've just learned there's a bottleneck of people trying to get into the dorm," he said to the man. "Go sort them out. And stay inside with them to make sure they don't leave. Nobody should be out here."

The young man paused for a minute, then nodded eagerly. He'd recognized Thomas and was more than relieved to have some official permission to get away from the lab and into the safety of the dorm. He turned and sprinted towards the path.

Thomas smiled. "I figured he'd jump at that chance."

I felt myself breathe for the first time in a full minute.

"Why are you here?" Thomas said, trying to keep his voice low despite his shock. "They'll kill you. Again."

"We're going to blow the lab," I said. "Eliminate every sample."

Thomas looked at me doubtfully. "Me and you?"

"No, there are some people in the lab right now wiring explosives. We've only got a few minutes."

"That's insane," Thomas said. "It won't work."

"Trust me, it will," I said. "Just come with me." I led him back away from the lab, and into the bush, checking to make sure nobody was watching, but the area was now empty. I checked my watch. Marco and René were supposed to be out of the building in three more minutes, giving René time to set off the explosions before the biohazard team entered the complex.

René appeared a minute later exiting through the same door he'd entered. He headed over to join us. He glanced quickly at Thomas, then back to me. He peeled off his mask. "Where's Marco?"

"No sign of him," I said.

288

René had the remote detonator in his hand. "That's quite rude of him," he said. He tried to keep his usual light-hearted tone, but there was a bit of worry in his voice. He pulled out a walkie talkie and hit the call button. Marco did not answer.

Thomas motioned back toward the dorms. A bend in the path kept the lab and the dorms from being in direct view of each other, but through a break in the foliage I could see what he was pointing at. A group of figures in biohazard suits were starting to organize, strapping on backpacks and spray guns that no doubt held sterilization solutions. They'd be headed our way in a matter of minutes.

"Stay here," I said. I yanked Thomas's ID off his belt and jogged out of the bush, ignoring the surprised shouts from Thomas and René. There were no guards in sight, and I figured all I needed was the magnetic stripe on the card to unlock the door. It worked, and I pushed through the doorway and into the building. The wailing was even louder inside the structure. I tried to remember Tshala's briefings. *Third right* stuck in my mind, so I sprinted down the hallway, counting the intersections. I got to the third one and raced down the hallway to my right. I reached another intersection and stopped. To my left was the corridor I'd been dragged down when they took me to the quarantine rooms. A moment of panic and anger washed over me at the memory of that day. I pushed both emotions aside and looked frantically for any clues as to which way to head. I saw a sign that said "Administration" and decided to head that way, figuring the IT rooms would be near the offices.

I was right—halfway down the hall was a sign that read *IT—Authorized Personnel Only* in French and English. The door was propped open, and as I approached it I could feel the wash of cooler air needed for the servers flow out of the room and into the hallway. I saw Marco inside, huddled over his PC, a cable leading from his device to the rack of servers in front of him. He looked up quickly as I stepped in but didn't move away from the keyboard.

"We need to go," I said.

"Almost there," he said patiently, as though I'd told him we had an Uber waiting, and not a squad of hostile men approaching in a building wired with explosives.

I tried again. "The hazmat team is coming. We're out of time."

"René will figure out something," he said. "I'm not leaving until I'm done." His fingers flew on the keyboard.

"We have Thomas. He'll know enough to help," I said. I could imagine the team of responders moving into the building now, fanning out to look for any stragglers.

"He won't have what I need," he said. I could feel his determination and knew nothing I said was going to get him to change his mind. He clicked a few more keys, then waited for what seemed like an hour, but was probably about 10 seconds. "There," he said, finally satisfied. He disconnected the cable and snapped the laptop shut.

We jogged back down the hall. The smell of natural gas was almost overpowering, and I expected to run into the suited biohazard team at every turn, but we made it to the doorway without meeting anyone or passing out. We burst out into the fresh air and kept running.

We reached the rally spot where I'd left René and Thomas, but they were nowhere to be found. Then I heard shouting from ahead on our right, on the path near the dorms. I saw René through the foliage, walking *towards* the biohazard team, who were clustered around someone on the ground. We moved through the bushes in their direction.

When we got closer, I could see the person on the ground was Thomas, his regular clothes looking out of place against the white suits of the biohazard team. Two other people in suits were holding Thomas down. He was screaming and thrashing for them to let him go.

"We're screwed," I said to Marco. As I spoke, René closed the distance to the team and pointed to Thomas. "Keep him down," René barked to the group, in his best sergeant's voice.

"I told you he'd think of something," Marco said. "C'mon." He stepped out onto the path, into plain view. Swallowing my terror, I followed him.

"What's going on?" Marco shouted to the group, still in his own biohazard suit.

As one, every goggled face turned toward the sound of his voice.

"It's about time you got back," René said. He held up his right hand, still holding the remote detonator. I saw a brief motion of his finger.

I didn't even have time to react before I felt everything behind me dissolve into fire and sound.

The blast knocked me down, and I felt searing heat wash over me. I prayed that the biohazard suit would protect me from the worst of the brief inferno. The roar of the explosion was louder than I'd expected and came in waves. I was still on the ground, struggling to catch my breath from the shockwave, when I felt a tug on my arm. "C'mon, move." It was Marco. He was already standing, and he dragged me to my feet with surprising strength. Ahead on the path I saw René doing the same with Thomas. The Genistar biohazard team was still scattered about on the ground, in shock, struggling to understand what had just happened. The four of us moved back into the jungle, Marco and René guiding Thomas and me along.

"It'll be a while before they figure out we're gone," Marco said. "They've got enough else to worry about right now."

I snuck a look back and saw the entire lab complex engulfed in orange flames that seemed to reach impossibly high into the sky. René had disconnected the natural gas lines and pumped the gas into the labs with the hoses he'd brought, even as he set the explosives. It was a dangerous move, as a spark could have set the building off with him and Marco still in it, but it was a risk he'd needed to take. The dynamite alone would have caused damage but combined with the gas, the air itself basically lit on fire when the explosives went off, annihilating anything biological in an instant. A homemade fuel-air explosive, René had called it.

We pushed our way back through the jungle and emerged onto the road in 10 minutes, breathing hard. René had radioed ahead to Henry to get the truck ready. We were back in the vehicle and rolling in a matter of minutes, the biohazard suits rolled up and covered with brush near the side of the road.

Now three of us were under the tarpaulins. It was even hotter and sweatier than before, but this time I paid no attention to it. We still had to get back past the checkpoint above Makoua and make it back to the mine. The soldiers would be surprised to see us again, and suspicious after hearing the blast, but we had no choice.

Curiously, we didn't slow to a stop any time in the next hour. Then René finally pulled over. He lifted the tarp off us. "Checkpoint was deserted," he said with his usual lopsided grin. "Apparently the soldiers also knew what was in those labs. They're probably ten miles away by now."

We made it to the mine an hour later. The operation was high on a hillside. Smoke from the explosion and subsequent fire were visible on the horizon, hanging over the tree canopy. The streams of workers carrying the heavy bags of ore down the slope to the processing lines ignored the sight, too deep in their own misery to even be curious about such things. The foreman took the truck keys back from us. He looked in the back, and his eyes settled on the open, empty explosive crates.

"Lost it on the road," René said, following his gaze. "Sorry, mate."

The foreman just nodded. Clearly, he'd been told not to ask a lot of questions about his strange visitors.

Alphonso was hanging out near the plane, smoking a cigarette. He snuffed it out and jumped into the pilot's seat as we approached. We loaded our bags into the back and climbed in.

"I'm not used to doing this without somebody shooting at us," I said to René as I boarded the plane. He laughed. "You did good. Keep it up and maybe Marco will hire *you*, for a change."

"I remember this one." Alphonso said, spotting the familiar face and jerking his thumb towards Thomas, who was in the cramped third row with Henry. "Didn't he try and kill us?"

"He's sorry for that," I said.

"Let me guess. He works for Genistar, too."

"Not anymore."

"Too bad. Now I can't give him the corporate rate," Alphonso said, as he turned the nose of the plane to the south, heading back to Kinshasa. From the window on my side, I could see the fire still burning in the distance as we passed the complex, the wind driving the black smoke east towards Makoua. I felt a wave of elation. We'd done it. I was sure the heat of that explosion and fire would have destroyed all the living matter in that lab. The samples were gone, as was the capability to make any more.

I turned to Thomas. "I told you it would work."

He shook his head sadly. "That's not what I meant. You're too late. They already produced all the virus they need for distribution. Stanley and his crew left with it yesterday afternoon. You haven't stopped them at all."

I felt a pit in my stomach, suddenly realizing that all that risk might have been for nothing. "How are they going to distribute it?"

He frowned. "I don't know. They stopped trusting me after I argued with them about...you." He reached forward, over the back of my seat and put a hand on my shoulder. "I'm sorry, Alan. For all of it."

I closed my eyes, the elation bleeding away as fast as it had come, leaving an empty hole in my chest. I felt a growing despair, once again, that Andrea had died for nothing.

Marco already had his laptop open in the copilot's seat. He was scrolling through a list of files.

"Marco, did you find anything?"

"Not about that," he said.

"I thought you said you got what you were looking for.".

"I did. That's not what I was looking for."

He didn't seem to want to share more, and I was too despondent to press the topic.

Below us the green canopy of the jungle spread out to every corner of the horizon. The Congo River glimmered to our right. The river and the far-reaching network of tributaries that fed it were the real highways of the Congo. The rivers carried more traffic than the decrepit roads that had been carved into the jungle by men to access the riches buried in the rock. Those roads had become nearly unusable over time, neglected or destroyed in wars as other men battled for the control of the Congo's mineral wealth. But from this height, the river was just a thin, tenuous line of silver, a thread that looked ready to break from the slightest pull.

The roads, the people, the land—none of it had been sacred to the men who had spread death and ruin in the Congo for centuries. But what Stanley planned to do was in some ways far worse. He was going to take from the people the most intimate characteristic of their bodies, by seizing control of the genetic language that had spoken life and uniqueness into each of one them.

That he'd execute such a plan at all was crime enough in my mind. That he'd misuse Andrea's work in that way and claim to be bringing it to fruition in her name was even worse.

I pushed away my despair at Thomas' words, forcing myself to get my mind back to the problems at hand. I told myself I had to find a way to keep that from being Andrea's legacy.

I racked my brain for a way to figure out Stanley's next step and stop him, but nothing came to mind. All I was left with was a prayer that Andrea, somehow, had left me the answers I needed in the pile of papers buried in my suitcase, which was stuffed under the bed in a teenager's room on the edge of Kinshasa. And that I could open my mind and heart to her once again, enough to hear what she'd given her life to tell me.

Chapter Thirty-Seven

WE WERE BACK at the house by the afternoon. Two of Marco's men were down by the gate and the end of the driveway, and they waved us in, closing the gate behind us. The house really was a fort, I realized. That was not too unusual given the high crime rate and almost non-existent police presence in Kinshasa. But it was comforting.

Tshala and Atombe were sitting close together on a bench in the garden behind the house. They'd gone back to the university in the morning so Tshala could make more of the failsafe compound. They had arrived back at the house only a short time before we'd pulled in.

"Did she tell him?" I asked Marco. He nodded.

Once they were sure the house was secure, Marco and René left. I took the wedding materials into the kitchen, covering the table with them. I'd been through them a dozen times before but now I stared at each document as if it were new. The table layout. The menu. The guest list. Samples of the invitation and the program. She'd even included the receipts for the flowers and the place settings. Nothing jumped out at me. I felt helpless and frustrated.

Time was ticking by.

Tshala and Atombe came back inside while I was at the table. They both looked warily at Thomas. I explained what had happened at the lab.

"What changed your mind?" Tshala asked him, an edge still in her voice.

"I realized they'd lied to me. The vaccine was no vaccine at all. At first, they were infecting more people, to test the virus's potency and effect. Then when it started to spread out of control, they were trying new versions of the killswitch. But they never got it to work."

"Andrea did," I said. He looked at me in surprise.

"I figured she must have, or you never would have survived that room," he said. He took a breath. "Stanley just got more reckless. He wouldn't listen to me or anyone about slowing down or getting more help. He was sure he knew better than anyone else."

"A lot of pain has been caused by people who thought they knew better than everyone else," Tshala said.

Thomas nodded. "And I saw what they did to Alan. They have no regard for life. I argued with them." He turned to me. "I would have tried to get you out of there, but I thought it was already too late."

I nodded again, still deciding how much I was willing to trust him.

Henry arrived back at the house with bags of food from a nearby restaurant. Atombe and Tshala started to organize the meal, pulling out plates, silverware and glasses. They stayed near each other and moved almost in unison, as if bound by an invisible rope. They spoke quietly, in short sentences that needed no elaboration. Whatever pain, grief or rage they'd felt had been expended outside. All that was left now between them was gentleness and love.

I felt like an intruder, but other than the bed there was no other flat surface big enough for the papers, and I wanted to see all the pages at once, as if having them in my sight would somehow let an answer leap out. So far it hadn't.

We ate in the living room, sitting on the couch in front of the television, watching Sky News. The anchor talked about the Ebola outbreak spreading in the east, and the inability of aid workers to reach the worst impacted. "But there is hope," she said. "A company working with the government has funded two hundred more aid workers to join the effort. Those health professionals started arriving in Kinshasa today and will be deployed throughout the countryside in two days. There's word the health ministry has reached an agreement with the main rebel groups to give those workers safe passage." As she spoke, the camera showed an image of a group of men and women carrying duffel bags through the N'Djili arrivals terminal. They all wore windbreakers with the Genistar logo on them.

What a farce, I thought. Stanley Reston was sending in an army of aid workers to the Congo to combat the problem he helped create. No doubt none of those idealistic doctors and nurses even knew that while they were trying to stamp out one epidemic, he'd be spreading another silent one that would be doing something far more dangerous.

Atombe checked his watch. "My turn for rounds," he said. He tucked the blanket around Tshala. He shot another odd look at me and headed out to the front of the house to relieve one of the other guards. Tshala watched him go, then turned to me.

"You said the other night that you wondered if maybe Stanley was right," she said. "That maybe this wholesale editing of a population is okay, if it has the result he thinks it will."

"I know Andrea would have fought for more controls. More study. But I could see why maybe she had started to believe in that idea a little at least." I pointed at the TV screen. "I know how frustrated she was. Those two hundred people. They won't make much difference. The problem is too big. Even when they get the Ebola situation under control, there's malaria. And measles. And HIV. And a dozen others like them."

Tshala moved the food around on her plate, almost as if she was organizing the food as she organized her thoughts. "I think for a while, after you were gone, she did get that frustrated. She wanted to end the misery here once and for all—at least the parts of it she could. But that didn't last." She unfurled the blanket from around her shoulders and pushed away the boxes of rice and beans on the coffee table. "There's something you should see. Let me have your laptop."

She put the laptop on the open space on the coffee table and typed in a URL. "This is a lecture that Andrea gave last year in Basel. She'd travel there to lecture sometimes, and towards the end to visit her own doctor in Zurich. I went with her to this lecture."

I knew Basel—tucked on the border of Switzerland, German and France—was one of Europe's hottest biotech centers. I had no idea she'd been traveling there so regularly.

Of course, I told myself, there was no way I should have known that, since I'd gone out of my way to not know a damn thing about what she was doing anymore.

The clip began with Andrea delivering an analysis of the state of epidemics and controls in Africa. I was reminded instantly of how sharp her mind had been, how clear her thinking. Then Andrea talked about the emerging work using genetic engineering, either to create resistance to those deadly diseases, or to impact the diseases earlier in the chain. She cited John's Hopkins University, which had created a malaria-resistant mosquito; since it didn't carry the parasite it could not pass it on to humans. That sort of engineering had huge potential for positive impact, she stated, without all the ethical considerations around modifying human DNA.

After a few minutes, Tshala clicked the double arrow to fast forward through the remaining parts of the lecture. I almost put my hand out to stop her, not wanting to miss any second of Andrea's voice or her image, seeing her so alive and vibrant even on the small laptop screen.

Tshala stopped forwarding when she reached the Q&A period at the end of the lecture. "This is the part," she said, turning up the volume.

"So why don't we just edit the DNA of the people?" one young woman asked on the screen. "Make them all resistant. Isn't our science advanced enough to do that?"

Andrea smiled indulgently at the young woman, despite the rather arrogant tone of the question. "To me, this isn't just about science," she said. "The genetic code is more than just a bunch of chemicals. It's the language that ties all of life together. Think of it like this," she paused to take a sip of water. "Early civilizations had oral histories—stories and songs that carried their traditions, beliefs and their history. Each generation heard them from their grandparents and parents and passed them down to their children and grandchildren. But over the course of generations, the stories would change a bit. The legends might grow larger in the telling, the morals of their stories evolve to fit the changing times they lived in. The beliefs became more layered and complex. And

301

sometimes things just got misheard or wrongly interpreted. But if you listened closely to the story you would still hear the roots that held their culture together, the foundations of the stories and the most important events that had shaped their destiny, generation after generation. Those stories are what united them and made them who they were."

Andrea got off the stool and moved to the front of the raised stage. She sat on the front edge of the platform, her legs dangling over the lip like a child on a swing. "Our genetic code is like that. If those oral histories people created encompass the stories of who we are culturally, DNA tells the story of who we are biologically. It's literally the story of our life—we inherit it from our parents and generations before that, we pass it on to our children. Each generation is a new story, the words reinterpreted and recombined, sometimes by chance, sometimes evolving slowly to fit our changing environment. When two people have children, they create a new chapter in that story. They don't know exactly what it will be, because every child, every combination and expression of the genetic code creates a human being who is unique in all the world. But if you look closely, you can still see the features of the grandparents in the child. We don't get to decide exactly what those stories will be, but in some ways that's the most beautiful part."

She stood again, walking back to her chair to fetch her water bottle. "I *do* think we should figure out how to fix things when the story for a person gets told wrong—when there are catastrophic defects that threaten their life or well-being, or if we can use the tools we're developing to target cancer or other diseases." She turned again, and faced the crowd, a stern, almost severe look on her face. "But I *don't* think we have a right to decide what the story is overall, for any group of people. We don't get to change a population's future simply because we think we know better. Enough people have twisted the other kinds of stories, the myths and morals of a society, to achieve terrible ends. I don't think we have the wisdom, or the discipline, to start messing with the story of life itself."

The screen went dark.

Tshala closed the laptop and looked at me. "So no, she didn't have a change of heart. Not about that anyway. I think she was already suspecting what Stanley was trying to do. And she was thinking about how to stop it."

I nodded, not trusting myself to speak for a minute. Tshala sat back and wrapped the blanket around herself again, seeming to understand the impact the video would have on me.

"I need to look at the wedding papers again," I said. "I need to see what else she was trying to tell me."

"Alan, you've been through them a dozen times. There may not *be* anything else," Tshala said. "Andrea figured out a lot, probably by eavesdropping on Stanley or maybe she lifted his email password. But they kept her out of a lot of the planning. She was basically confined to her lab. She might not have *known* what the rest of the plan was."

I hadn't thought of that. That maybe there were no more clues to be had. No more messages. The room seemed to grow more silent as I considered that idea. I'd gotten used to the connection through the documents—the idea that Andrea was still speaking to me in some way. She was still alive to me somehow, in those documents. The possibility that there was nothing else to be found left me feeling alone in some indescribably deep way. I felt like I was losing Andrea all over again.

I went back to my room and looked through the materials. Then I flopped onto the bed, splayed out on top of the covers with the papers all around me, running through them in my mind. I started to accept that Tshala might be right—that Andrea had not known the final parts of the plan. We would have to figure out on our own how Stanley would deliver the virus into the parts of the country he wanted to target. He needed a vector. But nothing spoke to me from the pages to help me understand what that vector could be.

There was one page that did whisper to me; but it was a dark, poisonous whisper I'd tried to avoid since I'd first come across it. It sat on the far edge of the bed, folded in half, a bit apart from the rest of the materials. I tried to keep my eyes off of it, to keep my thoughts focused on the rest of the pages: the typed lists of attendees, the handwritten comments and doodles. But, almost against my own will, I found myself glancing again at that one square, the way the little girl had kept one eye on the cardboard box in the airport. At the top of the visible side of the paper, on the outside of the fold, was a single underlined word: *toast*. Below it, I knew, were the reminders Andrea had written to herself about the speech I'd witnessed on the video:

Thank Minister Kufua
Thank Dr Huang
Show the ring
Don't forget the song

I studied the list again, marveling at Andrea's cleverness. To anyone else, the list would appear to be a collection of obvious thoughts, reminders of the things she didn't want to forget in the heat of the speech. But in the context of everything I'd learned over the past week, I'd realized the list was her own final failsafe; her, *'If you didn't figure anything else out yet just read this list, you dummy*' note, intended solely for me. Hidden in plain sight, she'd crafted it as a pointer for me to some of the most important clues she'd left, in a way that would seem perfectly innocent to anyone else. The first three items were clear: the reference to the song was the only one I still did not understand. I wondered if it was just there to take the emphasis off the other items on the page; a diversion in case one was needed. But even so, I thought, why pick one so hurtful to me, and so personal?

That question needled my heart, but it was the other side of the paper that put a stake straight through me, threatening to still the beat of trust and love that had been rekindled by the messages she'd left, and cut once again the connections I'd felt re-stitched as I walked the same ground she'd stood over those past years. I'd folded that piece of paper in an effort to try and keep the other side, and the words it contained, away from my sight and out of my thoughts.

Despite my effort the back side of the paper held its secret poorly; I could see a good part of the two columns of words on the lower part of that page, revealed by the slight opening of the fold, even if I could not make out the letters from across the bed. Not that I wanted to read the words again. Those two half-hidden columns were names, written in pen, separated by a vertical line, all drawn, I knew, by Andrea's own hand. Each column was topped by a single word.

Above column on the left, she wrote *girl's*; on the column to the right, she'd written *boy's*.

They were baby names.

Thinking of that list transported me back in time, to a clinic further east. It had been a bad week, the week I remembered; it had been hot—too hot to sleep, almost too hot to move. The heat seemed to bring out the worst in the jungle; I'd been with Andrea at the clinic and patients had been streaming in, some with malaria and dysentery, some with chest pains or leg pains or headaches or various undiagnosable maladies. One old man had come in on a makeshift stretcher born by his two sons; gangrene had already taken his foot and much of his lower leg. He'd originally cut his toe, and a local healer had tried to treat it with a mix of herbs, charging the family more every day even as the foot blackened and the infection spread. Andrea told the boys that their father's leg would need to be amputated to save his life. They shook their heads. She argued with them. They picked their father up and left, walking back down the road towards whatever village they'd come from, one of the old man's arms dangling off the stretcher, almost dragging on the ground, going back to the healer who would no doubt promise them that their father would walk again for only a few more francs.

At the end of that awful week, shooting had broken out between two local mercenary groups 20 miles to the north, and three civilians got caught in the crossfire. Andrea's team had saved one of them, but two had died. A man came to claim one of the corpses; the body of a young woman—his wife. He cradled an infant, no more than a month old. The baby was wailing, clearly starving. The man had been trying to comfort the child, a boy, but he could not give him the one thing he needed most. Andrea had mixed a bottle of formula and showed the man how to feed the baby. As the boy quieted, the man looked down at his dead wife and then at Andrea, hopelessness written on his face. He had no local family, he said, and without his wife to feed the baby, it would only be a matter of time before the boy died as well.

306

Andrea tried to console him, and gave him a week's supply of formula, telling him to return in seven days.

He'd smiled, a weak, frightened smile, meant more to please Andrea than to show his mood, and left with the baby. We looked at each other, knowing the odds were that neither he nor the baby would ever return.

"I wonder," Andrea had said, "how anyone can bring a child into this world, in the face of all this."

We'd talked about it again from time to time. She'd been pensive, afraid the world was too painful a place, and there were too many children already suffering across its expanse, for her to bring one more life into it. I'd always wondered if part of that fear was tied to her childhood, and the knowledge that even the wealthy parts of the world could hold their own horrors.

Looking at the square of paper, seeing a triangular slice of the list of names, I could conclude only one thing: that she had changed her mind, that at some point she had started to consider having children of her own.

With Stanley.

I tried to keep my attention on the list of prompts for the toast, wondering again about the song and why she'd included it.

I failed.

I'd seen Andrea with a baby in her arms a hundred times as she delivered them or treated them. But now, as much as I tried not to, I found myself picturing her cradling a baby of her own, bright green eyes staring up at her, helpless, adoring.

I could not reconcile that image with the thought of her leaping to her death in Boston; how could she have become both so optimistic about the world that she'd consider bring

307

a child into it and make that list, but so hopeless that she could end her own life only months later?

I took the square of paper and slid it back into the envelope, doing my best not to read any of the names.

Chapter Thirty-Eight

I HAD JUST gotten into bed around 10 when Atombe knocked on my door.

"Marco's here. He wants to see you." he said. "He didn't tell me why." He was gone before I'd even got my feet onto the floor.

I threw my clothes back on and padded out to the living area. Marco was at the kitchen table, his laptop open in front of him. Tshala emerged from her room, wearing her lounge pants and sweatshirt. Atombe stood near her, scowling. Apparently, Marco had insisted she be woken up too, and Atombe did not seem happy about that.

"I need you both to look at this," Marco said to Tshala and me. "I can't guarantee anything, but... I don't know, I just figured I'd take a shot. Maybe we got lucky." It was the first time I'd never heard him sound tentative.

"I got into the backup systems for the lab. I needed the root admin password because of the encryption...." He was rambling and I realized he wasn't just tentative; he was nervous.

"I found the backups for the rest of the lab protocols, and some of Genistar's other R&D efforts." He turned the screen towards Tshala and blew out a long breath. "Anyway, is this what you need?"

She scanned the list of file names on his screen. At first, she seemed puzzled, but her look turned to interest. Then her eyes opened wide. Tears started streaming down her face. "That's the compound," she said, almost too quietly for anyone else to hear. "For my treatment. You found it."

Marco smiled, his face settling into a combination of pleasure and relief.

"That's why you went back with us to Makoua," I said to him.

He nodded. "One of the reasons. I couldn't do this remotely. I needed the root admin password. For that I needed somebody from the IT staff, and direct system access."

I didn't ask how he'd gotten the password from whatever poor IT technician had been on duty at the time. There hadn't been any bodies on the floor of the data center when I'd showed up, so I assumed he'd found a more peaceful way to get it.

"That's all the science," Tshala said, her voice falling. "But I don't have access to the formularies or the equipment. It was all cutting edge. I can't reproduce it."

Marco locked eyes with me. I realized that's why he'd wanted me to see the data too.

"I know people who can," I said. "I told you, whatever it takes. If you have the science, I'll get you the whatever labs or expertise you need."

Tshala sat down hard, too stunned to speak.

"Does this mean...?" Atombe asked, afraid to finish the question.

I nodded at him. "We can treat her."

Atombe didn't say anything, but I saw his throat working. He put a hand on her shoulder, and she covered it with her own.

"Send me the files," I said to Marco. "I'll get people working on this in the morning."

Atombe and Tshala headed back to bed. Marco and I stayed at the table.

"That's what you were waiting for when I showed up in the IT room," I said.

"There were a lot of places to look, and they're big files. Took a while to download."

"You cut it close. You could have died."

He met my eyes. "Like I said. If you want to know what matters to you…."

"…figure out what you're willing to die for." I finished the sentence.

He reached under the table and brought up a paper bag. He pulled out a bottle of whiskey. "I brought this along, thinking that bit of news was worth drinking to. What do you say?"

I'd already decided I'd never get another uninterrupted night's sleep in Africa. I went to the cabinet and found two glasses. "Best plan I've heard all day."

He poured, and we touched glasses. I took a drink, enjoying the pleasant heat of the alcohol all the way down my throat. I looked at the label on the bottle. "Pike's Creek?"

"Best whiskey in Canada," he said. "Which means best in the world, of course."

"How'd you get it here?"

"I like a few touches of home. Some friends at the Canadian Embassy bring it for me."

"You miss Canada?"

He reflected for a minute. "Yeah. I miss the snow sometimes, the mountains. My dad still lives on the farm where I grew up. Near Big Quill Lake. Middle of nowhere. But I like

311

it here, too. It's crazy here, but there's a feeling to it I've sorta gotten addicted to."

"I know what you mean," I said. "I'm glad I came back."

I took another sip. "I still don't know how Stanley is going to distribute the virus, though. And even if we solve that, there's the issue of whoever else had hacked their systems and has the data. That's a problem for the whole world."

"Maybe not," Marco said. "At least not for a while. The other reason I wanted to get system access was to upload some files of my own. Whoever else was in those systems already had root access, but from the logs I saw, I figured they only got it in the last few days. I was betting that when they heard about the explosion at the lab they'd rush to pull a final set of backups from the offsite storage. When they do that, my files will go with the payload." He seemed to do some quick calculations in his head. "In twelve hours, the software I added will encrypt every data file on every system it touches. With a bit of luck, it'll turn every server that has the data from the lab into a useless silicon brick."

"It's like ransomware," I said.

"Yeah, except I don't plan on offering anyone the decryption key for a handful of bitcoins. They may find a way to get the data back eventually, but it should slow them down a whole lot."

I clinked glasses with him again. "Congratulations for possibly saving the world."

"Thanks. Now let's figure out to save the people closer to home. We have two days."

"Thanks for the reminder. I think I need another drink."

"My pleasure," he said, reaching for the bottle.

Chapter Thirty-Nine

I WOKE UP to a whiskey headache and mixed feelings. The thought that we could reproduce the drug compound Tshala needed had lifted my spirits. But that euphoria battled with a growing dread that we were almost out of time, and we still didn't know what Stanley's plan was. I showered, using the hot water to clear my head and soak away the throbbing.

I emerged from my room to find Atombe and Tshala already in the living room, mugs of tea in hand. I made coffee, thinking we'd owe the owners of the house for their unintentional hospitality. My own steaming mug in hand, I fired up my laptop. Marco had sent me the files as promised and in matter of minutes I had them on their way to Simone and a few other folks I knew who could be of help.

I had a string of emails from Frank on the deal. His notes outlined the terms of the deal Zestra wanted. I read through the paragraphs and tables describing revenue multiples, escrow terms, stock option vesting. Only a few weeks earlier I would have been immersed in it, devouring every detail, looking for ways to wring the maximum value out of the deal for myself and my company. Now it was all an abstract pattern of words and numbers. The dollar figures being talked about were huge. A billion dollars would change hands when the deal closed, but the lawyers and bankers talked about the figures as though they were table change. Which, to some of them, they were; they'd no doubt worked on far larger deals.

I thought of the mine workers we'd seen when we dropped off the truck, living on pennies a day, if they were paid at all and not beaten or enslaved for not producing at the levels the mine owners required. It seemed impossible that both of those realities—the boardrooms in Boston and the mines in the Congo—could exist in the same world. But they did. And in one form or another, I knew, they always had.

The news was playing in the background. The morning broadcast was revisiting the story we'd heard the night before about the aid workers Genistar was funding. I barely listened, my mind caught halfway between the two extremes of high finance and basic survival I was trying to navigate. There was a pause, then I heard the same story again—Tshala had hit rewind on the satellite box and replayed the segment. Then she turned off the TV.

Her actions had hardly registered in my mind. Her next words however, got my full attention.

"Alan, I think I know how he's going to do it."

I turned toward her voice, all thoughts of mega deals immediately gone. She was sitting bolt upright, staring at me, the blanket having fallen away, unnoticed, from her shoulders.

"He didn't find a vector," she said. "He *created* one. The aid workers. They're his vector. He doesn't need to infect a whole population in the countryside. He just needs to infect those workers and send them out on their missions. They'll come in contact with enough people to spread the virus just where he wants it."

It hit me instantly. She was right. They were perfect. He was going to send 200 people into all the corners of the jungle—to the places where the diseases he wanted to prove he could defeat were raging. They'd carry the virus with them—and through their interactions in the clinics and villages they'd infect thousands more, and through those people tens of thousands. From that point, it would spread exponentially. By the time anyone figured it out, the virus would have done its work. He'd have edited the genetic code of hundreds of thousands—perhaps millions—of people. Once the ones of child-rearing age started having children, if he'd been successful, he'd have made his point—a wave of children genetically resistant to some of the region's biggest killers. But the virus would not stop at the borders of the Congo. It would spread silently all over the world. If he'd miscalculated in any way, he'd have unleashed a kind of epidemic from which the world may never recover.

"The news said Genistar is bringing them all to Kinshasa tomorrow for a briefing, then sending them out to their posts." she said. "I bet he's going to infect them here."

It made perfect sense. There wasn't a reliable way for him to distribute the virus so he'd created his own: an army of aid workers. All he had to do was get them in a conference room someplace in Kinshasa and release the virus into the air. In an hour they'd all be infected. They'd all be well on their way to their final destinations throughout the countryside before any of them were contagious. Some of the more sensitive might have some symptoms after a day or two—headaches or cramps. But they'd probably just chalk those up to the foreign food or poor sanitation. The virus would not go lytic, reproducing violently: it would simply find the cells it was designed for, then do its work.

315

If he'd gotten it right.

"We need to find out where they're meeting," Tshala said. "And find a way to get the killswitch there, too."

"I think I can do the first part," I said, reaching for my phone.

Marco had wanted to keep Thomas at the house where his men could keep an eye on him, but I'd convinced him to let Thomas return to his own apartment in the city. Thomas answered after a few rings.

"Yes, I think I know where they would do it," he said, once I told him what Tshala had figured out. "They've talked for weeks about a big meeting at the Kinshasa Grand Hotel. Minister Nyindu would be there. He and Stanley would have a press conference to announce the new aid workers."

"Makes perfect sense," I said. "There's no politician in the world who would miss a photo op like this—hundreds of professionals being sent out to end the nation's biggest health crisis."

I'd been to events in the Kinshasa Grand Hotel. It has a main ballroom that would be perfect for Stanley's needs. More than big enough for 200 people, with access easily managed, so the virus could be released in the room but still contained.

Two hours later we were huddled with Marco and his team, a Google satellite image of the hotel up on a large screen in Marco's conference room.

"Okay, that's half the battle," Marco said. "We know where they'll be. We just need to get the killswitch in there."

"They'll have a lot of security with the health minister there," René said. "We won't be able to get inside without starting a war."

"They'll have to come out the front," I said. "It's not that big a space out front. They'll have the buses in the parking area. The people will have to walk across the open space in front of the hotel to the buses. They'll want to march them out that way for the TV cameras."

"Odds are the security will be tighter inside," Marco said. "And concentrated around the minister. Once they've gotten the virus deployed, they'll want to get everyone out of there and to the airport. The police will be more relaxed outside."

"Doesn't matter. None of us will be able to get within a hundred yards of the place long enough to deliver the killswitch without being recognized at this point," Tshala said.

We all stared at the screen. "Maybe we can't," Atombe said. "But I know who can."

He laid out his plan. Tshala and I argued the there was too much risk. But Atombe just smiled, a sad, wise smile that should have belonged to someone well beyond his years. "Trust me. This is the least risky thing they'll do all day," he said.

We spent the rest of the day making preparations. At one point, Atombe and I were alone in the office. Marco had taken Tshala out to buy some supplies we'd need and René had gone to do a drive-by of the hotel.

"I'm grateful you will help Tshala," Atombe said. The words came out unwillingly, like a child forced to make an apology they don't really mean.

"Of course," I said. "I would never do anything less."

"I know," he said. "I see how you look at her, sometimes."

Suddenly it all clicked—the icy stare at the plane, and his reaction in the dance club. I almost burst out laughing, but I saw how serious he was.

I stood up to face him. "Tshala is an amazing woman," I said. I saw his eyes start to flash in anger. "But when I look at her like that," I said, speaking quickly and thinking of the knife strapped to his calf, "It's because I see somebody else, Atombe. She reminds me of my ex-wife in so many ways. Looking at her takes me back in time." I put my hands on his shoulders. "Listen closely to me. Tshala really likes you. You need to believe that. Respect it, and don't let your own fears or doubts get in the way of it. You need to trust."

I could see his shoulders relax. He seemed to be debating what to say next. When he finally spoke, the words were halting, almost shy. "When I was young, everything was taken from me. My family. My home. Even my name. She asked me where my name came from. How could I tell her no one had called me by my old name for so long, it didn't seem like mine any more. So, I made one up for myself. My name means nothing. I was invisible. I was a Shegue. Tshala..." He struggled for the words. "I don't want her taken away, too."

"That, my friend, is the hardest part," I said. "You may not get to decide that. But you have to decide to love her anyway."

"I keep asking myself how she could love someone like me," he said. "I don't deserve her."

"I've only known you for a little more than a week and I can see exactly why she would," I said. "And for what it's worth, I spent the last three years thinking that same thing about Andrea. That I didn't deserve to have her love me." I took my hands off his shoulders and turned to the window so he couldn't see my face. "I was too caught up in myself to realize that that was *her* choice to make, not mine. It was the biggest mistake I've ever made." I could see him nod in the reflection of the glass.

318

I thought for a moment, then turned back to him. "You say your name means nothing. I say that you made it up, so it can mean whatever you want it to. I'm thinking it means *courage*."

He nodded in thanks. "I am sorry for being suspicious of you," he said.

I laughed. "Don't worry. I'll consider it a compliment you could think of me as your competition. I'm sure you're the only one who does."

We returned to our work, and the rest of the team filtered back in from their various missions. By evening, we had everything in place. We all retired back to the house, and Henry made another food run for dinner. We ate without much talk, everyone thinking about what the next day could bring. I'd gotten some good news from my contacts in the States about the protocol for Tshala. Their best guess was that it might only be a week before she'd be able to get a treatment. I shared that information with everyone, which brightened the mood around the table.

"Thank you," Atombe said quietly. This time there was no resentment. I just smiled at him and mouthed the word "*Trust.*"

Chapter Forty

I WOULD SAY I woke up early the next morning, but the reality was I'd never really gotten to sleep. I'd tossed and turned, running over the plan in my mind, thinking about my conversation with Atombe and, most of all, seeing Andrea in the video Tshala had shown me, replaying it over and over in my mind.

I'd been to Basel a few times in the past couple of years, meeting with the startups and small biotech companies there. I wondered, as I twisted in the bed, if Andrea and I had ever been in Basel at the same time. Could I really have been that close to her? And what would have happened if we'd just run into each other on the street. Would we have realized that we were each waiting for the other, lost in our own guilt and regrets? Could things have been different?

At sunrise I climbed out of bed, trying my best to put all those thoughts aside. My part in the day was minimal, but I still wanted to be focused, in case there was something we'd missed. I couldn't bring Andrea back, but I resolved that I would do everything I could that day to make sure she didn't die for nothing.

By mid-morning we were ready. Henry had relayed instructions from Marco: we were to pack all of our belongings in case things went wrong and we needed to leave in a hurry. Of course, if it went right, no one would even know what we'd done.

Tshala had been able to make several small bottles of the killswitch. It didn't seem like much to me, but she was elated at the success. "It's plenty. Even a tiny bit will do the trick," she said.

"Frog poison," I said, nodding, thinking about Simone's description.

"And it's stable for hours," Tshala continued, one eye cocked as she tried to make sense of my comment. "So even if somebody just touches a surface that's been in contact with the compound in the past few hours, it will still work. Andrea did an amazing job perfecting it."

We split up then: Thomas headed off with Atombe and Tshala so they could finish their preparations, René and I drove across town to Marco's offices. On the way, René told me more stories of his time in the service with Marco, and I told him more about my years with Andrea. "There's a million reasons for all the terrible shit that happens in this region," he said, as if summing up both our experiences. "Ninety-nine percent of it comes down to a fight for control of the minerals. You see that Black Panther movie?"

I nodded.

"Cobalt, the stuff they mine here for batteries and such? That shit's the real Vibranium. And this country is loaded with it. But there ain't no secret cities with magic healing machines here."

"I didn't see you as a movie buff," I said.

"Not me. My kids."

I realized I'd never thought about his personal life. "You have kids?"

322

"Three. Married a Kinois, long time ago, and never left. She's home with them now."

"Why didn't you bring them to the hotel or the house? I'd love to meet them."

He shot me a wicked smile. "Most of the time you've been here you've either been getting shot at or dying from Ebola. Not the best example for the little ones, I figured."

I laughed. "It's been a busy week."

We reached the offices around 10:30. The press conference was at noon. Thomas had said that Stanley and Minister Nyundi would address the aid team gathered at the hotel at 11 to kick off their orientation. The press conference would be at noon. It made sense, I thought. Stanley and the minister would be outside, basking in the media attention, far away from the conference room while the volunteers who had offered their time and skills to help the people of the Congo were poisoned with the virus he'd engineered.

He'd said he trusted his science. Apparently, he didn't trust it completely.

The hotel layout actually made our plan easier. Marco was with Atombe and Tshala, so René and I headed over toward the hotel in a dusty Toyota Corolla. René found a parking spot where we could see the front of the hotel and the parking area in front of the building. We were still far enough away to avoid any interest from the police, who were starting to set up a loose perimeter in front of the hotel. As René had guessed, the police were positioning themselves to control access to the hotel where Minister Nyundi would be, but little regard was paid to the area away from the building itself. The parking lot had already been emptied of vehicles, and a pair of policemen in fatigues were waving away cars that tried to access it.

The buses arrived around 11. There were eight of them, gleaming white tour buses, crawling along the street to the parking area. They filed in, lining up neatly to await their passengers.

René handed me a pair of small binoculars. I scanned the steps in front of the hotel. A few camera crews and a knot of people were lounging there, apparently awaiting the press event.

Stanley and Minister Nyundi walked out of the hotel doors just before noon with a retinue of staff around them. I recognized a third person, too—the Belgian security chief who'd locked me in the quarantine room. He shadowed Stanley and the minister, keeping a dozen paces away, staying out of the view of the cameras, but his shaved head made him impossible to miss even at that distance. Stanley and the Belgian wore blue blazers despite the heat. The minister, a big man half a head taller than Stanley, wore a light-colored blazer with a purple shirt and black pants. The reporters and cameras clustered around Stanley and Minister Nyundi. I could guess what Stanley would be saying—bland words about Genistar's selfless commitment to the people of the DRC, and how some causes were more important than profits. The health minister would trumpet his ability to convince a world leading company to assist the DRC, and his ability to reach accommodation with the rebel groups to allow safe passage. I wondered how much Stanley had spent to bribe the rebels for a few months of access to the region.

The press conference ended after about 15 minutes. The minster departed, trailed by his gaggle of aides. Stanley and the Belgian moved away into the shade, careful to keep to the edge of the main entrance, away from the bank of doors leading from the hotel to the street. *That's right. You don't want to get too close to the people you're experimenting on when they come out of those doors, just in case*, I thought.

The police were already starting to look fidgety, shifting their location and finding pockets of shade, thinking their job was over. But they still hung around, waiting to be released.

A few minutes later, I leaned forward. "It's happening," I said, completely unnecessarily, since René had his own binoculars and was watching the same scene. A stream of people came through the doors, mostly Caucasian faces, a mix of men and women. Most seemed to be in their late twenties or early thirties; old enough to have gotten their medical training, still young enough to have the freedom and desire to want to save the world. They all had large duffel bags in hand and backpacks slung over their shoulders. They were smiling and laughing, chatting with the new colleagues they'd just met, excited for their mission and oblivious to the horror that had just been visited upon them. It was like watching a group of college kids exiting an auditorium after their freshman orientation.

They moved out of the shade of lobby's overhang as the hotel staff directed them with hand gestures towards the buses in the parking area, a few hundred feet away.

That's when they came.

Dozens of kids, appearing as if from nowhere. They dashed up to the group, holding out their items for sale. Hand-held misters, with small fans attached. Or spray bottles full of clear liquid. I couldn't hear the kids, but I knew what they'd been instructed to say: *Beat the jungle heat. Stay cool, pretty lady.* And a variety of other slogans. As they moved through the group, they demonstrated their wares, spraying cool mist in the air, onto the arms, faces, heads of the aid workers. The group, still in good spirits and already beginning to sweat

325

in the heat, laughed at the young children, who smiled back and complemented them in French or broken English as they scooted around.

The police started shouting at the children, trying half-heartedly to shoo them away. It was a common part of life for police in Kinshasa, chasing the Shegues out from the downtown area—a constant game of cat and mouse as the children disappeared, only to re-emerge in new locations, trying to make a few pennies selling bags of water, battery-powered fans, or cheap jewelry.

The police moved languidly in the heat. At this point the entire group of aid workers had reached the row of buses and was packed together around the vehicles, waiting their turn for their bags to be loaded into the open bays. This made the task easier for the kids, who moved around the dense crowd, spraying, spraying, spraying.

It's working. I thought, watching the Westerners laugh. Some stopped to take pictures of the kids. Unknown to them, every one of the spray bottles held a mixture of water and the killswitch chemical Tshala had reproduced. The children had been told to spray it on clothes, backpacks, and bare skin whenever possible. The taller kids just sprayed it into the air over the crowd. They were carrying out their task with enthusiasm. The whole mass of people was under a fine mist of the water and chemical—more than enough, based on what Simone had said, to shut down the virus before it had time to become contagious.

Another thought occurred to me seeing all the young faces in the medical group. Not only would those young men and women have become vectors for the virus, but it was indiscriminate in its work—it would have altered their DNA, too, hiding in their bodies and changing each one of them in a fundamental way that would impact their children and every generation after them. *You have no idea how big a favor these kids are doing for you,* I thought, watching the children dart about.

The police began moving in more aggressively, having had enough of the kids' interruption. But still all they did was shout and threaten. They saw the warm reaction the Westerners had for the kids, and they did not seem to want to be seen exhibiting their usual cruel behavior towards the Shegues in front of the whole world.

I turned my glasses back to the hotel. Stanley and his security chief were still there. Stanley was scowling, his arms crossed. He said something to the Belgian and they both rolled their eyes as they watched the kids, no doubt lamenting the sad state of culture in the country they were convinced they were saving. Then I saw Stanley's face change. The change was so sudden it was almost as if I could hear the thoughts clicking into place in his mind.

He'd figured out what was happening.

He snarled something to his security chief who immediately put a walkie talkie to his mouth. Stanley started running down the stairs, shouting at the police. His violent reaction spurred them into action. They started running towards the kids. Then I heard the whistle. The sound was Atombe's signal to the kids to flee. As quickly as they'd come, they faded back behind the buses, darting between cars and across traffic, more agile than the police chasing them. The aid workers looked around in confusion as the police pushed through them, trying to reach the Shegues. But the kids could fit into spaces between the buses and concrete barriers the police could not. In what seemed like an instant, the kids were gone, invisible again against the background of Kinshasa, a skill they all knew too well.

I scanned the area in front of the hotel again and cursed.

They'd all made it away. All but one.

One of the boys had apparently gotten cut off from the escape route by the advance of the officers. He'd tried to run the other way, off to the side of the hotel. Stanley's security chief had intercepted him and was holding him by the collar of his shirt. Stanley reached the two of them and said something to the Belgian man. They turned, dragging the boy with them towards the access road that led around behind the hotel.

"Shit, they got one of the kids," I said to René. Without waiting to see if he'd heard me, I was out of the car, cutting through the stalled traffic along the edge of the parking area. I had no idea what they would do with the boy, but I didn't want to give them the chance. And I didn't want to see Sephora or her houses identified to the authorities as being part of the plan.

I made it to the access road, already sweating. There was no sign of anyone. The side of the hotel was to my right. It was just a windowless concrete wall five stories high and running the width of the building. there was a tall barrier fence to my left, so the only way out was behind the hotel. I kept moving, rounding the corner of the building in time to see the Belgian stuffing the boy into the back seat of a sedan. Stanley was climbing in the driver's door. Clearly Stanley had left his car there to simplify his exit, avoiding all the commotion out front with the buses.

The Belgian was looking down, pinning the boy against the seat while he started to slide in after him. I kept moving, and hit the big man with all my force, slamming him against the still-open car door. We both bounced back onto the hot tar roadway. The Belgian wound up on his hands and knees, stunned by the unexpected attack. I saw the boy climb out of the open door and sprint away back up the access road. The Belgian saw him, too. I leapt forward again, catching the man flush on the side of his head with a right hook before he could make a move to follow the boy.

That was the last punch I made.

He stood up, looking at me more out of annoyance than pain. He flashed out a right fist that caught me on the jaw, knocking me backwards two steps. I shook my head to clear away the stars and rushed him again. The next blow was an uppercut to my diaphragm, blowing all the air out of my lungs and dropping me to my knees. Then he slammed an elbow into my back, driving me down onto the ground, the hot gravel on the hard road digging into my face. He rolled me over, and I saw him draw his hand back again.

"I should have killed you this way the first time," he said. Then a blur came from my left. I heard the collision of flesh on flesh, and the Belgian was knocked off me. I rolled to my side to see René complete a shoulder roll on the far side of the man, rising lightly back onto his feet. The Belgian was facing away from me now, looking at René. I saw the Belgian's right hand disappear behind him, under his sport coat. He started to draw out a pistol that must have been tucked in the small of his back. Still gasping for breath, I got to my feet and sprang forward. I grabbed the Belgian's wrist, jerking the arm upwards towards his shoulder blade. He shouted in pain and surprise, and the pistol clattered to the tar, but then he stomped down on my right instep. The flash of pain caused me to lose my grip. The elbow that followed knocked me to the ground again.

But by then René was back on him. They locked each other up like wrestlers, each trying to find an opening to exploit, grunting and cursing, feet shifting as they fought for leverage.

I heard an engine roar. Stanley had dropped the car into gear and was accelerating away up the access road behind the hotel, leaving his security chief behind to battle René. Then I saw a large chrome grill appear as another vehicle rounded the far end of the building, turning towards us. It was a white Range Rover. I realized it had to be Marco. Marco turned the SUV sideways, blocking the escape route. Stanley locked up the brakes, skidding to a stop. Then he put the car into reverse, picking up speed, backing fast in our direction. René and the Belgian had not loosened their grips on each other. I looked side to side frantically but already knew what I'd find. The wall of the hotel was to my back and a tall concrete barrier abutted the road on the other side; there was nowhere for us to go. I scanned the ground and saw the glint of the Belgian's pistol still lying on the road. I picked it up, clicked off the safety, and fired three shots into the rear window of the sedan as it raced towards us. The front wheels turned suddenly to the right, driving the rear of the car into the wall of the hotel. I thought for a second I'd hit Stanley, but then the driver side door opened and he stumbled out, dazed but not bleeding.

The sound of the gun and the crash of the car hitting the wall were enough to cause René and the Belgian to release each other. The Belgian looked at the sedan angled across the road and realized quickly that his boss had been about to run him down in an effort to escape. He screamed something in Dutch at Stanley, then turned to face René just in to meet a right hook that dropped him onto his knees. René drew his arm back again, but the Belgian raised his hands in surrender. He looked over at Stanley and spat some blood into the dirt. "This is not my fight any longer," he said, loud enough for both René and Stanley to hear him. René pointed down the road and the Belgian accepted the offer, climbing to his feet and sprinting back the way he'd come in.

I turned back to Stanley. He was just standing between the two vehicles, not sure which way to go. I swung myself over the hood of the sedan, landing on the other side and coming face to face with him. I still held the pistol. "Get down!" I shouted. He dropped to his knees, his hands up in the air. Marco approached from the other end of the road but stopped a dozen yards away.

I felt all the rage I'd been collecting since I'd heard about Andrea's death boil up in me, and a storm of images and emotions exploded in my mind. The gurney with Andrea's body on it, highlighted on the evening news, being lowered down the ladder from the roof in Boston. The thin, cold light of the quarantine room, and the first feelings of the Ebola virus raging in my body. Tshala's expression when she'd told us about her condition. And the laughing, smiling faces of the aid workers Stanley had been about to exploit. For a surreal moment, Stanley's image and the memory of the three men kneeling on that dirt road years ago seemed to merge, and I felt like I was in both places at once.

I stepped forward and pointed the pistol at Stanley's forehead.

"How'd that work out for you last time?" Marco said quietly. But he made no move to stop me.

"You going to say you did this for Andrea, too?" Stanley said, spittle flying out of his mouth as he spoke. "Out of *love*?" I could hear the fear in his voice. But there was something else, even in that terrifying moment. Resentment? Bitterness?

I shook my head. "No. I don't have that right." I lowered my arm to my side. "Neither did you."

"You should have done it. This guy's a pain in the ass," René muttered, climbing over the hood of the sedan from behind me and hauling Stanley to his feet. Marco looked at René, who was covered with dust, his eye already swelling. "You're a mess," Marco said.

"I know, you wouldn't have had a mark on you," René said. "Could be worse. I could be Alan."

They both laughed, and I realized how I must have looked. The right side of my face was throbbing and still flecked with grime from the oily tarmac, and every breath was a sharp pain in my gut.

"Frank's going to want a refund," Marco said, studying me. I started to laugh, then quickly regretted it when the pain in my ribs flared up.

"Let's go," Marco said. "It'll take the police a minute to figure out where the shots came from. But I don't want to be here when they do. I think I've run out of favors."

René hustled Stanley back to the Range Rover, one hand on his neck, the other on his forearm. He found a long zip tie in the back and used it to secure Stanley's wrists behind his back. My mind flashed back to the ride in the back of that car after being dragged out of the restaurant, the zip ties cutting into my wrists. It seemed like a million years ago. Stanley had given that order too, I guessed.

Marco straightened out the car and we got around to the front of the hotel without incident. He pulled out into traffic, calling Atombe to make sure everyone else was okay.

"It worked," he said once he got off the phone. "Tshala's confident of it."

"We're heading back to the house?" I asked.

"First stop, Canadian Embassy," Marco said. "I know the Ambassador pretty well. I spoke with her last night and told her what we'd learned. I didn't tell them what we were doing today. But I said I might be stopping by. We can leave Stanley with them. They'll sort him with the local authorities. She's also been talking to the World Health Organization. I sent them enough of the files to show them what Genistar was up to."

I looked up in concern at his mention of files.

"Not the files with the science," he said, guessing the reason for my reaction. "Tshala showed me which ones not to send."

I looked at Stanley. He was hunched up against the side window. "It would have worked," he said. "You just cost thousands of kids their lives—a generation would have been born free from the worst diseases."

"You forgot about the ethics," I said.

He glared at me. "The ethics are what the people here would call a first-world problem."

"The first world has spent enough time meddling in the lives of the people here," I said.

"You won't stop it. Too many people think like I do. The work will go on."

"We destroyed the labs. And the backups. It's all gone."

He lapsed into silence, but I had the uneasy feeling it was a smug silence.

We were at the embassy's tall steel gates in a matter of minutes. I'd spent the rest of the short trip fighting my own inner turmoil. Part of me wanted to put my hands around

Stanley's throat and choke the life out of him, doing to him, physically, what he'd done to Andrea's spirit and hope. But as I looked at him slumped against the window, all I saw was his weakness and bitterness.

Chapter Forty-One

AT THE EMBASSY, two members of the Canadian military police came out to meet us after we were given a quick inspection and waved through the security gates. The two policemen brought Stanley to a secure room under guard, with René going along as escort, and ushered Marco and me to a conference room deep in the building. The room was big enough to easily hold 10 people, with simple but comfortable padded chairs, a long wooden table and a paper map of the DRC on the side wall. Photos of the Ambassador at a variety of events in the DRC lined the wall across from us. She had long, curly reddish hair, and looked to be in her late forties. From the pictures, she seemed to have spent a lot of time actually out in the countryside at various health centers, schools and community projects. I got the sense of someone actually engaged in the country and its problems, not just a figurehead who entertained foreign dignitaries in the comfort of the embassy. A flat screen TV was mounted on the wall opposite the head of the table, with a camera and microphone above it, no doubt for her communications back to Ottawa.

While we waited, another officer came into the room with a first aid kit. He cleaned off the dirt from my face and gave me a cold pack for my cheek.

The Ambassador herself arrive a few minutes after that, sweeping into the room, still talking to someone over her shoulder about an event scheduled for later that day. We stood to greet her.

"Madame Ambassador," Marco said, with a smile. He introduced me to her.

"This is really something you've gotten into," she said, dispensing with any small talk, and plopping down unceremoniously into the seat at the end of the table. "We heard about the fire in Makoua. Was that you, too?" She seemed more curious than shocked, making me wonder more about the other kinds of work Marco and his team did for the Canadian government.

"We think we got the situation under control, at least for now," Marco said, ignoring the direct question. "That lab's gone. If you round up the Genistar people still in Makoua, we can wipe their laptops and anything else that survived. I'm pretty sure the backups are not going to be accessible to anyone."

"I spoke to the WHO folks this morning," the Ambassador said. "They said they've just started looking at samples from Ebola victims around Makoua, but so far everything you and that woman…" Her pause served as the question mark.

"Tshala."

"Yes, everything you and Tshala said to them seems to be holding up. One thing, though." She flashed a look of concern. "This doctor you mentioned. Doctor Huang, or Liu, or whichever. Nobody can find him anywhere under either name. "

"Tshala said he was working out of a Genistar lab, but she didn't know where. He won't know yet about what happened here today," I said. "Can you have police raid *all* the labs?"

"That'll take days to set up," Marco said. "He'll definitely know by then that we've got Stanley and that we've figured out what they were up to. He'll disappear back to China, I'm betting. He may even have a third identity to travel under. We need to get him now."

"We can't just guess. If we start raiding labs one by one, he'll get wind of that, too," the Ambassador said.

"Would Thomas know?" Marco said to me.

I shook my head. "I asked him. He had no idea either. It was a closely held secret."

"This would be a good time to pull one more trick out your Andrea hat," Marco said.

I'd thought that same thing. I'd been racking my brains as we spoke. I'd been over the documents so many times I pretty much had them memorized. I also wondered if maybe it was something she'd said, perhaps. Not something in the files themselves.

The song.

The band had played our song. She'd said everyone should think of where they were when they'd heard that song. I remembered how hurt I'd been that she'd used that song. And I knew where I'd been. With Andrea, in a coffee shop in Zurich, waiting on train to Paris.

It had to be a clue.

"Zurich," I said, getting excited. "See if they have a lab in Zurich." Marco took out his phone to search the web. I got out my phone to call Tshala as well.

My excitement didn't last long.

"No," Tshala said, when I reached her. "There's no facilities there I've ever heard of." Marco shook his head as well. No listings online for any Genistar facilities in Zurich.

"What made you think of that?" the Ambassador asked.

"A song we both loved," I said, sinking down into the chair. I'd felt sure that would be it. The final clue from Andrea. But I realized that was probably asking too much of her.

"Not sure love has much to do with this situation," the Ambassador said.

I thought about how right she was. Then I smiled. I opened the browser on my phone and searched for a company name. It came up, just as I expected. Then I laughed. *No*, I thought to myself, *love had nothing to do with it.*

"Right country, wrong city," I said. I called Tshala back and put her on speaker. "He's in Bern," I said. I didn't even pose it as a question.

"There's a small lab there," she said. She sounded doubtful. "But I'm not even sure it's an active one. It's left over from an acquisition we did a year ago."

"He's there," I said. "A smaller lab would be perfect. Easier to control, and isolated from all the other projects."

"You sure?" Marco said. "If we're wrong, we'll spook him."

I thought of the wedding notes. And Andrea's insistence on chocolates on every table. *Lindt*, she'd written in the margins, with an exclamation point. Andrea hated chocolate. She'd never have asked for it, especially by name. Lindt Chocolates was founded in Bern, Switzerland, the webpage I'd brought up on my phone said.

It had to be the place. "I'm sure," I said.

The Ambassador looked doubtful too. "How do you know that's it?"

"Trust me. I'm sure."

"You get that from Andrea?" Marco asked, looking at me.

I nodded.

"Who's Andrea?" the Ambassador asked.

"His ex-wife."

"She's here, too?"

"She's dead," I said.

The Ambassador looked at Marco, the "*Is he crazy?*" question obvious in her eyes. Marco shook his head. "Andrea's gotten us this far. I'd believe the man."

The Ambassador considered that for a moment, then shrugged. "If it's good enough for you, it's good enough for me," she said, and reached for the secure telephone on the table in front of her.

Chapter Forty-Two

I PUSHED OPEN the door to a different conference room, part way down the hall from where I'd just left Marco and the Ambassador. Stanley looked up at me, hands still bound behind his back, eyes hollow and defeated. I wondered if that's how I'd looked to him, when he walked into that room in the lab to find me in that plastic chair.

I met eyes with René, who was sitting across from Stanley, his chair tipped back, boots up on the polished wood of the conference table.

"You want me to stay?" he said.

I shook my head.

He climbed to his feet and moved to the door, glancing at Stanley. "You need anything, call my name. Otherwise I don't think I'll hear anything that happens in here in the next few minutes, if that's what suits you."

Stanley watched René leave. I sat down in the chair the big Canadian had just vacated.

"You've killed thousands," Stanley said again. But the conviction was gone from his voice.

"We've saved millions. You have no idea how that virus would have performed in the wild, or what the mutations you'd planned on would really have done to those people."

341

"Not mutations, *corrections*," he said, a bit of glare coming back into his eyes.

"Mutations," I insisted.

We stared at each other in silence for a minute.

"How did you know?" he finally asked. "How did she tell you?"

"The wedding documents she sent me. The clues were in there. In ways you would never guess. The papers. The video. All of them were meant to help me know where to look."

He pursed his lips, processing this thought. "She said she wanted you to see what a real wedding looked like. She said that's why she wanted to send them to you."

I thought back to that day with Andrea in Lufua's church, our toes curling in the cool dirt. "I know what a real wedding looks like."

"You blew it up, you know." He said it in an odd way. Less combative. Almost gentle. Like he was sharing some kind of secret thought with me.

"The lab? Damn right we did."

"No, the urn. I had it in my office. I picked it up from the runway. Cleaned it up. Put it on a shelf there. It's gone now, of course."

He rocked uncomfortably in the chair. "I wondered for a bit which one of us she would have wanted to have it. In the end."

"I didn't."

He was silent again, working his way towards the question I knew he meant to ask. "So it was all a sham? What she said about how she felt about me. The big wedding in Boston. It was all a lie?"

"I think you already know the answer to that."

I let him dwell on that thought and let myself enjoy the silence while he did it. Finally, he spoke again.

"Why did she have to kill herself?"

"I think she knew it was the only way to get my attention. To drag me out of my own hole. And I think she felt so much guilt. For what she helped you create."

He nodded. I stood to leave, realizing there was nothing more to be said.

"You shouldn't have left her," he said, when my hand was on the doorknob.

"I know," I said. I stepped through the door and closed it behind me.

Chapter Forty-Three

WE NAVIGATED THROUGH the Kinshasa traffic one final time. Marco was driving, and I sat next to him. Tshala was in the second row with Atombe. René followed behind with Henry in a second car. They had come along just to say good-bye; there was no more risk of trouble now. President Kabila himself had ordered the arrest of Minister Nyundi, after being briefed by the Canadian embassy. Knowing Kabila's history, I wasn't sure if the minister had been arrested for jeopardizing the integrity of the human race or simply because he hadn't brought the president and his fellow ministers in on the opportunity for huge profits. But it didn't matter; Genistar would now be investigated worldwide. We'd deployed the killswitch to stop the spread of the engineered virus, and the two hundred aid workers Genistar had flown in were now doing what they'd come to do, helping to stem the natural outbreak in the east. I'd already said goodbye to Sephora. The kids had been in class when we'd stopped in. They'd been sitting at their desks, working earnestly, heads down. I wondered if they really knew what they'd helped accomplish only a few days earlier.

The Gulfstream's engines were already turning when we reached the airstrip. René helped load the bags. Mine were meager; one less set of clothes than I'd come with. And one less cardboard box, which I realized I already missed.

Tshala had two suitcases. She'd been allowed access to her room at the dorms two days earlier and had been able to collect all her things. Atombe had only one bag, but I knew there was a shopping trip in both of their futures anyway. It was approaching Halloween in Boston and I knew neither he nor Tshala had warm enough clothes for those temperatures. Tshala's treatments would begin in Boston the day we arrived, and she'd need to spend a month there until the regimen got fine-tuned. Atombe would have a chance to see Boston. And they'd have time to really get to know each other.

I started to shake Marco's hand one we exited the car, but then changed my mind and gave him a bear hug instead. "Thanks for everything," I said, stepping back.

"I'm glad I got to be part of it," he said. "For once, I felt I was using all my old skills for a cause I could really believe in."

We walked slowly towards the plane, in no rush to hasten the goodbyes. "I do have one question though," I said.

"What's that?"

"If I hadn't figured out how Andrea had given me the killswitch, and I'd died in Makoua, would you have my name tattooed onto your arm?"

"No," he said, smiling. "That's just for people I like." He put his arm around my shoulder. "But look on the bright side. I did put your name on the invoice I sent to Frank. So that should count for something."

I laughed. We reached the plane. I hugged René as well. He patted me on the back. "Don't worry about him," he said, smiling. "If you didn't make it back, I'd have tattooed your name on my arse. You've been enough of a pain there already."

I boarded, still laughing, and the door closed.

I realized I felt like I was leaving home.

The plane took off to the north. I'd given the pilot one special request. He held that heading a bit longer than usual. I looked down to my right. In a matter of minutes, Lake N'tomba slid into view, rolling in over the horizon from the north. The air was clear, and sunlight sparkled off the water.

I watched the lake as long as I could, tears in my eyes. Even though I felt like I was leaving home, I knew Andrea was not. She was home. And I realized, despite my sorrow, how proud I was of all she had done. In life and death.

I'd been right about the chocolates—Doctor Huang had been at the lab in Bern, his laptop and files already packed. He and all his files were now safe and in custody.

So, unlike last time I'd left the Congo, I let myself believe I was leaving it a little better than I'd found it.

Chapter Forty-Four

Epilogue

I SAT IN a coffee shop in Zurich, still holding the piece of paper in my hand. The May sun was starting to provide warmth even in the northern latitudes, so I'd taken a table outside. My seat not only let me soak in the sun, but also gave me a better view of the building across the street. The heat on my skin still made me think of Andrea even then, eight months after giving her ashes to Lake N'Tomba. Behind me, I heard an occasional roar as trains came and left from the Stadelhofen train station.

My coffee cup was empty in front of me. The waiter eyed me, but I shook my head. I'd been sitting for too long already, studying the two-story, white stone building, with its peaked entrance way and tall, barred windows. I'd watched people come and go from it. Some couples, some singles. The singles were mostly women.

The piece of paper held an address but no name, either individuals or companies. I hadn't looked it up ahead of time. I knew pretty much where it was. And I'd decided I didn't want to know the reason for this final mystery from Andrea any sooner than I had to—the open question reminded me of those days in the Congo, unravelling the clues she'd woven so brilliantly into the unlikeliest of places.

I knew the coffee shop, too. I'd been there once before. With Andrea, while we waited on a train to Paris, to catch a flight back to the DRC. We'd been on a panel together at a conference in Zurich, speaking about the challenges of delivering medical care in the Congo. We'd finished each other's sentences on the panel, even though we'd really only realized our interest in each other a few months earlier.

A song had come to life on the speaker system while we sat, one we'd never heard together before. We each started singing it, quietly, then laughed when we caught the other in the same act. The words seemed to fit our mood while speaking to something larger—something exciting and unknown that was still unfolding between us.

It had become our song. We played it everywhere we went, in some of our darkest moments. And every time it had made me think of that day in Zurich.

Now it made me think of a different day. The day Andrea had ended her own life. Because she'd played it then, at the reception, and asked everyone in the room to think of where they'd been, the first time they heard it with the one they loved.

It had puzzled me for months after I'd left the Congo. All the clues she'd left me in her wedding files had been put to use. But her decision to play that song still tugged at my mind. I'd decided that it was not meant to hurt me. But I'd never quite figured out what significance it may have had, unless it was simply another way for her to reach out me and remind me of what we'd shared.

Then I'd gotten a call from her lawyer. Her estate had finally cleared probate. There were two pieces of information the lawyer had been asked to relay to me.

One was the fact that, in a side note left to her lawyer, Andrea had asked that her marriage to Stanley be annulled because the marriage had been coerced—a result of the unending surveillance around her, and the threat to Tshala if Andrea had refused to cooperate with Stanley's plans. A judge had agreed, after viewing the evidence in a sealed proceeding. Andrea was no longer Andrea Reston. And, in the eyes of the Commonwealth of Massachusetts, she'd never been.

But if she'd never been Andrea Reston, that meant she had always been Andrea Wright. We were still married, according to that simple ceremony in Makoua, in the only way that had mattered to either of us.

The other piece of information was the address I held in my hand at the coffee shop. Andrea had asked that it be given to me only after the annulment was complete.

I left a 10 franc note on the table, took a breath, and walked across the street.

The street address was clear on the side of the building. As was the name of the facility, in German. *360° Kinderwunsch Zentrum.*

It was a woman's health and fertility clinic.

I walked past the concrete plant holders out front, which were sculpted enough to be decorative but clearly solid enough to be a defensive perimeter. I pushed my way through the front door and identified myself to the young woman sitting behind a glass window in the lobby. She buzzed me into the waiting area. Ten minutes later, a woman in her fifties came out to greet me. I said hello in French, but she responded in English. She brought me into a small room off the lobby comfortably appointed with couches and a coffee table. The center provided regular medical services

351

but also counseling and coaching services, and the room we sat in was clearly designed for those purposes.

She thumbed through her notes.

"Yes, Andrea's gynecologist for the past year was here. Andrea had come regularly. She was also here several times more recently once she'd elected to have her eggs frozen. She is—was—in her thirties so we had suggested that she provide a higher number of eggs. They are frozen safely. And yes, your name is on the files. They are now your property. And I am sorry for your loss."

I just nodded, still trying to comprehend everything I'd heard, and how clever Andrea had been. As Tshala had said, Andrea had gone to Basel to speak on a regular basis. More recently she'd identified a clinic in Zurich that provided regular medical services as well as reproductive health offerings and switched to there for her checkups; she could make regular visits there after her lectures without raising anyone's suspicion.

I thanked the woman and left, blinking as I found myself back in the sunlight. I walked the streets of Zurich for an hour. My numbness turned to sadness, but then to peace. And finally to joy.

Walking the wide avenues, I didn't know what I would do with the choice she'd given me, frozen, in the vaults of the clinic. She'd left it for me—the most personal story of the woman I'd loved, in the form of her DNA. It was her half of a story that she and I could still tell together, should I so choose. It was her final gift to me. And I knew, even without her there to tell me, that it was an offering without obligation—any choice I made would have been one she would have accepted. At one point I stopped and took a square of paper out of my pocket; the one remaining puzzle from the materials Andrea had given me. I saw the list of clues she'd left in the form of reminders for her toast. But this time I flipped the paper over without hesitation and looked at the list of names. The baby names Andrea had left, not for Stanley, but for me, in case I decided to create that new story with her.

I smiled to myself as I walked again; ever the planner, she'd made sure to have her say in that decision, even after death.

I had added a name to the bottom of each list, scratched in my own block lettering. On the girl's side I'd scribbled Tshala. On the boy's side, Atombe.

I was pretty sure Andrea would be happy with those choices, too.

I knew that if I did move forward, I would be starting a story whose chapters I could not predict, because only part of the story would be mine to tell. Andrea would always own her part, and the vagaries of nature and fate would have their say as well. Only the decision to take that initial leap was something I could really control. Which, I suspect Andrea would tell me, was the true magic of life.

* * *

353

Brian Fitzgerald

www.brianbooks.com

OVER THE COURSE of a career in marketing and technology Brian made his living through storytelling, communicating in print, online and national broadcast TV. During that time, as head of communications for a billion-dollar information security firm, he had a role in some of the most tumultuous events in cybersecurity including major breaches and global privacy issues. Brian has worked with (and at times been at odds with) the media, academia and even America's intelligence and law-enforcement agencies. These experiences have informed his fiction writing, as he strives to bring to life the human consequences of advances in technology, medicine and social media.

CPSIA information can be obtained
at www.ICGtesting.com
Printed in the USA
BVHW080735251021
619802BV00016B/543